Always Us

LIZZIE MORTON

Editor: Black Quill Editing
Cover Photographer: Marcel Klangwart
Cover Model: Marvin Elliott

ISBN - 978-1-7391175-4-2

3

For Poppy – Thank you for always being patient while Mummy worked. I love you more than you will ever know.

One
Abby

"What's German for vomit?" I ask. Looking around hopelessly, I pray someone will answer, but all I get in return are vacant stares.

I'll give you a clue. Déjà. Fucking. Vu. It's unbelievable that at the age of twenty-six, we're still here reliving similar scenarios, just in different locations and with a different audience.

I mutter under my breath, "We're not even in our home country and they still can't behave like normal humans."

"Got it!" shouts Sooz excitedly from behind. Her eyes are glued to the screen of her cell as she frantically scours Google Translate. "*Erbrechen!* It's *erbrechen.*"

"Are you sure?"

The last time we were in a situation like this, we failed, big time. We're lucky we didn't get arrested we messed up that bad. Life lesson: don't always believe what you read on the internet.

"Would you like to check yourself?" she snipes back, pissed that I still doubt her after all this time.

"Nah, I trust you," I reply calmly.

Turning back to the bouncer, I rub my hands up and down my dress nervously. I'm sweating an obscene amount and it has nothing to do with the summer heat. It's known universally that all bouncers are intimidating giants, but German ones— they take it to the next level. This guy is huge, and his face is cold as ice as he looks down at me with one eyebrow raised.

Swallowing, I finally find my voice, even if it does come out a squeak, "*Erbrechen*?" I flinch and await the repercussions of what I've said. God, I hope I didn't say *dick*.

All he does in response is stand and stare blankly.

Just in case he hadn't heard me thanks to the noise of the club behind him, I repeat myself louder this time, "Erbrechen."

He shakes his head looking thoroughly annoyed. I don't blame him. Sooz and I have been standing for ten minutes wasting his time, trying to explain why we need to get into one of the most exclusive clubs in Berlin.

Finally, he replies, "*Ich verstehen nicht.*"

We may have figured out how to say a single word to him, but now we have the new challenge of figuring out what the hell he's saying back.

I don't know how I end up in these ridiculous positions. I thought handling them in America, on home soil was bad enough, but nothing beats being in a foreign country, chasing after my waster friends and not speaking a word of the language.

I turn back to my South African friend and only ally. "Dammit. Sooz, have you still got that translator app on your cell?"

"Yes! Thank God. Why didn't I think of that? It isn't the most reliable thing in the world, but it should give us a better idea of what's being said than the nothing we've come up with so far ..."

"At this point, what have we got to lose?"

Taking her cell in a shaky hand, I hold it up toward the bouncer.

He looks bewildered, but then somehow seems to understand what I'm trying to do and repeats, "*Ich verstehen nicht.*"

The translator repeats back robotically, "I don't understand."

"That makes two of us." I sigh. Looking to Sooz, I resign myself to the fact this whole thing is a lost cause. "I think it's time we give up."

Her eyes widen and she replies, "We can't just leave them in there. If we've struggled to find them, how on earth are they going to find their way back to the hotel?"

I throw my arms up in the air in sheer frustration. "I don't know. This isn't like it is normally. We don't speak a word of the language and even with your translator thing we're not going to get anywhere fast. They could be gone by the time we get in there. That's *if* we even get in there."

We continue bickering and as we do a cab pulls up at the entrance. Three girls spill out of the back. They're tall, blonde and more glamorous than I could ever imagine being. My spidey senses crank into full force, when I hear one of them speaking with an English accent to the others. Confidently, they make their way to the bouncer, greeting him in German and kissing him on both cheeks.

The asshole looks like a pig in shit, blatantly watching their asses sway from side to side as they walk into the club. It suddenly dawns on me that my golden ticket has just slipped by.

Without thinking, I quickly shout, "Yo, blondie! Over here!"

The blonde at the rear turns back around abruptly, eyes narrowed. It's not surprising, as I've literally hollered at her. Desperate times and all that.

Her stance is defensive as she looks me up and down suspiciously. "Excuse me? Do I know you?" she asks.

I hold my hands up in a peace offering and attempt to explain, "Sorry, that was rude of me, but we need your help."

Still annoyed by how I gained her attention, she shakes her head and turns to follow her friends into the club.

Seeing my moment slip away, I shriek at the top of my voice, "Please!"

Turning back, she hesitates before replying, "Make it quick."

"My friends have somehow managed to get into the club, but they're wasted, and we have no way of getting in touch with them. They have no idea where they are, and none of us speak a word of German." My shoulders slump in defeat after what has turned into a wild goose chase around the capital of Germany.

Thankfully, I have Sooz to back me up. "We just need you to help us get in, so we can find them and get them home."

It feels like forever, as we stand waiting for the blonde to make a choice. Without warning, she turns to the bouncer and speaks something garbled I'm past the point of attempting to understand. The bouncer appears to be listening intently to whatever it is she's saying, although I suspect what I'm actually seeing is him staring at her breasts in the low-cut dress she's wearing. Pervert.

The blonde finishes talking, then the bouncer faces us.

He removes the rope barrier before saying abruptly, "*Komm rein.*"

Sooz and I just stare. He's obviously not grasped that there's no clear wave of communication between any of us.

Fortunately, the blonde intervenes and says, "He's letting you in. I'd be quick before he changes his mind."

With that, she waltzes into the club, leaving me and Sooz to stumble behind. We follow her down a long, dark passage that seems to go on forever. Besides being creepy and giving off some serious horror movie vibes, it smells musty, and the floor is sticky and gross. If you ask me, it's a bit of a dive considering it's meant to be an 'exclusive' club.

When we get to the end of the passage there's a large metal door. As it's opened slowly by two other bouncers, my jaw hits the floor. If I thought we'd overcome our biggest hurdle of the night by getting into the club, I was wrong. Sooz and I stand, mouths wide open, gawping at what looks to be the biggest club either of us has ever seen.

"Oh, sweet mother of God," says Sooz.

"Shit. How are we supposed to find them in here? It's huge!"

I want to scream, stomp my feet, smash a glass. Anything to let out the anger that has been building throughout the day. I'm in the wrong career, I should be filming a fly on the wall documentary of the crap my two best friends get up to instead.

Tonight, has been our own, real life version of *The Hangover*. Since around 2 PM, Sooz and I have spent our time piecing together Zoe and Sophie's antics. We only left them for an hour while we finished up a job in the center of Berlin. I repeat, *an hour*. One. Singular. True to form, neither of them updated their payment plans to international on their cells, so we've been chasing them from location to location, following them wherever they could get Wi-Fi and post on Instagram, in the hope of catching them. Things went downhill when they checked in at an absinthe shop and the posts have been minimal since. Of course, they have no idea where our hotel is, having relied on me and Sooz to get around the whole time they've been in Germany with us.

Just when we were at the point of giving up, we got lucky, and a stranger tagged them in this club around thirty minutes ago. It was our only glimmer of hope and I've been praying they're still here, that we could get to them before they decided to move on to somewhere else. That was until exactly a minute ago when we entered the club. It's an old, abandoned warehouse on the outskirts of Berlin. But looks can be deceiving. Inside, this place looks bigger than a football stadium. We don't stand a chance of finding them any time soon.

"Yes! They've put up a post!" shouts Sooz, waving her cell around frantically.

"Let me see." I quickly grab it from her, but when my eyes make contact with the image on the screen, I throw it back abruptly. "Oh my God, my eyes. Why did I have to see that? Sooz, don't look." If I could erase what I'd just seen I would.

"That bad?" she shouts over the music.

"Worse. We're looking for a trapeze with a naked, fire-breathing man and two wasted girls hanging off him."

Braver than I am, Sooz looks at the image and then back at me, barely able to contain her laughter. "Wow. So why are these your friends?"

"I ask myself the same thing sometimes. And they've claimed themselves as your friends too, making them equally your responsibility."

Trying not to look at the picture again, we show the screen to the first person within reach, and they point us to the center of the club. We make our way through the crowds and I frantically push past men of every shape and size, dressed in every color imaginable. It's like a rainbow vomited everywhere.

Something begins to niggle away at me as Sooz slows down and says, "I think I'm in love with this place. I've never been somewhere with so many hot guys. It's like an all you can eat man buffet." She flutters her eye lashes at a group of guys, watching as they dance against each other.

It's then that it clicks what feels off about this place. "Sooz, we're in a gay club." I let out a sigh at all the potential on offer that will never be ours.

"Dammit. It's always the good ones," she says, voicing the opinion of most of the women in the club.

"I know what you mean, but less drooling. We need to find the girls and get out of here before they do something inappropriate."

It's a sight to behold when we get to the middle of the club. There must be at least twenty naked men floating above us and breathing fire. And there, swaying backwards and forwards with their new friend, are Sophie and Zoe.

"Give me your concealer, Sooz," I demand.

She looks horrified. "What? Why?"

"It needs to be sacrificed. It's for a good cause."

Looking up to where the girls are hanging above us, I begin to calculate the angle of my throw

"But it's MAC!" she shrieks at a pitch that could deafen cats.

"I'll replace it, I promise."

Reluctantly, she hands it over, only to watch in horror as I launch it up, as hard as possible, in Sophie's direction. The trapeze moves just at the wrong moment and instead of hitting her in the side of the head, I nail her straight in the eye, hard.

"Damn," I say.

Even from down below, with the loud electro music booming around us, I can hear her drunken howls clearly. At least she'll have a memento of the night, besides their drunken Instagram photos.

When she eventually stops howling and looks down for the culprit, her eyes settle on mine. She swallows nervously as I signal abruptly for them to come down. Hell hath no fury like an Abby that has raced around Berlin, chasing their sorry asses. Over the years I've come to accept my motherly role, but today has pushed me to my limit.

"They look scared," says Sooz, wiping away tears of laughter for the second time in ten minutes.

"Good."

They're lowered down slowly, finally waving goodbye, albeit sheepishly, to their naked friend.

I'm blunt when I say, "Do not say a word. We're leaving now, and you will come without causing any more problems. I've had enough of your crap today to last a lifetime."

Making our way hastily out of the club, Sophie and Zoe scuttle behind like two scorned toddlers. Sooz lingers at the back, taking her fill of the club's occupants one last time. When we're outside, we make our way to what appears is a cab-rank. I spend a few minutes doing a version of Pictionary with one of the drivers, in an attempt to explain where the hotel is. Eventually he seems to understand, and I turn around to find Zoe and Sophie chatting with a group of seedy looking women. It baffles me that in less than five minutes they've managed to find the only English-speaking people around, yet it took Sooz and I over half an hour, and a big dose of luck.

"Guys. In. Now." Holding open the back-passenger door, I signal for them to get in fast.

When we're settled, the driver pulls away, making a hasty journey through the streets of Berlin.

"They were nice," Zoe slurs, completely unaware of who she's talking too.

"They were hookers. They'd be nice to anyone they thought they could get money from."

Sooz snickers at my reply from the front, while pointing the driver in the direction of the TV Tower and hopefully towards our hotel.

Zoe is oblivious as always. "Oh. Really?"

"Yes. If you spent less time getting wasted, you'd see the things around you clearer. I thought we were past all this?"

"And I thought we were past you acting so bitchy all the time," she grumbles under her breath.

I narrow my eyes. "I heard that."

"You were meant to."

The cab driver swerves, taking an abrupt left. Even in the back of the cab, in the darkness, there's no mistaking the shade of green Zoe's face changes to.

"Zo ..."

I thought we'd gotten away lightly and there might not be a puking incident, but clearly, I was wrong. The streets prove too much for Zoe's absinthe-lined stomach to handle, but before we have time to tell the driver to pull over, she pukes all over my lap.

In case the day hadn't been long and tiring enough, the last part is spent cleaning up Zoe and the cab while trying not to vomit myself, and then there was the fine. When we finally collapse in bed with the girls safely laying on their sides and a bucket next to them, all I can think is get me the hell out of Berlin.

***

After a night of Zoe and Sophie's escapades, normally we would spend the following morning lounging in bed and laughing off the night before. This isn't one of those mornings. I'm too annoyed. That, and the fact Sooz and I have landed a couple of last-minute appointments to finish up business in Berlin before we head back to Cape Town.

I could have let the girls wallow in their misery, but I force their sorry looking assess onto the U-Bahn bright and early, dragging them around the city with us. I'm not ashamed to admit I enjoy each sway of the train, watching as their faces turn green.

Later, sitting in a small café near our hotel, Sooz and I are consumed with work, which is piling up at an alarming rate, while the girls nurse what is left of their hangovers. We were originally sold the idea of Berlin by our boss, and it was described as 'just' a few pre-fashion week photoshoots. It was also supposed to be a 'quick and easy' trip. It's been anything but. We've chased from one appointment to the next for a week solid. I have hundreds of images to work with and edit, and not a clue where to begin. With my stress levels so high, I'm extra snappy and Zoe and Sophie's antics couldn't have come at a worse time.

Zoning out from my workload, I watch as Sophie attempts yet again to cover her black eye from the night before, ironically with concealer.

She looks up and catches me watching then asks hesitantly, "Coffee?"

It's an obvious peace offering, and I take it. I have too much going on to have the energy to hold a major grudge. Plus, the monstrous hangover I've watched them both endure was suffering enough.

"Please," I respond with a small smile, letting her know my anger from the day before is finally lessening.

It's not often they get themselves in such states anymore, especially after I had my drink spiked at a festival in Brooklyn a couple of years ago. It scared the shit out of them, and they felt hugely responsible and guilty. It seemed to tame their wild ways, but occasionally, they still like to let their hair down for old times' sake. Unfortunately for me and Sooz, it happened to be in the one country none of us speak an ounce of the language.

A few minutes later, Sophie returns with a tray of steaming coffees, and we all sigh with satisfaction. The main thing that unites us is our love of caffeine. Sophie and Zoe wouldn't be able to function through their hangovers without it and Sooz and I wouldn't be able to function, period.

"How are you getting on?" asks Zoe.

"Nowhere fast. I feel like I'm going around in circles. I'm gonna call it a day." I close my laptop and pack it away, opting to give my coffee my undivided attention instead.

"What's the plan for the rest of the day then? Drinks?" asks Zoe, with a hopeful tone that can't be missed.

"You're an animal, I swear. There's not a chance I'm letting you two near alcohol while we're still in Berlin. We have early flights tomorrow and I'm not missing mine because I'm trying to hunt the two of you down," I say.

"Party pooper."

17

I leave Sophie and Zoe in their own little world, watching as they speak quietly, trying to piece together yesterday's events. I don't miss the fact that Sophie is beginning to look green in the face again. Instead, I focus my attention on Sooz, whose brows are furrowed as she stares intently at her laptop.

She really is beautiful with the South African beach babe vibes she has going for her. It's no wonder guys fall at her feet, although she's far too career-driven to notice. When I accepted the job in Cape Town a couple of years ago, I warmed to her instantly. She was the exact sort of person I needed in my life. Someone with the same drive and dedication, who didn't care about guys or romance. Perfect considering I was mending a broken heart. We clicked, and when Sophie and Zoe met her, they got along great. It sealed the deal that we had another friend for life. So, we went from being a trio, to a crew.

It takes me a few minutes of watching to realize she isn't doing anything, just sitting, staring. I wave my hand in front of her face to catch her attention, before saying, "Earth to Sooz. Everything ok?"

She takes a few moments to gather herself together, before looking up and clearing her throat awkwardly. "Don't hate me for what I'm about to ask."

You know that feeling you get sometimes, when something bad is about to happen, or your life is about to take a whole new direction? That feeling where your skin prickles, your senses heighten and dread washes over you. I have that feeling as I say reluctantly, "Go on ..."

"What was the name of Jake's band? You know, *Jake* ... The Jake—"

I don't mean to interrupt, but I'm getting impatient and want to know what's going on. "I get it, Sooz. You don't need to say his name again. The band's name is S.C.A.R.A.B. Why?"

Another few minutes pass and I'm still no clearer as to what is going on. Sooz continues staring at her laptop. This time, it's not only me who watches as she sits frowning. At the mention of Jake's name, Sophie and Zoe join the conversation.

I don't speak about Jake much with Sooz, but she knows our history, knows I left everything behind, including him, when I moved to South Africa. She also knows to proceed with caution. There's radio silence, and I'm beginning to get agitated, wondering what awful news she's about to deliver.

It's Zoe who attempts to break the silence next. "Is everything ok?" she asks.

After what feels like an eternity, Sooz finally replies, "The thing is ... yesterday I got a really important email from Ange ..."

"Right?" I urge her to continue.

"Yeah. So, we spent most of yesterday chasing these two loons around and I never got a chance to check them. Let's just say the email was urgent and required an immediate response."

With absolutely no idea where she's going with this, I feel completely bewildered. But nothing could prepare me for what comes out of her mouth next.

She speaks rapidly, as if by doing so, it will make things better and change my reaction, "I missed an email asking whether we were free for a huge project. The sort of opportunity that would give the company global exposure. Rather than missing out simply because I hadn't responded, Ange checked our diaries, saw they were clear and said yes. There's no easy way to say this ..."

Dread seeps into every part of my body making me feel sick. Whatever she's about to say, it involves him. Everything stops and my mind goes blank, as I hear what comes out of her mouth next without really hearing it.

"... we're going on S.C.A.R.A.B.'s European tour. We're going on tour with Jake. *Your* Jake."

Two
Jake

"We smashed it man!" I get a slap on the back, before Sam jumps all over me like a little kid. I flinch slightly when he makes contact with my back, which is drenched in sweat after being under the glaring lights for a full set. One of the perks nobody tells you about performing on stage. It's sweaty work and the last thing I want is this asshole crowding me. I need a shower, like yesterday.

I shove him away, removing my earpiece and grabbing an ice-cold bottle of water before replying, "You say it like you're surprised."

He shrugs and I know it's pissing him off that I'm not more enthusiastic.

"It gets me every time. That we're here, doing this. Living the dream," when he speaks it's with excitement and makes him look younger than the twenty-six years we've managed to reach. He looks the way I remember my best friend from high school looking, before life on the road spent boozing and

21

using women, left, right and center began to take its toll.

"This is where hard work and perseverance gets you. And talent," I sound cocky, but we didn't get here by chance and we deserve every success we've had. We've worked hard since leaving high school, covered multiple jobs, taken risks. We've sacrificed more than anyone will ever know, more than any of us thought we'd have to, and now, it's all finally been worth it.

"Yeah, yeah. I don't need one of your speeches again. Anyway, it's our last gig on home turf, celebratory drinks?"

Truthfully, I'm beat, but there's no way I'm letting the guys down so they can bitch at me for days after. This is the part they live for: the afterparty and the women. Looking at Zach and Ryan, I wonder if maybe, just this once they'll back out and decide to do the sensible thing, calling it a night. But when they nod their confirmation in Sam's direction, I resign myself to it being at least a few more hours till I can crawl into bed.

"Sure," I reply. He doesn't need to know that my plan is to grab a couple of beers and then ditch without them realizing.

Completely oblivious to my foul mood, he continues, "Man. I caught a glimpse of some of the ladies in that crowd. They were so wet for us."

"Ever the gentleman."

"Hey, come on. You can't say you're not tempted. Not even a little?"

He looks at me hopefully, wanting my answer to be different than it has been in the past two years, as if overnight I might have had an epiphany and decided it's finally time to move on. But if my actions in the past couple of weeks haven't convinced him otherwise, I don't know what will. I'm as close to moving on as I am to rekindling things with my estranged mother: not at all.

I can't be bothered going into it all again, so I say, "Maybe."

It pacifies him, for now. He's too amped from our set to focus on me any longer.

Heading to our dressing room, I'm ready for a shower and change of clothes before we greet the fans. It needs to be a quick turnaround. We've become known in the industry for being professional and always on time, it's not a reputation I'm willing to sacrifice. Despite the guys being guys, it's the one thing we've all agreed on, not to become assholes with the fame.

When we've cleaned up, we make our way to the press room which has been reserved for meet and greets. A member of the stage crew ushers us to the door quickly and I brace myself for the fans. As the door opens, the screaming hits us and the feelings of euphoria kick in. This is it. This makes every sacrifice we've ever made worth it. It makes losing *her* worth it.

***

"It's settled then. Are you excited? This summer is going to be huge."

I glance up from the spot on my jeans, which I've been staring at for the last ten minutes, to where John West is sitting at the end of the exec table, beaming back at me. I can't look at him for long, especially when he pulls a face like he is now; he looks too much like *her*. I give a simple nod of confirmation, along with Zach and Ryan, then return to staring at the spot on my jeans.

Sam, unable to contain his excitement, hoots out, "Hell yeah!"

It's so loud even the sound proofing of this swanky meeting room can't stop his voice making its way into the offices surrounding us. The group of female employees walking by giggle at his response.

Mr. West continues smiling, not remotely phased by Sam's reaction. "Excellent. This is it, what you've been working for. You think what you've been doing up until now was making it big? We've tracked the figures in Europe and they're insane. They love you. Boys, you're about to step it up to a whole other level." Even with his cheesy record label spiel, his excitement is infectious, and I find myself nodding back enthusiastically with the other guys. Then he asks the question that's on all our minds: "Are you ready?"

It sobers us immediately and it's like we've been transported back to two years ago, sitting in the same room signing our first record deal as he asked the same question. Now, the daunting feeling of what's to come, the pressure of putting everything on the line is bigger than ever. It's crossed my mind more than once and I know, although they would never admit it, the other guys have thought the same. Can we step up our game and take this thing to the next level? Can we each give it everything we have and commit one hundred percent?

Sam, Zach and Ryan are ready, I know they are, they always have been. They live for this shit and over the years have let nothing get in their way. But me?

On more than one occasion, Sam has vocalized that he's worried I'm holding back, that I'm not giving the band my all. He might be right, but damn if I'm not trying my hardest. It's not my fault, there's a piece to the puzzle missing, and there's only one way to get it back.

We wrap up our final meeting before the tour quickly. Everything else left to do is for those behind the scenes to deal with—we do the easy bit. We show up and live our best life, or at least try to make it appear that way.

As we make to leave, John West holds up a hand in my direction stopping me in my tracks. He says, "Jake, can you hold back a moment?"

I thought I'd gotten away with it, clearly not.

The guys scuttle out, knowing what's coming. They're my best friends and have put a lot on the line for me, like I have them, so it seemed only right to let them in on what I wanted to do. They were supportive, kind of, at least they didn't say no.

Giving John a small nod, I sit back down in my seat, bracing for what's to come. His reaction might not be negative, but it certainly won't be positive. Working together over the past couple of years, we've gotten to know each other well, but I can't always read him, in the same way I can't always read his daughter.

"So ..." he sighs.

"So?" I say.

Leaning over the table, he clasps his hands, shifting uncomfortably in his seat. "Funny story, Jake. I got an angry phone call before this meeting. It was from a certain daughter of mine. She demanding to know why she'd been signed as part of S.C.A.R.A.B.'s PR team for the tour."

I don't flinch; there's nothing I can say to get out of this. He knows it and I know it. I'm also assuming he knows how it's come about. Perks of being the boss, he has eyes and ears everywhere.

Rubbing a hand through his hair in frustration, the record exec mask comes off and he looks older than he did five minutes ago, his face full of concern. "Are you sure you want to do this?"

"It's already done," I reply.

He frowns. There's a bunch of other things going through his head he wants to say, but he goes for the simple option. "Be kind to her."

"I will if she is."

He's fighting a losing battle and he knows it.

"What do you suggest I tell my daughter then?" he asks.

"Nothing. Please," my voice falters, almost pleading. It pisses me off that he's caught a glimpse of my vulnerable side, the side I don't have any control over when it comes to her. Clearing my throat, I attempt to give my voice more certainty when I continue, "Don't give her the full truth for now, give her a tamer version."

"Which would be?"

"That she's the best and we need her."

***

After winding things up with John, I take a breather, wandering the streets of Brooklyn before finding the guys in Riffs. Surprise.

"He didn't tear your balls off?" asks Sam, pushing a beer across the table in my direction.

I shrug, not really wanting to get into it. "Not quite. But he wasn't happy."

Zach chuckles. "What did you expect man? You had his daughter signed into an iron clad contract to work with us for seven weeks. I've read it … The President couldn't get out of that shit. You must really want her on this tour."

Sam howls with laughter, before threatening to kill me if I ruin things for us.

Ryan being a typical drummer, simply responds, "More pussy for me."

"What are we talking about?" Shaun heads over from behind the bar with a fresh pitcher of beer.

"About how Jakey here has royally fucked us all over. He had Abby signed up as part of our PR team for the tour," replies Sam.

Shaun's face flashes from confused, to understanding. Of all the guys, he's the one most likely to get where I'm coming from, why I have to do this. If anyone knows what unrequited love feels like, it's him.

"You sure that's a good idea?" he asks.

"Are you sure carting your ass all the way to Spain, chasing after a certain blonde is a good idea?" I reply.

He holds his hands up and says, "Touché man. Just be good to her. It's been two years, and this is the band's time to shine. Don't let that old crap ruin everything you've worked for."

I nod. "I'll do my best."

"Seriously though. Why are you really doing this? What do you expect to get from it?"

"I don't know." It's the truth. I have no idea why it seemed like a good idea, or why I worked so hard to make sure there was no way she could get out of it. I just did. Since the day she kicked my sorry-ass to the curb, walking straight out of Brooklyn and hopping on a plane to South Africa, I haven't been the same. I've been here, functioning, but that's about it.

"You need to figure it out and don't fuck with her. She's been through enough."

The last bit pisses me off, because all of this is her doing. We could have had it all, we could have finally been together with nothing in the way to stop us, but she was too scared and walked away.

"She did this. Whatever happens this summer, she brought it on herself." The day she walked away from us, she took a part of me with her and I want it back. It didn't have to be like this. I want her to fix what she broke without a care in the world.

Abby West and I have unfinished business.

Three
Abby

"Do you feel like you're ready?"

"Soph, I'll never be ready to see him again. I can't believe there's no way of getting out of this. I don't know who came up with the contracts but they're tighter than Zoe's ass." I look around my room and let out a sigh, trying to relieve the building frustration I've been fighting for days.

The rest of our time in Berlin was a blur. I think I was in shock. After Sooz gave the news, things got a bit out of control. Zoe's suggestion of a strong drink to get my head around everything may not have been the smartest idea. One thing led to another and I wound up wasted, puking in the restroom of some random bar at three in the afternoon. Not my finest moment.

Sooz and I parted ways with Sophie and Zoe the next day, as they headed back to Brooklyn and us to Cape Town. They promised they wouldn't abandon me in all this, and if ever there was a time I was thankful for their slack lifestyle, it's now.

Sophie, being the 'perpetual student,' has the summer off, while Zoe stated it was an excellent opportunity to influence the American people to jump on a plane and experience the European music scene or some crap like that. Luckily, they have the banks of Mummy and Daddy to fund them and will meet us at the first stop of the tour, ironically back in Germany.

"I guess it wouldn't help if I suggested you just try and treat it as work?" Even through my cell I can hear she's unconvinced by her own words.

"We've tried that, remember? Look where it got us."

"Good point," she agrees.

Two summers ago, I returned to Brooklyn after six years of self-inflicted exile, thanks to a broken heart from the one and only, Jake Ross. When I first returned, I convinced myself everything would be fine, and we'd make it through in one piece. I thought I could avoid him, but I was wrong. Our old group was as tight as ever after high school, and it proved impossible not to see each other, no matter how hard I tried.

When we both wound up working for my dad's record label it was a disaster. We ended our current relationships at the time and had one blissful night together. I don't allow myself to think much about that night or I'll inevitably wind up down the rabbit hole never to return. Thinking about the memories of that summer makes my chest physically ache. My heart, that had begun to heal in its own way was put through the ringer once more when I returned to Brooklyn, only this time it was through my own doing.

But was it really?

Sometimes, in the dark of night I indulge myself and allow my mind to wander back to what happened with Jake. Why I walked away when I could have had everything. But that's the thing, it wouldn't have been everything because he wouldn't give me every part of himself. All I'd asked for were answers as to why he left me the first time, closure so I could solidify in my mind what we had and why he made me feel the way he did when we were teenagers. But he wouldn't give me either.

Asshole.

He was scared it would change things and I'd walk away. What he didn't realize was that by not having faith in me, I would walk away anyway.

Breaking me from my thoughts, Sophie's voice rings down the line, "You still there?"

"Yeah, sorry." I look around my room, blinking and taking in my surroundings, trying to ground myself back in reality. "My mind jumped on the Jake train."

"I thought as much."

I sigh and say, "What am I going to do, Soph? I can't be around him for a whole summer, not again. It isn't going to be like it was back in Brooklyn; there will be no escape and it will be intense. Plus, I don't stand a chance avoiding him when we're supposed to work together."

"I wish I could ask what you want to do, but I can't. You can't not go. You're stuck in a contract. Unless you quit—"

"Thanks for pointing out the obvious," I snap, before she has a chance to continue.

"Will you let a girl continue before jumping the gun?"

"Sorry. I get ratty when it comes to all things Jake related."

31

"It's ok. And after you put up with everything from me and Zoe, I need to up my tolerance of crap from you."

The memory of Berlin makes me smile, something I never thought I'd say. It seems like child's play looking back, compared to what I'm having to deal with now. If only I'd known that night what was coming for me.

"Anyway, you were saying ..."

"Before you rudely interrupted," she replies. "I was trying to say, that you do have a choice over something: how you handle the whole situation. You've already bumped uglies, so at least you don't have that on the brain constantly. You know ... wondering what it would be like, et cetera, because you've already tapped it—"

"I get what you're saying, and that would have been a great way of thinking about it all if the sex hadn't been mind-blowing ... The kind where you go straight in for round two, then three. The sort where you can't walk for days after."

She looks at me almost dreamily and says, "That does mess things up a little. But he's not the only guy who's good in bed, Abby. The world doesn't start and end with Jake. That's how you've got to start thinking. Luckily for you, you get to spend a summer backstage with bands full of hot rock guys."

What she's saying makes my ears prick. Having been so focused on the negatives of the summer, I've neglected to see there will also be positives. "I guess I didn't think of it that way."

"You know what Zoe would say ..."

She doesn't need to finish. We repeated it so many times after we broke up the first time it became my mantra.

"The best way to get over someone is to get under someone," I mimic in Zoe's voice.

"Exactly. I'm not suggesting you try to be friends because we all know that didn't work last time, but maybe the two of you could be professional? To do that though, you need to go into this with an open mind. All those gorgeous guys are going to provide plenty of distractions and Jake might be hot, but he isn't the hottest guy to walk the planet, while you my dear are sexy as hell. Guys are going to be dropping at your feet. There will be so much going on to take your mind off him … and you have us, the crew. We will make sure you don't lose your mind and wind up in bed with him again."

Out of her and Zoe, she's the one who offers the more reasonable advice that doesn't tend to be solely focused on sex. The positive vibes she's giving off are helping things seem clearer with a fresher perspective.

"You've almost persuaded me to think this could be easy," my voice might not sound one hundred percent convincing, but she has.

"That's because it could be easy. I hate to break it to you, but sometimes you can be the queen of negativity. Let's get excited about this. A summer touring around Europe, doing what you love and living the dream. You need to see Jake as a speed bump, a minor blip."

Earlier this evening there was something inside me telling me I needed to call her and I'm glad I did. "I feel better," I say, hoping she can tell how grateful I am.

"Good. Now what time's your flight tomorrow?"

"Lunch time. At least it's not super early, so if I don't sleep it gives me chance to catch up."

"Have you packed?"

"Erm ..." I look over at the empty case on the floor I should have started on days ago.

"Seriously, Abby? You're about to head off for seven weeks and you still haven't packed? Get your ass moving.

"Oh, and if you value your sex-deprived body, let Sooz help, or so help me God I will burn all the clothes you pack on the spot. Frumpy is not sexy."

I roll my eyes knowing she can't see me. "Nice to see we're back on to a normal conversation."

"Somebody has to tell you how it is. There's no need for some of the monstrosities you wear, not when you have a body like yours. I'm not saying flaunt it to the level Zoe thinks you should—she'd have you walking round naked permanently—but at least show a bit of skin. Work those curves."

I look at my closet skeptically. I'm not sure where she thinks I'm going to poof a new wardrobe from at this time of night. "Right, I guess I have some work to do. So much for an early night ..."

"Love you." She makes a kissing noise. "Let me know when you get there safely; we'll be meeting you after the first set. Oh, and Abby ..."

"Yeah?"

"Do not kill Jake on the spot. That is not part of the plan."

"I'll try," I reply, reluctantly.

After hanging up, I go to my closet and stand staring, trying to figure out what I'm going to take on this trip. The girls are right, my fashion sense isn't brilliant, and my choice of tomboy clothes won't help me "get under somebody" this summer. Maybe I should have spent my time back home doing something productive like shopping for a summer wardrobe, rather than sitting, raging in my room, and cursing all things Jake like I have done.

"Need some help?"

I don't need to look to know it's Sooz at my door. We've been living together for the best part of two years.

As luck would have it, when I arrived, I managed to bag the dingiest apartment in possibly one of the most dangerous areas of Cape Town. It was around the same time Sooz returned home to an empty apartment after her crazy roommate at the time just up and left. It worked out perfect for the both of us, seeing as though we hit it off straight away, so we jumped at the chance to live together.

It started on a trial basis, but within a week we both knew it would be a long-term thing. So that's how, four months into my job in Cape Town, we wound up being roomies.

I let out a groan, knowing it's hopeless looking any longer. I turn to Sooz and reply, "Can you make a full summer wardrobe appear out of thin air?"

"Well, actually ..."

My eyebrows shoot up in surprise. "Sooz, do you have magical powers you've been holding back?"

"No. But a certain friend of yours preempted this and pulled a few strings."

Only Zoe would be able to pull this off.

"Maybe her freelance blogging career isn't a waste after all."

"Far from it. You should see some of the things she's managed to get you, they're amazing."

"Let me guess, they have minimal material?"

She waves a hand in the air dismissively. "Minor details, Abby. When you have a body like yours what does it matter?"

I don't stand a chance with any of them, it's pointless even trying, so I reply, "Show me the goods."

35

She spins and leaves the room. She's gone a good five minutes before I hear her grunting and huffing as she makes her way back with the biggest pile of clothes I've ever seen.

"Holy cow. I thought you said a few things?"

She dumps them on the bed then stands up straight and says, "I actually never specified. It was you who assumed as always. Anyway, let's look through and get packed. Any bits you don't want I'm totally stealing. If they fit. Not all of us have a skinny ass like you."

"Behave." I swat her away.

She always does this, puts herself down because she doesn't see how gorgeous she is. Totally absorbed by work she's unable to see the male attention she attracts left, right, and center.

Over an hour later, we've managed to make our way through the huge pile of clothes and gather together a mix to fit most occasions, not knowing what the summer will entail.

"Of course, there's going to be down time and we'll be in some of the hottest cities in Europe, which means we can go shopping!" screeches Sooz. "I can't believe we're going on tour. I knew the company was ready for branching out, but this is taking things to a whole other level."

The job I took two years ago was with a fashion PR company in Cape Town, as their lead photographer. Sooz was the one who hired me, and she's the head of PR. She's amazing at what she does and has a laser focus most people would kill for. But with that comes drawbacks, like her nonexistent love life. Not that I can talk as mine is also nonexistent. We've spoken over recent months about how we'd like to branch our skills out further than what the company has to offer, so this opportunity to move into the music scene and go on tour has come just at the right time. It's just a shame who we're going on tour with.

Just thinking about him again, even for a second, is proving a struggle.

The expression on my face must have changed as Sooz asks, "Do you want to talk about him?"

I dismiss her quickly. "Not really."

"Ok?"

"There's nothing to say. I'm going to be stuck with him for seven freaking weeks."

The optimism Sophie inspired earlier has quickly disappeared and I can feel myself slipping back to the wallowing Abby I've been since Sooz gave me the news of the tour.

"It might not be as bad as you think."

"Come on Sooz. Really?" I sigh. Sooz has yet to witness the disaster that is Jake and I together so of course she would be optimistic.

"At least we don't have to travel with them or stay with them," she offers, trying to be reassuring.

It eases some of the tension because I know she's right. It was a relief when I found out there would be at least a little bit of distance between us over the summer, if she had delivered any other news it might have just tipped me over the edge. I'm still skeptical though. "We just have to spend most hours of the day with them."

"It won't be that bad, Abby. There will be so many other things going on, other bands and more importantly, hot guys."

It's like listening to Sophie all over again. I wonder how much they've been communicating since we left Berlin. I can't deny that the thought of being backstage with some of the biggest names in music is a perk. But there will always be a certain someone there in the background.

As much as I'm trying to keep my mind away from him, my thoughts constantly stray back and being near him isn't going to help. The first time we broke up I had to leave the state to get over him. The second the freaking country. It sounds extreme, but Jake and I do not work well in proximity of each other.

Resigned from my mind running on a continuous loop, I say, "We need wine."

"Are you sure that's a good idea? We've got a long day tomorrow."

I frown, showing it's not open for discussion. "We are having wine, otherwise there's no way I'm going to sleep tonight, I'm too wound up."

"Okay. If you're sure. But when you're ratty tomorrow, I'll be reminding you of this."

"Whatever."

I leave her behind in my room, making my way to the kitchen in search of the blissful drink before she has a chance to change my mind. When I stumble into bed later that night, after drowning my sorrows, I don't feel any better and can't help thinking maybe Sooz was right.

Four

Abby

It would appear I have a thing with airports. I just love to stand in them amidst life-changing moments, while full of dread usually related to Jake. The first time I left Brooklyn, I practically ran out of the city on my own two feet after the way he treated me. I skipped right out and didn't look back for six years. Then two summers ago, I returned to Brooklyn, leaving behind Florida and my boyfriend at the time, Michael.

The second time I left Brooklyn, at the end of that fateful summer, it was different. I literally had to rip myself away as every part of me screamed to stay with my family and friends who had managed to break down the walls I'd put up over the years. I sobbed the twenty-four hours it took to get to Cape Town, and still feel guilty for the poor people sitting next to me on the plane. I was a sniveling, snotty mess and wound up wasted for a large chunk of the journey. If it wasn't embarrassing enough, twice an air steward had to wake me as I was snoring so loud, I was disturbing the other passengers.

This time, I'm leaving Cape Town behind—a place I've grown to love despite a rocky beginning—and once again I'm full of dread at the thought of seeing Jake. The best part of the day so far was being manhandled by Sooz as she dragged me through Cape Town International when I got cold feet. We drew a lot of attention but surprisingly security didn't get involved.

Now we're settled in the departure lounge, waiting for our flight, but my mood hasn't improved despite her best efforts. She's tried everything to cheer me up and make light of a bad situation, treating me to my favorite airport meal and two double-strength vanilla lattes to help with my wine-induced hangover. I'm full, as wired as a raver and still undeniably miserable.

"I can't believe we're having to go back to Germany," I grumble.

"You love Germany," replies Sooz.

She's right but I'm not about to agree with her. "I hate everywhere he is. So now I hate Germany." I sniff.

She raises an eyebrow, one of my habits which rubbed off on her, a sign we spend too much time together. "Irrational much?"

"Sooz he broke my heart ... again."

The departure lounge probably isn't the time or the place to be having this conversation, but my hangover has me in a doom-and-gloom mood and I'm a sucker for punishment.

Rather than telling me to snap out of it, Sooz humors me by continuing the conversation, the sign of a true friend, "Actually, if I remember the story right, it was you who walked away this time."

"Minor details."

"No Abby, crucial details. You can't hate the guy. He didn't do anything wrong."

A small, more rational part of me knows what she's saying is right, but for now, my irrational side is winning. "He didn't give me what I needed."

"Did you give him a chance? Was it necessary for him to give you that information right away?"

"Six years it had been, Sooz. I think that's more than enough time."

She huffs at my response. "Maybe we should agree to disagree, for now."

We've had this conversation on more than one occasion, always coming to the same conclusion. No conclusion.

Sooz begins checking work emails on her cell. I don't envy her job. All I have to do is press a button on a camera; I can hide behind my work. Sooz basically runs the show when it comes to all things PR. You name it she's done it, or she will find a way to, and she'll make it look effortless in the process.

In case this summer wasn't daunting enough, it's such a big project that we've grouped with another company from New York, so the rest of the team we have yet to meet. Why the other PR company couldn't bring a full team for the band and why they need us is beyond me. Something I've spent the past few days simmering over.

I'm getting bored, having been sitting in the departure lounge stewing in my bad mood for long enough. I angle some small talk at Sooz, anything to distract my mind. "Remind me, where are we headed?"

"Seriously Abby, you haven't even looked at the schedule? I get moping, but this is ridiculous."

And that is why Sooz and I work so well together, both as friends and in business. We keep each other accountable. Often, it's her calling me out on my bull shit, but I like to think I bring something to the table too.

"What can I say? I may have stuck my head in the sand."

She looks at me sternly. "More like buried yourself under concrete. You need to get clued up. Now. I'm forwarding all the tour details to you, again. Lucky for you the journey is over twenty-four hours, so you've got time to get yourself up to speed. If you don't, I swear you will get no help from me with any Jake-related scenarios. I'm not putting up with any shit. Got it?"

"I love it when you're feisty." I blow a kiss.

She rolls her eyes and glances back down at her cell. "Fuck!" she yells, to which we receive a round of disapproving stares from our fellow passengers at the gate.

"Bad news?" I ask.

"Catastrophic. Fuckety fuck, fuck."

"Care to share? Or are you just going to keep swearing at the object in your hand?"

"S.C.A.R.A.B.'s flight has been canceled. The next one they can get means they land the day after tomorrow. Three hours before they're due on stage." She throws the offending cell to the ground and places her head between her knees doing some weird deep breathing technique in a bid to calm down.

My mind works at a million miles an hour, as what she's saying begins to fall into place. "Damn. That means—"

"No soundchecks, no settling in, no wardrobe checks. And if there's traffic or any further delays ... Shit, shit, shit."

"Let's not get ahead of ourselves. We have the whole flight to do what we can and make sure things are sorted. Like you said, it's over twenty-four hours which is more than enough time to sort any problems."

Letting out a long sigh and raising her head, she replies, "You're right. Plus, there's nothing we can do about it now."

"Exactly. I promise I'll get my act together and I won't leave you to sort this on your own." I sound more confident than I feel, but she doesn't need to know that.

She manages a meek smile and says, "Thanks."

With excellent timing our flight is called, so we make our way onto the plane and settle into what is going to be a painful journey for both of us.

Sooz is right, I need to get my act together. I haven't spent the past two years working my ass off to mess it all up over Jake. I left two years ago to advance my career, not throw it away at the first sign of trouble.

Now my racing heart needs to catch up with my brain.

***

The journey went relatively smoothly and as promised, I used my time to catch up on all things related to the tour. It's hard to believe we're going to spend the summer at some of the locations scheduled, hanging out with the biggest names in rock music. I have to pinch myself a few times as a reminder it's real and not a dream.

All I need to do is get my head around working with Jake. In the grand scheme of things, I'm only taking a few photos of him, so there shouldn't be an issue, right? Besides, I get to spend the rest of the time with my friends, surrounded by hot guys and good music. It's a life most people would kill for and it's what has me sitting with a stupid grin on my face as our cab makes its way through the streets of Nuremberg.

The city is breathtaking, what I always imagined Germany to be like. Quite a contrast to what we experienced in Berlin just a couple of weeks ago. Taking in the traditional German culture, I can't imagine there's any way Sophie and Zoe can cause any chaos here.

It's late evening when we finally pull up to a cute hotel in the center of the city. Thankfully, the company managed to pull a few strings last minute so Sooz and I could share a room. If we'd had to camp with the rest of the festival population, there's no way any work would be getting done. We make our way into the hotel and there's only one thing on my agenda for the night: sleep.

Having managed to iron out most of the details on the flight for the band's set tomorrow, I get to wallow in my two-day hangover without being disturbed. If I was worried earlier about not sleeping due to the nerves of seeing Jake tomorrow, I needn't have been, as I fall into a deep slumber instantly.

***

Jake 2 Years Earlier

"This is it, boys. It's everything you've worked for. Are you ready?"

It's all anyone keeps asking, "Are you ready?" I'm ready as I'll ever be. I think. Since high school, we've worked our asses off, focused on nothing but the band. All the late nights, traveling and missing out on normality, while living and breathing our music have been worth it. Nothing can beat this feeling of success.

Mom and Grandpa put tons of pressure on me to go to an Ivy League school. They never accepted me for who I was and what I wanted to do with my life. It was always about keeping up appearances, heaven forbid I taint the family name. I'm surprised they didn't piss themselves when I got my acceptance letter to Columbia.

After everything that happened with Abby, the last thing I needed was my Grandpa finding out what I was up to. So, I went to the fancy college to keep them happy. It was a small price to pay, but what I didn't tell them was my plan to carry on with music.

The beauty of music has always been that it's on me; it's been my choice and he couldn't take it away if I was clever with what I was doing. The sneaking around part was easy, I could blame my absence at home on class schedules and study groups, with him being none the wiser. Really me and the guys were running around Manhattan, living the dream. It was like living two separate lives, the one I had to live and the one I wanted to live. Somehow the guys and I managed to keep what we were doing a secret. In the beginning, it was hard juggling everything, I managed to keep my grades high enough to be acceptable and not raise any suspicion. There were days that were hard, but it was worth every damn minute, and still to this day I wouldn't change a thing.

It might make me sound like an asshole, but when Grandpa passed away, it was a relief. Sure, we were family, but really, he was an oppressive dick who just couldn't let me be. So yeah, when he died, I was happy. Happy I could finally live my life the way I wanted. I almost suggested to the guys we play at his wake, a tribute to him, our maker, the one who spurred me on to push as hard as I did.

In the end I decided it wasn't the best idea or my mom would have shortly been in the grave next to him. She blew a gasket when she found out I'd dropped out of college, but she was always the easy one of the two to defy. She didn't have the balls to follow up the threats. She didn't quite follow in her father's footsteps.

When he died, my first thought wasn't that I would be free to follow my music, it was Abby. Abby and music were all that mattered in life. All I'd ever wanted.

I didn't think I'd get another chance with her. I didn't think it was possible. Not when she lived so far away. Then this summer happened. When we came back from our tour on the East Coast, I never expected things to take the turn they did. My mind was pre-occupied by the possible deal with the record label; it should have been the only thing that mattered.

Then Abby turned up that night in the club, rolling around in a puddle of beer and I was screwed. Screwed from the moment I looked down into those bright blue eyes, eyes that made me feel the kind of things that inspire people to write poetry and shit. And yet I spent half the summer being an asshole, not knowing how to take being around her again after all this time and frustrated by the fact our paths had finally crossed but we were both with other people.

I'm not sure why I haven't told her we're signing the record deal today. Maybe it's because of that question, "Are you ready?"

Am I ready to give it my all, to finally have everything I've worked for and ever wanted? But it's not just about me, I keep asking myself is she ready? Is she ready to let go of what happened in the past so we can move forward and make a go of this?

With Abby by my side, I'd be ready to take on the world. She's all I've ever wanted and now, maybe we can finally be together. There will be hurdles to cross and things we need to work around, like both of us being on the road with work, but they're just minor details. If we love each other, what difference would the distance make? No matter what, no matter how hard, I'll do what I have to, so we can have the best of both worlds.

When it comes to Abby, nothing will get in my way, not now I know what it feels like to have her in my arms again, have her in my bed. Six years have gone by without us seeing each other, and I still need her like I need air. That's got to mean something. It's got to be worth fighting for.

Looking up at John West, I wonder for the last time, am I ready? Then I make the choice.

"Yeah, we're ready."

Five
Abby

The first time I saw Jake, we were in high school and the group was out together. I was so shy at the time, I barely spoke to anyone, which is luckily something I grew out of. I remember the moment clearer than anything else in my life. It was one of those life-altering ones, where something inside you shifts and you know deep down, this is it, life will never be the same.

We were hanging out, relishing the end of summer, when time seems never ending and the days are lazy as the heat hits its peak. We'd been chatting on and off since Zoe introduced us online. We'd even chatted on video calls, but nothing compared to the moment I finally met him in person. I was lying on some grass, soaking in the late sun when Sophie whispered in my ear, letting me know he'd finally arrived. When I looked up, it felt like all the breath was sucked from me as I stared straight into deep brown eyes. Little did I know at the time, those brown eyes would be the undoing of me, over and over.

I knew seeing Jake again would be hard, but I didn't expect the full whammy to the gut and tears springing to my eyes at the mere thought of having to face him. In the two years we've been apart, I thought I'd moved on, just a little, but the way I'm reacting makes me feel like I haven't moved on at all.

I've spent the morning gearing myself up for the band's arrival, with Sooz telling me off on numerous occasions for being antsy. She sent me on trips away from the hotel room to source coffee, snacks and other random items, at hourly intervals which started around 7 AM. Anything to get me out of her hair.

I don't blame her, I'm a mess. A useless mess at a time when she needs me to get my act together. Eventually it's time to get ready to make our way to the festival, thank God. It provides an hour of my mind being occupied, rushing around using up the excess nervous energy that's been building while I get myself together.

I thought I'd see him before the band went on stage. It would have helped to soften the blow, preparing me so I could work with a clear head, knowing the worst bit was out of the way. But no, things never seem to work out with me and Jake the way we need them to. Things are always messy. Sooz demands I make my way to the frontstage area with my gear so I can get set up. Once I'm there, a whole new set of nerves take over that have nothing to do with Jake.

I've never done anything like this before, or at least anything of this size. The place is huge, with thousands of fans standing behind me waiting for Jake's band to come on. The noise level makes it hard to concentrate and the music hasn't even begun. Don't get me started on the lighting. The changing light as dusk begins to set in, combined with the stage

49

lighting constantly altering, makes me realize in all of this, Jake should have been the least of my worries. I wring my hands nervously, as my mind runs on a continuous loop. I ask myself can I really do this?

The crowd roars its approval as a stage crew member comes on checking the mic, meaning their performance is imminent. I should be worrying about my lack of experience working in this area, but still, I find myself buzzing in anticipation for the guys. I know they've done bigger gigs over the past couple of years, Sophie and Zoe have vaguely kept me up to date without mentioning Jake. But now, they're branching out and pushing harder than they ever have before.

When I looked over the tour notes Sooz sent me on the flight, I was shocked and excited at what was to come. Some of the places where the guys will be performing are the biggest and most prestigious rock festivals in the world. They're not always going to be performing in some little tent off to the side, some sets will be on the main stage, like today. It's going to be epic for their careers and I don't doubt they're going to blow everyone out of the water because that's what they do. They engage and draw you in with their lyrics and melodies before you even realize, making you want to hear more.

In the few moments before the guys step on stage, there's a buildup in the atmosphere. The crowd knows the next act is coming and the energy is electric. I can feel it around me, skirting over the exposed skin on my arms causing goosebumps, and I begin bouncing back and forth on my feet gearing myself up ready.

In the last minute, music rings out into the night. I can see movement at the side of the stage and attempt to swallow down the slight feeling of nausea.

This is it. The crowd begins counting down the seconds until the band steps out, and when they do, the music amplifies to a whole other level.

On autopilot I raise my camera and begin snapping instinctively, being careful to zoom in on the band without anything like mics and speakers getting in the way, praying that somehow, I manage to capture some decent images even though I feel completely out of my depth. My vision feels blurry and I'm struggling to keep my focus, but as the outline of Sam captures my eye, I remember this isn't just about me and Jake. It's about the other guys as well. There's so much more on the line than just my history with Jake, and it's that thought which helps to bring me back down to earth and regain my composure.

When I've managed to capture a few decent photos, I give the guys some time to settle into their groove and get comfortable on stage before I take any more. I still haven't acknowledged Jake's presence. I don't even know if he's aware I'm working on the tour.

I look up from my camera for a moment, and without meaning to, my eyes trail up the frame I've grown to love and hate all at the same time. Unguarded for just a second, I look into those deep brown eyes that stare straight back, narrowed, and it feels like the world stops.

***

Jake

"Jake. Jake man wake up. We're almost here."

I'm beginning to stir, when I open my eyes and look around, Sam is sitting next to me, shaking me vigorously.

"How long was I out?"

"A few hours. No worries though, it's not like we had anything else to do. We're landing soon so you need to get yourself together."

I sit for a moment, blinking, trying to shake off the dream Sam pulled me out of. When Abby first left, all I did was think back over that summer, replaying everything in my head, wondering if there was any way I could have changed things. No matter how hard I tried, I couldn't get her voice and the memories out of my head. She haunted me.

I turned my focus to one thing and one thing only, music. It took time, but eventually, I managed to phase the voices out. Recently though, those voices have been harder to silence, sometimes they've been impossible. That's why I made the decision I did. She might not like it, but she'll have to deal. I didn't like the decisions she made that summer, but I didn't get a say in the matter, she just up and walked away.

That dream though ... it's dredging up old memories, painful ones I could do without. Remembering is making things harder, causing me to lose focus rather than adding fuel to my fire. It's not what I need right before our first show.

Nothing seems to be going to plan and we could have done without the flight delay, but here we are. We've got a reputation to keep up, so we will show up and get the job done. That's if Abby doesn't get in the way and make things any worse. I thought everything would be fine. We were meant to have a day before our set at the festival, giving us a chance to see each other and get that awkward first meeting out of the way. But fate has its own way of dealing with things, and if our first time performing in Europe wasn't nerve wracking enough, the first time I see her in two years, I'll be standing on stage in front of thousands of people. Shit.

There's no time to overthink things.

As soon as the plane touches down in Germany, we sprint our way through arrivals and straight to our tour bus. Yes, we have our own fucking tour bus. What should have been a rite of passage, something we should have been able to enjoy, was tainted thanks to the mess up with the flights. It's not worth the risk, standing in front of the bus and taking a few shitty photos when the turnaround time to get to one of Germany's biggest rock festivals is so tight.

As soon as we're on the bus and en route to the festival, in theory, we should have been able to chill out and get our heads in the zone—something we normally would have done backstage—but there will be no time when we get there. Sam is acting like a hyperactive toddler, buzzing up and down the bus, and there's no way of calming him down, meaning there's little chance of us getting any peace. He needs to get his shit together before we step on stage or we're going to bomb.

"Living the dream baby!" he shouts, passing us each a cold beer.

Normally I'd say no. Drinking before gigs isn't something I often do, but damn, I need something to chill me out. My knees are bouncing so high I'm at risk of launching myself off the bus. I never get nervous like this, I'm usually the one to hold it all together. Here I am worrying about Sam when it's me who's the flight risk.

It's not the music making me nervous, it's seeing her again. It's only now in the last hour I'm considering what everyone was saying could be true.

Maybe this wasn't such a good idea. Great timing Jake. Who would have actually planned to see their ex right before one of the biggest gigs of their career? Only an idiot, that's who.

Thirty minutes left.

The bus swerves into the VIP parking zone and I'm struggling to keep up with what's going on. Time feels like it's suddenly sped up. It's a relief we've made it here, cutting it fine would be an understatement. We've never arrived at a venue so close to starting a set, never not had a sound check or seen the stage where we're performing. I chug back the rest of the beer Sam gave me, hoping it provides some Dutch courage and kicks my nerves in the ass.

Within minutes I can feel it working its magic, taking off the edge and relaxing me enough I find the strength to stand and make my way off the bus with the rest of the group.

Twenty minutes left.

There's no time to mess around. We're whisked away quickly by some members of the stage crew who speak urgently into their headsets as they drag us to wardrobe. Clothes are thrust at us and some woman barks for us to get changed as quickly as possible. So much for pleasantries.

Ten minutes left.

We walk into the area where our gear is being held. People mill around who I've never met, touching up makeup and straightening us out. They get in our personal space not giving a shit. It seems pointless for them to go to so much effort as we're going to be sweating buckets within minutes.

Someone shoves my guitar in my hands and I quickly pull the strap over my head, getting it into place, enjoying the feel of the only thing familiar in this crazy scenario. I attempt to tune it as best I can but with all the noise surrounding us it's not easy. It's surprising what you can manage under pressure. Everything disappears and we all zone out; we have a job to do.

Five minutes left.

I can feel my heart thudding a steady rhythm, finally settling. The closer we get, the calmer I become. This is it what we've worked for over the years, it all comes down to this.

Four minutes left. Gathered with our heads bowed low, we stand silently. We don't need to say anything, we all know what the others are feeling 'cause we're feeling it ourselves.

Looking up, with a nod, we confirm to each other: it's time, we're ready.

Three minutes left.

One of the stage crew members leads us to the wings. It's the first time we've caught a glimpse of the stage and it's huge, like nothing we've ever performed on before.

I shake my head to get rid of the intrusive thoughts. There isn't room for doubt, not now.

Two minutes left.

We hear thousands of fans, standing in front of the stage, screaming as the countdown timer on the screen begins. I do my best to block them out. Me and the guys look between each other giving reassuring nods. Nothing matters but the music, playing the best set of our lives.

One minute left.

The lights on stage dim and my heart feels like it stops. I swallow before letting out the first strum of music on my guitar, teasing waiting ears.

Thirty seconds left.

Stepping out onto the stage with the rest of the group, I strum the first chords to our opening song on repeat. The crowd roars their approval, the surge of noise almost knocking me off my feet.

"Good evening, Nuremberg!" screams Sam, while I continue strumming in the background, waiting for him to signal for us to properly begin. When he finally does, we let rip, hearing the music echo out for all to hear.

Since the moment we stepped out, I've avoided looking down into the frontstage area, knowing who I would find.

Finally, I look. It was inevitable. All I see are big blue eyes.

Six

Abby

"Holy shit, that was amazing!" squeals Zoe. She comes towards me, pulling me into a hug as I make my way into the VIP tent backstage.

Her and Sophie had scheduled their flights later, but luckily made it in time for the guys' first big set.

"They were so good," agrees Sophie with a smile. "I'm so proud of them."

The VIP area is buzzing because it's the place the afterparty begins after each band finishes their performance. It's a large tent, full of people milling around. There's everyone from stage crew to musicians, including some press. Sooz and I have worked our fair share of celeb studded events, but never quite to this level and it's intimidating to see some big names casually walking around. Most of the time the people we work with have little significance to my life, but the people I see now are who I grew up listening to, idolizing. I can't begin to imagine how the band feels, surrounded by the people who have inspired them, and are now considered to be on par with. It must be surreal.

Sooz wanders over, looking like the weight of the world has been lifted off her shoulders. Despite the circumstances everything ran smoothly. We pulled it off and there is no doubt in my mind it was largely down to her crisis management. She really is good at what she does.

"We did it!" she screeches, doing a little dance on the spot. "Now, where's the alcohol?"

"That's my girl. Nice to see you're human after all," says Zoe, looking ecstatic that Sooz is finally up for drinking. She's usually so focused on work it doesn't happen, however, today is a cause for celebration.

"Some of us know how to control ourselves and what our limits are," retorts Sooz.

Zoe rolls her eyes. "Chill out. I wasn't trying to insult you. It's just nice to see you letting your hair down, that's all."

Still not one hundred percent convinced, Sooz lets out a huff. She reminds me of myself, when I first returned to Brooklyn and was so consumed by work I rarely came up for air. I like to think I have a better work-life balance these days, that or I've formed a close friendship with alcohol that is just about acceptable. Either way, I agree with Zoe. Sooz could do with letting her hair down a bit more often, which between us all, we'll make sure she does tonight.

"What's the plan now then? And more to the point, have you seen Jake?" asks Sophie loudly.

I signal with bulging eyes that I'm not impressed at the volume she's speaking with.

Speaking equally as loud, Zoe joins in, "Of course she hasn't seen him. Do you think she'd be standing looking so relaxed if she had?"

A rough, familiar voice startles us all from behind, "Are you trying to say it wouldn't be a happy occasion to see me?"

Sophie and Zoe visibly pale, realizing they've made this more awkward than it needs to be. Meanwhile, the blood in my veins runs ice cold. I'm struggling to figure out, how between the four of us, nobody noticed him approaching.

There are two options. I can run away, or I can pull on my big girl panties, turn around and pretend I'm happy to see him and the history between us is just that, history. I'm favoring the former but the sensible part of me decides I need to turn around and at least acknowledge his presence.

I will myself to move, but my body is like lead and my feet remain in place. Zoe, Sophie and Sooz stand awkwardly, looking between the expression on my face and Jake. They all look bewildered and for once, Sophie and Zoe have been stunned into silence. Typically, that doesn't happen.

When I manage to turn, it's painfully slow. I look at the ground, trying to avoid looking at Jake until the very last minute. He clears his throat impatiently, making it obvious he's as happy to see me as I am him.

My eyes move up from his Converse covered feet, trailing over his body. His shirt is drenched with sweat from playing on stage and clings to his chest and arms. It's torture taking in each muscular part of him, muscles I spent one heavenly night getting to know intimately, after six years of waiting. A night that no matter how hard I try, I can't forget. But one night was never going to be enough to settle my need for him. I could spend a lifetime of nights with Jake and never have my fill.

He clears his throat again. I must have been staring longer than is socially acceptable and the blood rushes to my cheeks at being caught. The smirk on his face shows he knows exactly what I'm thinking and feeling. That's the thing about me and Jake, we know each other too well. We know each other's tells better than we know our own. The soft smiles I'd grown accustomed to back in Brooklyn, have been replaced with cold masks, proving I'm in for anything but an easy ride this summer.

"Finished staring?" he asks.

I want to respond quickly, show I'm unfazed by him, but my brain comes up blank when I try to think of something to say. Anything has to be better than standing in silence gawping, but when I open my mouth to speak, I stammer and close it again. I'm doing a fantastic goldfish impression, although a goldfish might show more intellect.

Jake looks puzzled at my behavior. "Has Abby West finally been silenced?"

My eyes burn. I try again to think of a smart response to put him in his place. I come up with nothing. This is utterly humiliating. Every part of me that dreaded this meeting was one hundred percent justified even though everyone told me otherwise. It's going worse than I could have ever imagined.

"Jake why are you over here anyway?" interrupts Sooz, coming to my rescue. She pushes forward and stands in front of me protectively. Her tone is firm yet professional, letting him know she means business without crossing any boundaries that would jeopardize our work for the company. "You should be getting changed and ready to do interviews with the press, then meet and greet with the fans. I know these sorts of festivals might still be new to you, so if you need me to, I can take you through each tour date's schedule and explain what everything means. Some of the terminology can be hard to get your head around."

She places her hands on her hips, a sassy smile on her lips, knowing she's put him in his place. Meanwhile I'm hating that my friend has had to come to my rescue. Zoe snorts down laughter, biting the inside of her cheek while Sophie looks around the tent awkwardly.

Jake narrows his eyes and I notice he has a slight flush to his own cheeks after being reprimanded by Sooz. He knows he's been caught and doesn't have a leg to stand on. Rather than taking the bait, he simply replies, "Not necessary. I understand the schedule."

"Then off you go. We know how you hate being late and the band has become known for being on time. It would be a shame to ruin it now." Sooz shoos him away, following closely behind.

As they leave the tent, she looks back over her shoulder winking at us. I swear I can visibly see steam coming out of Jake's ears. But it would be foolish to think the worst is over, we've been cut short and it's obvious he has a lot more to say.

"Well, that went well," says Sophie, wrapping her arm around my shoulders. "Come on, I hear the bar here is amazing, and even better, it's free."

But it doesn't matter how many drinks I have. Nothing could get rid of the sick feeling in my stomach. I've just witnessed firsthand that this summer is going to be anything but easy and this is just the beginning.

***

Jake

When we're a safe distance from the other girls, I turn and snap at Abby's friend and work colleague Sooz. "Who the hell do you think you are?"

"I don't have a clue what you're talking about," she replies with a soft, sweet, South African accent.

If I was any other guy, I'd be pussy whipped. She's fucking gorgeous and that accent seals the deal, but I only have eyes for one person.

I frown, letting her know she's not getting away with it that easily. "Yes, you do. Abby can speak for herself you know. At least I thought she could, although it appears she might have lost the ability in the past couple of years."

Sooz folds her arms across her chest, making it clear she's not going to back down and let me speak crap about her friend.

I've got every respect for her standing her ground. Our professional relationship confuses things, but she's refusing to let that interfere with doing what's right. I was an asshole back there, and I'm glad Abby has found someone who's got her back, although it doesn't make my life any easier having another female bitching at me and pulling me up on my shit.

"It's funny ... Abby told me what a nice guy you were, but fame seems to be going to your head. So far all I've seen is you acting like a prick." She's pushing the boundary hard, testing to see if I'll bite back.

I take a couple of deep breaths and try to show her I'm a good guy, despite the performance she just witnessed. A gentle reminder of the hierarchy here wouldn't go amiss though. "Maybe you shouldn't speak to me like that? Technically, I could have you fired," I say.

"But you won't because our issue is personal, so, 'technically,' you don't have a leg to stand on. If you didn't want any drama this summer, it might have been a good idea not to personally request Abby be recruited onto your PR team." She smiles and takes a breath, no way near finished putting me in my place. "I did my own investigating. I'm not an idiot and knew it couldn't be a coincidence that out of the blue, we were being requested just a couple of weeks before the tour. These things are organized months in advance. I know you're the one responsible for all this, but don't worry, I'll play nice if you do. This summer could do big things for her career and I'll be damned if I watch you ruin things for her, or yourself for that matter."

Her career. The reason why I didn't chase her down when she left Brooklyn. It's not just my ass on the line this summer. "Don't tell her." I might be ready to fight for us, finally, but it's going to be on my terms.

Sooz shakes her head. "She's not an idiot, Jake. She's going to figure it out eventually."

"I know she's not, but I'm tired of other people getting involved in our business. All it's ever done is make things harder between us. Let me be the one to tell her, she needs to hear it from me. *Please*," I practically beg the last part then soften my expression, so she doesn't feel the need to be so on guard.

It works.

Her stance becomes less defensive. I'm not sure which side to her I prefer because now she's looking at me like she feels sorry for me and I don't need her sympathy

"You still love her, don't you?"

"It's not like it matters, she doesn't give a damn."

"You would know that how? My understanding was you two haven't spoken in two years."

I shrug. "She was the one who moved to the other side of the world."

"And did you chase after her? From what I heard you didn't put up much of a fight."

I rub a hand over my face and let out a sigh. "It's more complicated than that. You don't know the full story."

"I know I don't, but neither does Abby. If you love someone, you have to put everything on the line. If you really believe they're The One, it's worth taking that risk. Let me tell you, Abby is worth every risk and every mountain you'd have to climb. If the purpose of this summer is to win her back, then you've got some serious work to do to earn her trust back."

"I get it." I don't need to say anything else.

We give each other a look of understanding. For now, we're on the same wavelength and if I play my cards right, Sooz could be my accomplice in this.

She nods and heads to where the rest of the band is standing, making sure they're organized and ready to head to where they are supposed to. I need to get myself together and follow them but take a few moments to reflect and process seeing Abby again.

What did I expect to come from this summer, from forcing us together like this? Was my original plan to try and win her back? No. My first thoughts were that I wanted to mess with her head the way she had mine, the way she is still doing after two years. Who am I kidding? She's been doing it since we were seventeen.

I don't know what I'm doing, we've only seen each other for a few minutes and I'm already questioning everything. Do I *want* her back? I have no idea. What

I do know, this is a time when my mind should be consumed by the band and the career I've worked hard for, but it isn't. Instead, it's consumed by all things related to Abby goddamn West.

Sooz was right earlier, this is both our reputations on the line. After everything we've worked for, I can't let our history get in the way. I'm the one who put us all in this awkward situation, now I need to man up and deal with it.

Seven

Abby

Last night was a doozy. We could have stayed at the festival and enjoyed the music, but after my first meeting with Jake went epically wrong, all I wanted to do was get away from there, rather than risk two rounds in one night.

I try not to feel guilty that I haven't seen the other guys yet, but once they catch wind of what went down, I know they'll understand. It's been two years since I've seen them. I should have put on a brave face and acted professionally like I told myself I would, but rather than seeing them, I ran in the other direction. All because of Jake.

A groan comes from Zoe. "My eyes hurt. Why's it so bright?"

The hangover from last night is going strong for all of us.

"At least you didn't vomit this time," says Sophie, taking a sip of coffee.

Out of all of us, surprisingly, she's the one looking the freshest. I don't doubt the memory of her Berlin hangover is still ripe in her mind and may have influenced her choices to be more sensible last night.

"Maybe I'd feel better if I had," replies Zoe. She rubs her stomach at the same time she pushes the breakfast pastry around her plate.

"You'll feel better if you eat that rather than playing with it," says Sooz.

"I'm too scared."

"Here's an idea. Why don't you stop being so melodramatic and just not drink as much?" I don't mean for it to come out as bitchy as it does, but unfortunately, thanks to my raging hangover, my brain doesn't connect with my mouth like it should.

My comment riles her up and she's clearly in no mood for my crap. "Like you're one to talk."

"I had an excuse—"

"There's only so long that's gonna fly," she interrupts and she's right.

I can't spend the whole summer being a bitch after every meeting I have with Jake, or it's going to be painful for everyone. There would also be a strong chance I'd be returning to Cape Town without many friends if I did. "I'm sorry. Seeing Jake again has affected me more than I thought it would," I admit.

"You don't need to explain. Your goldfish impression was rather impressive."

I sit, a little shell shocked. Even after how I spoke to her, it's a low blow.

Sooz attempts to intervene. "That was a bit harsh Zoe."

"No, she's right." I nod, letting her know it's ok, thankful that once again she's attempted to come to my rescue. "Last night was so embarrassing. It was like being back in high school again. I literally lost all ability to speak."

"I guess things have changed a bit between the two of you," agrees Sophie. "You have seen him naked though. I think I'd lose the ability to speak if I bumped into a guy a couple of years later, who I'd seen naked and broke up with the next day."

"That's because you don't get much practice," snipes Zoe.

"Keep your hungover opinions to yourself. I'd much rather have less experience than be known as the Brooklyn Bike," Sophie snaps back.

Her response shocks us all. It's out of character, but sex can be a sore subject with her. She's timid compared to the rest of us when it comes to guys, claiming she would rather spend the night with someone she can see herself in a relationship with, over scratching an itch like Zoe.

"How about, we stop bitching at each other because we all feel rotten and do a bit of sightseeing? It seems a shame to let being in a new place go to waste," volunteers Sooz, trying to calm the rising tempers.

"Sounds like a great idea," I say, but I would agree to a lot of things if they asked.

I'd do pretty much anything to avoid talking about Jake again.

***

"I need a Bratwurst, stat." My stomach growls loudly in agreement.

"What's a Bratwurst?" asks Sophie.

Zoe smirks. "A giant sausage ... Of course, she wants a giant sausage. How long's it been Abby?"

I roll my eyes. "Can we go at least an hour without relating something back to sex?"

"A big sausage sounds delicious," says Sophie innocently.

We all look at each other and burst out laughing.

"Where on earth are we? I feel like I'm in *Chitty Chitty Bang Bang*," says Zoe.

I look over at her and shake my head, knowing her comment isn't meant as an appreciation of the beautiful architecture surrounding us. We're in the old town area of Nuremberg, surrounded by traditional half-timbered German buildings which are incredible and not what I expected of our first tour date destination. If we visit more beautiful places like this we're going to have a great summer. Well, all of us apart from Zoe, who couldn't care less as long as there's alcohol and hot guys.

"Surprisingly, you're not far off the mark," mumbles Sooz with her head stuck in a guidebook. "It was actually filmed in Bavaria."

"Yawn. That's my history lesson over with." Zoe walks ahead, then shouts over her shoulder, "So where do we get us some giant sausages?"

"According to the guide, there's somewhere close that also does great steins. They're giant beers." Sooz directs the last part at Zoe before she gets a chance to complain once again that she doesn't understand any German.

"Now we're talking," says Zoe and pulls Sooz ahead eagerly.

Two hours later and our hangovers are long gone. We've managed to peel ourselves from one bar to the next. Heavily drinking two days in a row, we're setting the mark high for the rest of the tour. Luckily, we don't have too much work left to do with the band besides their performance dates. There's the odd photoshoot here and there, and some other small PR events, but so far, it's all proving to be pretty relaxed.

69

If it wasn't for having to deal with Jake drama, I'd be yelling for everyone to hear that I love my life.

We stumble our way into what we all agree will be our last beer stop. It's a small, intimate bar on the outskirts of the old town area and not too far from the hotel where we're staying. It's perfect for our last drink.

At least it was until we notice the band sat at a table, including Jake.

"Oh no," groans Sophie, coming to an abrupt stop at the front, causing us all to crash into her like dominoes.

It causes a scene and any chance we might have had to back away, out of the bar without the guys seeing us disappears. We've been noticed and now we have to face the consequences.

"I'll be damned, she isn't an enigma after all," says Sam loudly. He has a smile on his face, but I can tell by his tone he's annoyed I haven't sought him out yet. That and neglecting to give him any form of communication in the two years since I left Brooklyn, no big deal. "Too good even for our big famous band, are we?"

My feet feel like they're stuck in concrete, but Zoe pushes me forward, whispering into my ear, "Just go with it. The worst thing you can do is run away."

I know she's right, even though my stomach is churning. No matter what, I cannot walk away from the guys this time. They're not just any old band we're working with, they're some of my oldest friends and I need to prove to them, that after all this time, it still means something.

Sophie and Zoe make their way to the bar to order us drinks, greeting the band properly on their way past. Sooz is more professional, opting for the fake-it-till-you-make-it approach. It could also be a bit of

Dutch courage, especially after her run in with Jake yesterday. For the sake of the company, it's a relief one of us is managing to keep our head screwed on.

I follow slowly behind Sooz, who's approaching Sam standing with the other band member, Ryan, I don't know very well.

"Long time, no see!" I say with a sheepish smile.

"That's one way of putting it," mutters Sam. He furrows his brow and stands to his full height.

We lock eyes and I wait for him to unleash his wrath on me, but then he breaks the awkwardness when he bursts out laughing. "Just kidding, Abby bear."

He carries on howling with laughter and engulfs me in a bear hug, so tight I can feel the vibrations of his laughter running through his body.

It's comforting being in his arms, reminding me of the safety net he became when I returned to Brooklyn. I try to subtly breathe in his warmth and familiar scent, at the same time, trying not to make the hug overly friendly. I need to keep in the forefront of my mind that for Sam, there may be unresolved romantic feelings between us. This summer is becoming like *The Matrix*—similar story lines in different realities. If only I knew what the ending was then maybe things would be easier.

Zoe clears her throat. "Here's your drink." She leans forward, passing me a giant beer stein as she says under her breath, "I think you'll be needing this. Jake's watching and he doesn't look happy."

Glancing in his direction, I decide it's time to make a choice. I can either become a shadow of my former self in his presence, erasing every ounce of what I worked so hard to be over the years, or I can remember who the hell I am and not let a guy bring me down.

Deciding on the latter I plaster on a smile, turn to Jake and say, "Is there a problem?"

"Here we go," groans Zach from beside Sam.

He signals for the bartender to bring a round of shots, knowing how this is about to go down.

"There's no problem. I'm just watching you fall back into old bad habits," replies Jake.

"I'm gonna try not to be insulted that you lumped me into the bad habit category," says Sam, through a clenched jaw.

"Not you. I'm talking about Abby latching on to anyone she can. There's a name for that you know—"

"Which wouldn't be very professional ..." interrupts Sooz.

They glance between themselves and for once, Jake backs down. Whatever it was Sooz said to him when they disappeared yesterday worked.

"I'm out of here. The night's taken a turn for the worse." He doesn't wait for a response before leaving the bar.

"I'll go with him," says Zach. He offers me a sympathetic smile and then gives his drink, which remains on the bar untouched, a longing look. "Don't want him getting into any trouble."

"Nice to see you guys are still being friendly," jokes Sam. "Is this how the rest of the summer is gonna go?"

I shrug and say, "I'm trying, Sam, but he's not exactly making it easy. He's worse than ever."

"Do you blame him? You left him hanging and literally ran out of the country. You haven't been in touch for two years ... with any of us."

"This isn't the time or place for this conversation," says Sophie. "Why don't we try a proper reunion when we haven't all been drinking?"

"And when did you grow balls?" asks Sam snappily.

This night is spiraling out of control for everyone involved. It's not quite the bonding we all had in mind for our first group meeting.

Sophie squares up to him and replies, "Watch the attitude, Sam. It's not me you're pissed off with, but I'll happily give you a reason for it to be."

Sam stands, blinking. Fleetingly, his expression changes, like he's seeing Sophie in a different light. He shakes whatever it was off and takes a long drink.

"This night was an epic fail," says Zoe, pointing out the obvious. "I vote we head back to the hotel. We've got a long day tomorrow."

We all nod in agreement, as we really do have a long day, moving on to the next tour destination, Barcelona. The girls pack up their stuff and wave goodbye to the guys before walking to the exit.

I hold back, in a last effort to win Sam over. "I really am sorry."

"I know you are, Abs. But I don't know if that's enough."

Eight

Abby

I'm having a major pinch-me moment as I walk around the streets of Barcelona. Sometimes I have to stop and question, is this really my life? I live in one of the most beautiful cities in the world, have amazing friends and family (albeit weird), and I get paid to travel doing the thing I love the most: take photographs. It might have its ups and downs, but for all I bitch and moan about some of the situations I wind up in, I've got it good, and I know it.

After the disaster that was our last night in Nuremberg, we've avoided the band and it's been a couple of days since we've seen them. Not one hundred percent professional, but we all needed the space after some of the things that were said, and technically we don't have any work commitments until tomorrow. We will also get to finally meet the rest of the PR team who were delayed in New York when the band were and have only just been able to get a flight out.

Tomorrow's a big day and we've decided to lie low, avoiding anything alcohol-related that could prevent us being on top form. We might be in one of the most exciting, infectious cities there is, but even Sophie and Zoe know their limits and voted it was a good idea to play it cool for the night and chill in their room.

Despite being tired, the last thing I wanted to do was sit in the hotel room dwelling on what's happened so far, so I opted to take some time alone and reassess, leaving the others to rest. I've spent the past couple of hours walking around with my camera, exploring the beauty of Barcelona and trying to avoid thinking about anything to do with Jake.

The sun begins to set and there's a buzz in my veins which can only be tamed by the click of my camera. I should probably head back to the hotel and get some rest, but I just don't want to. I stop randomly, realizing I'm not sure where I've wandered to.

Thank God for Google Maps which hasn't failed me yet. Opening it, I try to find somewhere interesting to go, and see I'm close to an area called Las Ramblas. I haven't got a clue what it is, but I've heard snippets of other tourists' conversations in which it's been mentioned a few times.

When I get there, I'm not disappointed, thankful I didn't decide to head back to the room. It's a boulevard that runs through the center of the city, lined with lush green trees. It's full of street performers, market stalls and delicious looking eateries that fill the air with incredible smells. The place feels alive, as tourists bombard the area, taking in the surroundings. The atmosphere is infectious, and I take photographs of everything and everyone around me that captures my interest.

Eventually, the smells reaching my nose prove too much and my stomach grumbles loudly. I acknowledge it, allowing myself to come back down to earth, realizing night has fallen. I've been out longer than I thought. A quick glance at the time on my cell confirms it's after nine, so I've been gone for over five hours. I see there are a few messages from Sooz checking I'm ok, but that was a couple of hours ago. How I didn't notice my cell vibrating is beyond me, so I quickly shoot a message back, letting her know I'm fine as she must be getting worried.

With the new task of finding food, I'm overwhelmed by choices: cafes, restaurants and small pop-up food stalls everywhere. The heat of the day has been intense and even though I'm starving, the thought of a proper meal doesn't appeal. What does, is ice cream, especially when my eyes are drawn to the bright signs of an ice cream parlor ahead.

As I approach, the smell of freshly made waffle cones, mixed with the sweet vanilla scent of homemade ice cream has my mouth watering. The parlor itself is not what you would typically expect. The walls are covered in black-and-white photos of bands and rock music blares out into the street. It ticks all the boxes and is incredibly cool. The thought that Jake would love it here enters my mind, but I try to push it away, determined not to let him ruin what has been a perfect evening. I stay in the moment, stepping in and relishing the coolness on my skin from the air conditioning.

There is a huge ice cream display with so many flavors the choice is overwhelming, especially now my stomach has decided to crank its level of hunger up a notch. I spend a few minutes trying to decide and a Spanish girl behind the counter asks what I'd like, chuckling when I ask for some more time.

A friendly male voice with an English accent, startles me from my concentration, "Need a hand?"

Glancing to my side, I take in the tall guy standing next to me, wearing black jeans, a band T-shirt, and Vans. He's just my type and has thick, brown hair, styled long on top. His jawline is covered in stubble, adding to his sexy, rugged appearance.

The thing that captures my attention the most are his crystal blue eyes. They're breathtaking, bluer than the sky, and when he smiles, they twinkle with amusement, drawing me in. There's a flutter in my stomach as I stare into them, it's as if something is awakening inside me. It's been a long time since anyone has stirred a reaction from me in this way and it's exciting, however, I can't help feeling like I know him from somewhere but can't put my finger on where.

It doesn't matter for now, so I offer him a small smile and reply, "There's too many choices and I'm too hungry."

"My mum told me never to shop for food on an empty stomach."

I raise an eyebrow. "Does this count as shopping?"

"Possibly ... I'm not sure. Maybe I've just made an idiot of myself. I'm Dan." He offers his hand to shake and the smile that accompanies his gesture sets the awakening butterflies in my stomach into full force.

I offer my hand back. "Abby."

"Do you want some recommendations?" He nods towards the display, reminding me I came in here for a reason and he had offered to help decide.

"Are you a regular?"

"It's one of my favorite places to come to when I'm in the city."

"Ah, you come to Barcelona often?" I'm surprised as he doesn't strike me as the traveling type.

Internally I curse myself for doing the sort of thing Zoe does, judging him by his image.

"Sometimes for work I do." He's being vague and I can't decide if it's on purpose.

"Right ..." I only met the guy a couple of minutes ago and decide it's far too early to pry, so decide to move the conversation back to the reason I'm here. "What would you recommend then?"

"The chocolate," he replies without any hesitation.

"Out of all these flavors, you recommend *that*?" It's a simple choice. I would have pegged him for something a bit quirkier.

"It's all about the underdog. When there's so much choice, sometimes the simple flavors are the best and the ones that get overlooked."

I widen my eyes at his in-depth reply, not entirely sure whether we're talking about just ice cream anymore. "Hmm."

"You can trust me, Abby. It's just ice cream."

His eyes bore into mine and I'm almost certain despite his reassurances, we're no longer talking about the icy dessert.

The girl behind the counter heads back over, giving Dan a shy and longing look. Watching as she gazes in awe at him, it reinforces the feeling that I know him from somewhere, but I'm too tired and hungry to care. When she eventually looks at me, I point to the chocolate, signaling with my hand for two large cones. Dan's face lights up when he notices I've taken his advice.

"Seeing as though you've bought me an ice cream, would I be wrong to assume you might like to take a stroll with me?"

He looks uncertain, but combined with his hard rocker image, it's endearing.

My brain tells me to walk away, that it's late and I need to get back to the hotel and get some rest before tomorrow, but there's something about this guy pulling me in. It's been two years since I've felt this sort of draw to anyone, any sort of attraction and I can't say no. My heart is telling me it would be wrong to ignore these feelings and that life is too short. The girls would go mad if I missed an opportunity like this, so I don't.

We spend the next hour wandering around Las Ramblas. There's a soft glow of light from the restaurants and bars which, mixed with fairy lights hung around the small market stalls, creates a romantic atmosphere that causes my skin to tingle with excitement. He was also right about the ice cream, it's so delicious I could have eaten his as well.

We keep the conversation light, but interesting, and find we have a lot in common which is refreshing. We both love music, and he finds my photography career fascinating, especially when I tell him I'm working at the festival tomorrow. He gets excited and lets me know he'll be there as well. Everything with him seems easy and simple, plus, there's definitely an attraction between us. I might be out of practice, but I can still read the signs.

As the night draws to a close, we swap cell numbers and I plan to get in touch with him once I've finished working the band's set. It takes me by surprise when he pulls me in for a friendly hug. Besides, with the guys from the band, I'm not an openly affectionate person when it comes to the opposite sex, but there's something about this guy that's breaking down my defenses and we've only been together for a couple of hours. Rather than resisting, I find myself nuzzling into his chest breathing in his musky scent which fits him perfectly, trying to memorize it along with this night.

Pulling away, he looks down, lingering a moment longer than would be considered friendly. My instant thought is kiss me, but reluctantly he steps back and offers a small wave goodbye. His body says one thing, but his eyes look torn, like he's fighting everything inside himself not to pull me back in and kiss me.

As I watch him turn back to find his friends, I can't wipe the stupid smile off my face. It carries me all the way back to our hotel room and into bed, where I lay for a while mulling over the magical evening I've just had, relishing in the warm fuzzy feelings Dan left coursing through my body.

It's only when sleep is almost in my grasp that I notice I've barely thought about Jake. For once I made a choice and did something without even considering him, and I go to sleep with the hope that maybe this summer might not be so bad after all.

***

The buzz of the night before lasts well into the next morning and Zoe asks at least four times if I was gone so long because I fucked someone. She's disappointed when I inform her I spent the majority of the day walking around Barcelona with my camera, although her attention piques when I mention the guy I met towards the end of the night. When I state it was entirely PG, she loses complete interest.

There are a few hours before the guys perform at the festival, but this one is bigger and harder to navigate than the last, so we need to leave early. Luckily, the rest of the PR team who we will be working with on the tour arrived last night, so Sooz and I have extra hands.

The hard work begins as the volume of press interviews and scheduled magazine shoots increases dramatically. The tour isn't just about the music. At each new location there are interviews with local media, magazines, radio stations, etc., to help stir interest in the band all around Europe. Sooz has been coordinating everything with the PR team in New York, which consists of another three women we will be meeting in precisely an hour. That's if Zoe hurries her ass up.

It would be easy to be fooled into thinking a tame night might help make her more prompt getting ready, alas no. Sooz is spitting fire. Barcelona isn't the easiest of places to get around even at the best of times. Throw into the mix needing to pick up the guys' outfit changes and we're running out of time.

Eventually, Zoe confirms she's ready, but just as we're getting into the cab, remembers she left her bag in the room. Sooz looks like she's about to blow a fuse. Zoe remains quiet for the rest of the ride.

We're a few minutes away from the back entrance to the festival when it hits me that I don't know anything about the PR team who will be joining us for the rest of the tour.

I look at Sooz and ask, "Will the PR team be in there already?"

"Yeah," she replies. "They're getting everything sorted for us. They agreed they would do all the setting up and help with the sound check if needed, to take some of the pressure off us after Nuremberg."

"Do you have any idea who they are?"

She shrugs. "Not a clue, but Ange said they're some of the best in the business and will be great to work with. I guess we've got to go with it."

I can tell she's skeptical about working with people we don't know, but when it comes down to it, we have no choice. "Okay."

There's something not sitting quite right with me, a sort of sixth sense. I've always trusted my gut and it's giving off major vibes, telling me I need to be wary. It feels like whatever I'm about to walk into at the festival isn't going to make me happy. Something is about to go wrong.

"How do you feel about seeing Jake again?" asks Sophie.

"Shit," is my straight up response.

The thought of seeing him after the last night in Nuremberg fills me with dread. All I want is for this summer to go without a hitch, but that can only happen if we're both on our best behavior, which is something we both seem to be struggling with. If I thought the tension a couple of years ago was hard, now it's unbearable.

We don't have a chance to expand on the conversation, as the cab pulls into the back entrance of the festival. I might have felt like a fish out of water in Nuremberg, but this is next level. It's bigger than big, meaning the crowds are going to be huge. We already know some of the bands performing are bigger names than from the last gig and I spent the morning squealing with Sophie and Zoe over some of the people we might bump into. It feels overwhelming but exciting at the same time and the man candy is going to be something else entirely.

Then there's the underlying excitement of seeing Dan. It felt like we shared a connection last night and I can't wait to see him, to see whether this could become something more. But something is niggling away at my brain that just won't settle. I feel like I already know him, or I've seen him somewhere before, I just can't figure out how it's possible. He seemed so confident I would see him again, yet judging by the size of this festival, finding each other in the crowds is going to be near impossible. He mentioned something to do with work, so it's possible he's part of the stage crew that move around with different tours, which is maybe why I recognized him.

Loaded with clothes and gear for the band, the heat hits us after the luxury of the airconditioned cab. It's hot and uncomfortable, adding to my anxiety about working this festival. Between the heat and my gut churning its way into overdrive; I feel off kilter.

"You good?" ask Sooz looking concerned.

I can't hide anything from her, so I don't bother trying. "Something isn't sitting right."

She looks confused. "How so?"

"I feel like something's about to happen and it isn't going to be good."

"It could just be the anxiety over seeing Jake again?"

She's trying to be helpful, but mentioning his name makes the situation worse.

"Maybe you're right."

I resign myself to the fact I'm not going to get any answers standing around. After how long the journey took, we don't have the time to be messing about, which Sooz confirms with her jittery body language.

Managing to fill our arms with all the gear, we slowly make our way to one of the many tents behind the main stage. It's a much bigger setup than the last performance. Besides the main stage, this has smaller tents and stages where other bands perform. The guys won't be on the main stage today but judging by the size of the crowds and the level of noise, it won't make any difference. This is going to be one of the biggest performances of their careers.

Luckily Sooz has her head screwed on, directing us to where we're needed. I wouldn't have a clue where to go otherwise, but my role is only to support her, and the main work I do is with the camera. It relinquishes me of a lot of responsibility. All I need to do is capture moments.

"I feel like a cart horse," grumbles Zoe, pulling her hair back with one hand and fanning her face with the other.

"At least you've found a real job for the summer," says Sophie.

She grins and receives a swat to the head in return. Zoe's influencing career is often the butt of jokes and can be a sensitive subject at times.

It feels like we've walked for miles when we make our way into the tent where we're due to meet with the band. It's a buzz of activity and my heart begins racing, knowing I'm about to see Jake. I'm nervous after our last encounter. Nervous for what other hurtful words he has to say to me and how we're going to make this dynamic work, because we need to make it work, for everyone. I can only hope he's on his best behavior. If he isn't, I still wouldn't blame him after I walked away. Although it's not like he hasn't done the same thing to me.

It takes a while to find the band as they blend in with everyone else, but eventually we spot them in a corner. I see Sam standing on his tiptoes, looking around, and when he clocks us, he waves.

"Over here!"

As we shuffle over, with all their gear in our hands, the group moves position and there are three young women with them, two of which I can see clearly. They fit the typical New York PR image—pampered to perfection. If you ask me, they'd be better suited to a weekend at Coachella than a rock festival. I snicker, then scold myself for being a bitch. I don't even know them.

Getting closer, the third person becomes visible and my skin prickles as I take in the long blonde hair that cascades perfectly down the girl's back. I know the silhouette. Of course I do, because I spent my time feeling insecure and jealous around her when I was in Brooklyn two years ago.

This summer is turning into one giant round of déjà vu.

"Please, no," I murmur to myself.

Not quietly enough apparently: Zoe zones in.

"Is that who I think it is?" she says.

"I hope not, or this summer is about to go from crap to utterly shit."

She stands with me, looking annoyed. Meanwhile, Sooz and Sophie continue walking towards the group, not noticing we've stopped. Sam looks over to where we're standing with concern written all over his face. I know in that moment my suspicions are right, especially when the blonde turns around and I recognize each tall, leggy, big breasted part of her.

She shoots us the fakest smile I've ever seen, but from the angle she's standing only Zoe could notice the face she's pulled, bitch. Thanks to Sam waving us over, the rest of the group now know we're there, which means there's no way I can run back out of the tent.

"Breathe," says Zoe quietly, knowing I'm about to fall apart.

"I'm trying. What the fuck is she doing here?" I hiss back.

There's no time for her to reply, we're so close to the group they will be able to hear what's being said. Unless we want to start World War Three, we need to shut up and smile.

Doing as Zoe says, I take a deep breath in and out, then somehow find the strength inside me to say nicely, "Amanda ... Hi. Long time, no see."

It would be optimistic to think I might get a welcoming response, but what could I expect after the last summer I was in Brooklyn? Amanda is Jake's ex-girlfriend. The girlfriend whom at the time I was in Brooklyn, sadly took the brunt of my reunion with Jake, along with my ex, Michael.

All I get is a seriously dirty look, but then she must suddenly remember where she is and why we're here. Recovering, she plasters another fake smile on her face, before saying in a sickly-sweet voice, "Abby, *hiii.*"

She couldn't sound faker if she tried, but it's what I deserve after I technically stole her boyfriend. What she doesn't understand is he was never hers to have.

I shake my head trying to get rid of the ridiculous thoughts running through it. Jake isn't mine and never has been, the sooner I get my head around that fact, the better.

I focus on the ridiculous scenario that's been sprung upon us. There is no way this is a coincidence. How can Amanda and I both be on a freaking European tour with our ex-boyfriend who happens to be the same guy? There are coincidences and then there's *this*. My eyes find Jake, zoning in on him and I give him a cold look. I'm still pissed at his performance back in Nuremberg.

He looks sheepish, but then Sam leans in and says something in his ear. Whatever it is, Jake's demeanor changes, he straightens up.

He says, "Well look at this. My two favorite girls on one tour. Lucky me."

My mouth drops open and I blink. What the hell? This is not the Jake I know, not the sensitive, considerate guy I fell in love with. This is asshole Jake who doesn't deserve anyone's time or effort. My temper rises and my pulse rings in my ears. I take a step forward getting ready to unleash my wrath, but a busty blonde bombshell gets there first.

There's a resounding *slap* through the tent and Jake stands dumbfounded, rubbing his cheek where Amanda's hand made contact just seconds ago. Already it's bright red and I chuckle to myself, wondering if it will bruise. I remember how satisfying it was the time I hit him. Whatever—what he said was an asshole move and he fully deserved it. His talents in angering women haven't ceased in the years we've been apart.

The rest of the group stands with their mouths also hanging open. I feel myself coming out of my bubble of anger thanks to the satisfaction Amanda's bitch slap provided. We've gained an audience in the tent, which is slightly embarrassing, being that we're surrounded by some of the biggest names in the rock music industry and here we are hashing out teenage relationship drama.

It's Sooz who breaks the silence.

She screeches, "What the hell? The photoshoot! You can't go in looking like that!"

"Seriously man? You weren't able to hold it together for ten minutes?" asks Sam, slapping him playfully around the head.

"Shut up," Jake snaps.

His cheeks are flushed—besides the slap mark— making the humiliation of the situation evident. He would save himself the embarrassment if he learned to filter what came out of his mouth, it's what keeps getting him into these predicaments.

"Could you not have waited until the end of the day to do that?" says Sooz her eyes narrowed at Amanda.

From what I remember, back in Brooklyn, Amanda was sweet, and everyone seemed to get along with her. There was the odd occasion where she showed a feistier side, one I think we're going to witness this summer.

She doesn't bat an eyelid when she replies, "I'll act professional, when Jake learns to watch his mouth. I'd happily explain to my bosses why I slapped him and I'm sure they'll have something to say on the matter."

Sooz backs down knowing she's right.

One of the other girls from the New York team steps forward and offers a solution to the problem. "I have my makeup kit with me. Don't worry, I'll be able to tone the mark down. In this heat it will just look like he's hot."

Letting out a relieved sigh, Sooz says, "Right, let's get to work. The changing area is in the other tent and we need to hurry. We have interviews and photos to do before you guys are due to go on stage in two hours."

None of the guys say a word. Surely, they know they're in trouble and sheepishly move forward following behind Sooz, who has become a woman on a mission, determined to move past what happened and get on with the day. The PR team, including Sophie and Zoe, who have decided they're officially part of the team, shuffle behind quietly. None of us expected our first meeting to go this way, the only upside being that things can't get much worse.

"That was fun," says Zoe loudly, not even trying to hide the sarcasm in her voice.

"It could have gone better," agrees Sophie.

I try to catch their attention discreetly, widening my eyes and attempting to signal for them to be quiet. Amanda and her team are right in front of us—perfect hearing distance—but the effort is wasted. It's too little too late.

Amanda spins around and says, "This summer is not going how I wanted it to and I'm sure you're as happy to see me as I am you. But let's make one thing clear. Jake is mine and always has been. We might have to work together, but don't think I've forgotten you're a boyfriend-stealing whore. If you know what's good for you, you will back off." Spinning back on her heels she sashays through the tent like she owns the place, with her minions smirking evilly behind.

Zoe bursts out laughing.

Sophie looks horrified and asks, "Are you ok?"

"I'm not really sure," I reply.

The embarrassment of this whole thing is causing tears to brim at the surface yet again. I've spent more time almost crying so far on this tour than I have done anything else. I hate that I'm allowing old, weak Abby from high school to come to the surface and be affected by all of this. I thought I'd left that girl behind. The meek one who let people walk all over her and dictate who she was and how she was feeling. The fact I've allowed people to treat me the way they have has shown otherwise.

Anger is bubbling away, and until this point I've been a shadow of the person I've worked so hard to become. There is only one person responsible for that and it needs to stop. This all reaffirms why I broke things off with Jake back in Brooklyn, because of the fear we would hold each other back and get in the way of what we wanted to do with our lives. Now, here we are after just a matter of days, tearing apart what we've worked hard for in the two years we've been separated.

"Are you sure you're alright?" asks Zoe. "You look like you're about to explode."

The reality of the situation begins to kick in and I feel like I'm beginning to understand what I need to do and who I want to be in all of this. I feel like I'm beginning to see things clearer.

I reply, "I thought I wasn't, but I'm going to be fine. I'm tired of letting my life be defined by Jake fucking Ross. His ass is mine."

Nine

Abby

We manage to get through the interviews and photoshoot while maintaining a professional appearance. But only just. For most, that wouldn't be something to celebrate but after the shit show that's been going down, we all deserve a medal for making it through in one piece.

The band's set is also relatively uneventful. I spend the time with my camera, clicking away, trying to concentrate on doing my job and choosing not to focus at all on Jake and what's happened. If I waiver and let my focus slip even for just a second, I know my resolve will crumble.

That's the thing about the two of us together, we can bring out the best in each other, but we can also bring out the worst. There's a part of me which hates him, hates how he makes me feel and how he draws me in after everything that's happened. But mostly, I hate that he couldn't give me the one thing I needed: to have faith in our relationship and its ability to survive whatever life threw at us. He didn't trust in us, in me, enough to believe that whatever he had to tell me, it wouldn't change how I felt about him.

But as much as we're not good for each other, there's a pull between us I can't deny. Even when he talks and treats me like he has since we arrived on the tour, I can't make myself fully believe I need to stay away from him, and that scares the shit out of me. It's why I'm using every ounce of strength I have inside to keep my distance and stay focused on the job in hand. I need the distraction.

When their set wraps up, they move backstage to get changed and ready to head to the meet-and-greet area to sign autographs with fans. I'm scheduled to shoot some of the meet and greets throughout the tour, but not today, which works out perfectly as I receive a message on my cell from Dan, asking me to confirm that we can still meet up.

There's roughly an hour until I meet him and already the butterflies are fluttering in my stomach in anticipation of the night ahead. As we don't have anything else scheduled work wise before we move on to the next tour location, tonight, anything goes.

"*Iiiit's* party time," hollers Zoe, echoing my thoughts.

"Too right," says Sooz, reappearing without me noticing. "I don't know how we've pulled it off with everything going down, but there has been some good feedback."

She looks relieved. The tension caused by my history with Jake has already caused her enough stress and the summer has only just begun.

"I love it when you're not being uptight," says Zoe and laughs, throwing an arm around her shoulders. "Now show me where the free drinks are."

They walk ahead, leaving me and Sophie to follow. Since the tour began, something has seemed off with her. She seems lost, not her usual, wild self. Thanks to work and other drama, I've barely had time to ask if anything is wrong. There's no time like the present and seeing as though we're alone and I don't know when we will get another opportunity to speak just the two of us, I jump at the opportunity.

"Soph, is everything okay?" I ask.

She startles, as if she's been in a world of her own. "Sorry. Yeah of course it is. Why?"

"It's just … you seem kind of distracted. Not yourself."

We've known each other our whole lives which does have its drawbacks, one being we can't hide anything from each other.

Sophie can't hide the sadness that transforms her face at my question. "I don't know. I think I'm okay … I'm just not sure."

"Want to talk about it?"

"It's nothing really. I just feel a little lost at the moment. I've spent the past few years bumbling around and this summer it hit me. I'm twenty-six, don't have a steady job, or a boyfriend. I don't have a clue what I'm doing, and nobody seems to care."

My voice goes a pitch higher when I say, "I care, don't be ridiculous."

She chuckles. "Of course, I know you do silly, but you're on the other side of the world. I mean outside our bubble. Especially being with Zoe so much, I feel like sometimes my time is so consumed by her and everything we get up to, that I've not really found myself."

I nod. "I get it." And I do. Even though I've got my dream career and a life most would envy, it's hard not to notice old friends from high school on social media, beginning to settle down and start families. We're at a point in our lives where we're expected to enjoy everything life has to offer and make something of ourselves, but at the same time settle down and set roots. It's all a bit contradictory if you ask me, but I can imagine for someone like Sophie who's never had a steady job, relying on her parents' money to support her, that it feels even worse.

"I'll be ok. I just feel like after this summer I need to get my shit together. I don't know how, but I need to do something. It feels like time is slipping away from me."

"Well, like you said to me when I came back to Brooklyn feeling lost, let's make this the best summer ever. How many opportunities will you get to do something like this? Not many, so seize the day and worry about that stuff when you're back home. We can't do much about it right now, can we?" I hope I sound reassuring. I don't feel like I sound convincing, as some of the things she's said have hit a nerve and played on my own insecurities about life.

"You're right." She smiles this time, which is better than no progress at all.

"Of course, I'm right."

We made our way to the VIP bar where Zoe hands over some dubious looking cocktails claiming they're free and we have to drink them. Thankfully, I don't see Amanda and the other girls anywhere. We could do without any more drama for the night.

Zoe returns to whatever conversation she was having with Sooz, and after taking a couple of sips of our drinks, wincing at how strong they are, Sophie and I carry on with our own conversation.

"Have you heard anymore from that guy?" asks Sophie.

"His name's Dan," I reply with a frown. Her head really must be up her ass. She would never normally forget minor details like his name, she's the queen of gossip.

"Yeah, Dan. So, when are we meeting him?"

"In less than an hour which gives us enough time to have a couple of drinks and let our hair down."

"Where are we meeting him?"

"The Triangle stage. He was a bit cryptic and didn't give an exact location, just said I'd be able to find him."

"Weird," she frowns.

"Totally," I agree.

It's odd because last night he didn't give off any sketchy vibes. He seemed cool, drama free and dare I say it, normal. But there's still the feeling lurking that I've already met him, that I know him somehow, which is ridiculous. I'd remember clearly if we'd seen each other before.

Shaking away the feelings of doubt, I get back to my drink. Sophie and I avoid any further conversations about Dan, or her life dilemmas, opting to enjoy ourselves and get excited for the night ahead. We join Zoe and Sooz, who have knocked their drinks back already and ordered another round for us all. They force us to catch up and I feel giddy as the alcohol courses through my veins. I'm too buzzed to even notice the band has joined us for a while. But when I do, my eyes trail round the tent, searching for Jake.

"He's not here," says a familiar voice, close to my ear.

I turn and look up into Sam's face, relishing at how comforting it feels having him near again. Nuremberg wasn't what I would define as a warm welcome and the summer hasn't gone to plan so far. I hate that we haven't had a chance to clear the air after I left Brooklyn so abruptly.

"Am I that obvious?" I ask.

I hate that everyone can read the situation with me and Jake so clearly, clearer than the two of us can ourselves.

"Only to those who know ..."

"The whole group then," I say with a slight huff.

"Give yourself a break, it wasn't an easy choice to make. I have full respect for you."

"Thanks."

I'm uncertain how genuine he's being and still can't read the situation, whether he forgives me for leaving like I did. We'd gotten close the summer I'd returned. It was almost like we were back in high school. But then there was the revelation from his brother Shaun that he was still harboring old feelings towards me and needless to say, I'd understand if he was upset I left without saying goodbye.

"Do the others hate me?" I ask.

I'm annoyed at myself for caring so much. New Abby doesn't care what people think. She bosses through life, not giving a shit, but I can feel all that unraveling just being around my old friends.

"Of course, they don't." Throwing an arm around my shoulders, he pulls me into his side. "If anything, they should be thanking you. After you left, Jake put everything into the band and his focus was amazing."

I don't miss the fact he's speaking in past tense. "Was?"

He looks unsure about whether to continue, but then after a few moments, shakes his head as if whatever internal battle he had going on has passed. "Let's just say, for a while he's been a bit lost and the band hasn't been all that important to him."

"Why's that?" I don't want to be intrigued, but I am.

"That's a conversation you should have with Jake."

I roll my eyes. "*Aaaand* we're back to being cryptic."

"There's some things the two of you need to discuss between yourselves. Remember what last time was like when things kept going between everyone? It got messy. Sometimes it's best to hear it straight from the horse's mouth."

"I guess you're right."

He smirks. "I'm always right."

"Are we good, Sam?" I ask, wanting to change the subject.

"We're always good, Abby bear. I shouldn't have said what I did back in Nuremberg, I didn't mean it. I get why you left, but next time, at least say goodbye."

I try to swallow down the lump in my throat, before replying, "I will. Where is he anyway?" My eyes flit around searching for Jake.

"No idea. He said he'd catch up with us in a bit. You know what he can be like."

Suspicious feelings creep in, as I imagine the different scenarios of where he might be. Meeting with groupies in quiet locations to do God knows what, or even meeting with Amanda. My mind goes back to the way she said, "He's mine." Does that mean they're together again? The possibility causes jealousy to rise which I attempt to dampen down by centering my attention on the fact I'm about to meet up with the gorgeous guy I met last night.

We knock back our drinks and make our way to The Triangle where Dan asked me to meet him. It's a bigger stage than the band performed on, being one down from the headliner, meaning the band about to come on is huge. We're all buzzing with excitement, having been so focused on work, but between all of us, we still don't know who the band is.

Thanks to the guys, we manage to push our way towards the front of the huge crowd, with drinks in hand to keep us going. The whole time we're moving, I scan the crowd looking for any sign of Dan, but he isn't anywhere to be found. Huffing to myself, I accept that there's no way I'm going to be able to find him in this crowd. At least I have his number and can message him later, when there might be the possibility of meeting somewhere quieter.

The stage is suddenly plunged into darkness and the crowd goes quiet, brimming with anticipation. A countdown clock begins on the backscreen and the crowd goes wild, chanting. Zoe and Sophie stand close by me squealing.

"I wonder who it is?" shouts Zoe over the noise.

Really, it doesn't matter, the atmosphere is infectious and whatever the group, I know we're going to have the best night. As the clock gets closer to one, I manage to grasp the band name the crowd is chanting over and over. The penny drops at the same moment the lights on stage come on, full blare, illuminating the band in the center.

My stomach flips and I stop jumping. All I'm capable of doing is standing and staring in complete shock.

"What's wrong?" asks Zoe, bewildered.

I try to reply but I'm in disbelief, struggling to accept that who I'm seeing on stage, is part of one of the biggest rock bands in the world. "Holy shit, it's him," I reply, still gawping.

Sophie and Zoe look between me and the stage.

"What's who?" they ask simultaneously.

"Dan White ..."

Their eyes follow mine, to the singer on stage, whose voice rings out above the roaring crowd.

"Dan White. It's my Dan."

Ten
Jake

I had a plan for tonight. I wanted to get Abby alone, spend some time with her and try to clear the air, somewhere neutral without everyone else around watching and adding pressure to an already volatile situation. The summer back in Brooklyn—it's what worked best and when we made some progress. I'm sticking with what I know. Well, that was the plan.

This summer is spiraling out of control, nothing makes sense, and I don't know what I'm doing anymore. I'm still no clearer in what I thought I would achieve by dragging her here. Did I think she would come running back, take one look at me and beg for me to give her a second chance? Maybe if I saw a shrink, they would say that on some subconscious level it's what I'm trying to achieve. But it's unlikely to happen, considering at the first sign of trouble she bolted out of Brooklyn faster than Usain Bolt, leaving me in the dust.

Now, I'm like a duck out of water and if my head was screwed before we came on tour, it's like a nuclear explosion now. Things weren't working in my favor anyway, and when Amanda showed up before our set, it well and truly messed things up. Everyone looked at me, pointing a finger, as if there was no way it could be a coincidence that my two ex-girlfriends were here on the same tour, 'by chance.' Yes, I might have been responsible for one, but the blonde—that was nothing to do with me.

I should have known there was a chance it could happen. We were together for four years and I knew which PR company she worked for. She was the one who helped get the band on the radar, because she's good at what she does. But if I'd have known she was scheduled on *our* tour, I would have put my foot down. Why would I want the girl I left for Abby, spending a whole summer with me and Abby? It's so messed up I can't get my head around it.

Sure, it's nice seeing her again, especially after how we left things when we broke up, but it would have been equally as nice bumping into her in a bar back home, when we could have said goodbye after sharing a beer together. Not having to spend the next six weeks with her on my European fucking tour, while cooped up on a bus. But it's too late, the damage is done. Abby was pissed anyway, and when she saw Amanda, she looked about ready to combust. Any hope of having nice amenable Abby to work with has gone out of the window.

As soon as the set and PR bits were over with, I shot out of there as quickly as I could, letting the guys know I'd catch up with them later. Heading over to Las Ramblas, I booked a table at the smallest, most intimate restaurant I could find. I was hoping if she was going to be pissed with me, I might stand a chance at winning her over with a bit of romance on my side.

What I wasn't expecting, was to turn up a couple of hours later at The Triangle where the guys messaged me to meet them and find her being serenaded by the lead fucking singer of Six Seconds to Barcelona. Only Abby West could go on a European Tour and unknowingly gain the attention of one of the biggest names in modern rock music.

I've met the guy a couple of times and always thought he seemed fine, just a normal guy considering how famous he is. But now, standing and watching her look up at the stage with adoration written all over her face, after he's just dedicated a goddamn song to her in front of thousands of people in one of the most exciting and romantic cities in the world, I want to rip his face off.

If I wasn't confused enough over what I wanted to achieve this summer, watching her watch him, the words *she's mine* run through my mind over and over. All I can think about is how I'm going to get the asshole to back off. There's no way I can compete.

"Hey man, you good?" shouts Sam over the music.

We're standing off to the side of the group, meaning there's no risk anyone will overhear us.

"Just great," I reply, my eyes bouncing back and forth between Abby and her new love interest.

"Did you get whatever you needed to do done?"

"Yeah. Not that it matters now ..." I grumble, looking down and kicking the floor.

Sam looks confused, but my expression must tell him not to push it any further as he doesn't pry. What would be the point in taking her somewhere after this performance? I'll be wanting her undivided attention and all she'll be able to do is think about him.

I wonder if she remembers the night at the party two years ago, when we dedicated a song to her, right before we made it big. The night I swept her off her feet and fucked her senseless all night long. Not that it made much of a difference, it seems to take more than a good lay to tie her down. I'm evidence of that as she still dumped my sorry-ass and shot out of Brooklyn the first chance she got. And what have I heard from her in two years? Nothing.

It's as if that whole summer meant nothing to her. If that's the case, I'll have to make it mean nothing to me.

Easier said than done.

**

Abby

"Oh. My. God!" shrieks Zoe. "Did last night seriously happen? Like seriously? A rock star dedicated a song to you, in front of thousands of people, and made googly eyes at you for the rest of the night!"

"*Eeeeek!*" squeals Sophie and Sooz at the same time.

"How on earth do you do it?" asks Sooz.

"For one, I take a break from work." I blow a kiss in her direction to show I'm joking, sort of.

"I cannot believe you ate ice cream with Dan White from Six Seconds to Barcelona," says Sophie and laughs. "Only you would be able to do that and not know who he was, especially meeting him *in* Barcelona. I wonder what he thought when you didn't realize who he was the other night?"

"I did say I felt I knew him from somewhere," I say quietly, slightly embarrassed at my blunder. Everyone spent the night laughing at my expense, but I was too shell shocked to care. "Now I know where."

"Obviously!" the girls all shout together, before collapsing back on the bed in hysterics.

"Did he say when he would see you again?" ask Zoe eagerly.

My face drops and I shake my head. "Not for a couple of weeks."

We only met a couple of nights ago and already I'm like some love-struck teenager.

"Why so long?"

"Their tour dates don't coincide with ours until we get to France."

I wish they did though. I wish we had more time to explore this thing between us. We had a little bit of time after their set last night to grab a drink in the VIP area, but it wasn't the same as being in Las Ramblas where we had our own space to get to know each other without people watching. The night felt like it went all too quick, especially with people constantly interrupting, needing his attention, which he apologized for over and over. All too soon we were reluctantly saying goodbye.

"Makes sense. You have his cell number, right?"

"Yeah ..." I sigh, as my mind trails off into a daydream reliving the night, it was like living in a movie.

"Well, there's nothing like a bit of sexting, or even phone sex, to keep him wanting more." Zoe wiggles her eyebrows suggestively.

Sooz and Sophie snort in amusement.

"Not gonna happen," I reply bluntly, trying to convince myself of the same thing.

Zoe whines, "Oh come on. You've got to keep him on his toes, you can't just go radio silent."

"I won't, but that doesn't mean I have to tease him with sex. We are capable of using our time together to have real conversations, like normal people do."

"But that's boring. And Dan isn't a normal person, he's a world-famous rock star!"

103

"Well, it's what we did the first night. Maybe he likes normal." She's beginning to annoy me. The last thing I need is the pressure to start acting like a sex crazed groupie. That's not what drew him to me the first night here in Barcelona and I refuse to change or try to compete because he's the lead singer of one of the biggest bands in the world. Damnit. I'm in over my head.

"Anyway," interrupts Sooz, knowing the way these conversations between me and Zoe can go. "We best get packing, there's been a slight change of plan."

"What do you mean?" I ask. I don't like the sound of this, and the way the summer is going, it won't be anything good.

"Well ..." she says.

She's hesitating and I have a strong suspicion it's because she doesn't want to give me the news.

"Go on," I urge. There's no way she's getting out of this, I'm going to find out eventually.

"There may have been a mix-up with our flights. Don't ask me what happened. I have no idea. I found out last night and didn't want to ruin your Dan-driven high." She looks away.

"What does that mean? How are we meant to get from Barcelona to the Czech Republic?"

"That's the thing ... I rang Ange and she was reluctant to book another round of flights with the potential for them to be canceled again. Especially as the tour schedule is so tight, and with how many mess ups there have been already. She went ahead and canceled the rest of our commercial flights for the tour and said we had a more reliable option."

"What the hell?"

My breaths become short and I know what is about to come out of Sooz's mouth next, but I pray to God it doesn't.

She waits for me to signal when I'm ready to hear the rest of what she has to say. When I feel like I get my breathing marginally under control, I nod for her to continue.

"Yeah, so anyway ... for the rest of the tour the PR team is traveling with the band," her lighthearted tone doesn't match the strained expression on her face.

"On a private plane, right? That's not too bad, it could be worse." Sighing in relief, I smile again, but it's quickly wiped off my face when Sooz carries on speaking.

"No. They're not using a private jet. With it being their first tour, they wanted to experience everything true-rock-band style and requested a tour bus."

"Hang on a minute. You're telling me we're going to be living on a bus for the next six weeks? With Jake?"

"Maybe?" she squeaks, then darts off the bed and starts to frantically fill up her cup of coffee.

Meanwhile I remain where I am, trying to level my anger as I feel like I'm about to combust.

"You have got to be kidding me? Seriously? You can't make this shit up." I let out a groan and bring my hands up to my face, biting down on my palm to stop myself from screaming the hotel room down.

Sophie and Zoe both look down into their empty cups, not daring to say a word and risk disturbing the beast anymore. I'm starting to hyperventilate. The thought of just working on tour with Jake for a couple of months was bad enough, but now we are going to be living together for some of it too.

Me, him, and his ex-girlfriend. Not possible.

I'm talking to myself when I say, "Surely that's not legal? I mean, how many people can you fit on one bus?"

"Have you ever watched any of the rock star movies? How do you think they managed to get so many groupies in their orgies?" chips in Zoe.

I turn, eyes blazing. "Not helping, Zo. Not helping at all."

"Maybe this is a good thing?" says Sophie cheerily, trying to be reassuring.

"How can this be a good thing?" I ask dumbfounded. How she's managing to see the positivity in one of the craziest situations any of us has been a part of is beyond me.

"Maybe it's what you both need: some time to bond again?"

"Bond? Sophie, we screwed and I left the country. The guy hates me, and I don't feel too great about him either. And now there's Amanda too."

"Try not to overthink it. Why don't we just go with the flow and see what happens? You've got us all here for support, so it's not like you're going to be left alone with him." She rubs my shoulder, then stands to begin packing.

"How long is it going to take for us to get to the next place?" I ask Sooz.

She looks up from where she has begun packing.

"With rest stops for the driver, food stops, overnight stops and a couple of PR setups on the way ... we're looking at around three days. When we get there, we have our own hotel though. Fortunately, Ange didn't decide to go overboard and save money for the whole trip by canceling our accommodation as well. I think she realized a few days at a time traveling together between locations would be about all we could handle and still stay sane."

It feels like the world is closing in on me and everything is going black. I'm trying not to spiral down into the darkness, but the thought of spending the next three days in proximity to Jake is more than I can handle.

"Abby, are you ok?" Sophie seems to be the only one noticing the extent of my despair.

"I think I need some air." I jump up from the bed and walk out of the hotel. I couldn't give a shit that I'm still in my pajamas, that I should be packing, and we have a schedule to stick to. This summer is proving to be one giant pain in my ass, so for once I'm going to be the inconvenience.

***

Two hours later, we manage to get everyone together in front of the bus, with the luggage loaded ready to leave. I refuse to look at anyone and stand with my back turned to them, visibly fuming. I can't hide how I'm feeling and I'm too angry to care what anyone thinks of how I'm behaving.

"Not how you thought your summer would go?" asks Zach, standing beside me.

He's not as tall as the other guys in the band, but still taller than me, so I have to look up to see his face and when I do some of my anger waivers. Out of all the guys he is the most chilled out and we got along well when I was back home. He was supportive of me and Jake and everything that happened, which I was and still am thankful for.

"You could say that," I reply, trying to make my voice sound friendlier than I'm feeling. None of this is his fault so he doesn't deserve to have me take my foul mood out on him, especially when he's showing he cares how I'm coping with everything.

"It will be fine, Abby. You'll get through this because you're strong."

"I don't feel that way," I say honestly.

"Come on, you know you are. And I know Jake can be an asshole when he wants to be, but we both know deep down it's because he cares so much."

"Does he though?"

He smiles. "It's pretty obvious. He worships the ground you stand on."

"You didn't hear about our first reunion then? Oh, and the one after that."

He chuckles, then rubs a hand over his face. "I get what you're saying, but he's a good guy and you know he is. He cares about you ... more than I think you realize. Sometimes he just doesn't know how to show you. You guys didn't exactly leave things on good terms."

"Which wasn't one hundred percent my fault. He knew what I needed, and he wouldn't give it to me."

"You didn't exactly give him much time to come around."

Clenching my fists at my sides, I try not to get upset. This conversation doesn't need to turn into an argument, not between me and Zach. We've never been that way and I don't want to start now. "He knew what I needed from the very beginning, and that's all that matters. It wasn't just that night, he had more than one chance to tell me what I needed to hear."

"I believe you. Just don't give up on him, ok?"

"What do you mean?"

"I mean, don't give up. I know there's a new guy on the scene, but don't forget about Jake. Make sure you still give him a chance."

I don't know how to take what he's saying, but it hits a nerve.

It was easy to give up on Jake when we weren't in the same country, but when we're near each other, it's near impossible. Can I honestly say to myself I've moved on from him, when all I've done for the past two years is avoid my feelings and bury myself in work? Whenever I've been alone, I've allowed my mind to wander back to all those times with him, feeling him, kissing him.

I can feel a flush rising to my cheeks and try to distract myself back to the conversation with Zach. I hear Amanda giggling sickeningly in the background and looking over my shoulder. I see her hanging off Jake, and watch as he smiles down at her. Jealousy once again threatens to rear its head, so I quickly turn away, not needing to watch anymore.

Quietly, I reply, "I'll try."

Eleven

Abby

A high-pitched giggle stirs me from my nap. I'd hoped that by going to sleep I might be able to block out the sound of Amanda giggling incessantly at every little thing Jake has to say. I was wrong.

Back in Brooklyn, everyone would say how nice she was, that she was good for Jake and they worked well together. I'm guessing that was before anyone had to spend any long spell of time with her and before she was desperate to win him back. It's surprising what heartbreak will make you do and how it can change you and I empathize, knowing the pain Jake himself can cause and how she must be feeling. After all, I've experienced firsthand what a broken heart by his hands feels like. Still, it doesn't change the fact she's grating on my nerves and we're only a few hours into a three-day journey.

"Can someone please tell her to shut up, or at least shove a sock in her mouth?" groans Sam from the corner of the booth where we hid away together from the rest of the group.

It's been a failed attempt for the both of us to get some shut eye.

"I don't think that would stop her." Opening one eye, I find him smiling back at me.

"I could get used to this ..." he murmurs.

"What?" I ask.

"Waking up to the sight of you."

I swallow uncomfortably. It's no secret he has some underlying feelings for me from years ago. Back in high school there was a time when we were more than friends, but we never quite became more. Every now and again, even though I'm one of his closest friends, he lets the mask he tries to keep firmly in place slip.

"What would your rock star think if he heard him saying things like that to you?"

The smile I had is stripped away, as I look up to find Jake towering over us, the expression on his face showing he's unimpressed by what he heard Sam say.

"Whatever, Jake," I say.

At the same time, Sam says, "Leave it man."

The rest of the bus has conveniently gone quiet, blatantly trying to listen in to what is being said.

"No, really," Jake continues. "You have a habit of playing more than one guy at a time, why change the habit of a lifetime?"

He's trying to hurt me with his words, but I refuse to get into an argument for everyone on the bus to hear, I'm not a sideshow for everyone's entertainment. I choose to walk away before we can say anything else to each other, pushing past him angrily. The strength with which I shove him isn't one hundred percent intentional, but there's hardly any room, so it causes him to stumble back into the wall behind.

"What the hell?" he snaps after me.

I don't hear him. All I can hear is the ringing in my ears caused by rage at what he's said and insinuated, again. I'm trying to keep my cool and remember what Zach said earlier about him not meaning any of it, but it's a struggle.

I storm over to Sophie and Zoe, who are sitting on a sofa pretending to watch a small TV screen. "Where's the restroom?"

Neither says a word. They simply point to a door towards the back of the bus.

"Thanks," I say curtly and head towards it.

I need space from everything and if the only place I can get some is in a restroom on a bus, then so be it. There's no way I'm sitting with everyone while they look at me warily after what Jake said. It will make everything feel worse.

I shut the door behind me, sit down on the closed toilet seat and begin my deep breathing exercises. Immediately the anger starts to seep away, my heart rate following suit as it settles back to normal.

I'm not sure how long I sit alone but I savor the peace and quiet. I'd be insane if I thought I could have too much time to myself, so it doesn't come as a shock when there is a cautious knock at the door.

"Who is it?" I ask loudly so whoever is on the other side of the door can hear.

They don't reply, just knock again but firmer this time.

It's annoying. Who doesn't understand when someone clearly needs space? Plus, it's not like there's not another restroom on here. Why can't they just leave me alone?

Rather than ignoring it I open the door, only to be faced with Jake.

"What now?" I snap. "Didn't manage to get enough in before?"

He scowls and then pushes me back. Not so forcefully I would fall, but enough to move me back into the restroom before I realize what he's doing. He walks in after me, shuts the door and then locks it.

"What are you doing?" I ask breathlessly.

I hate that just being close to him causes this reaction, but I'd be a fool if I thought I had any control, it's always the same. No wonder he assumes he can say and do whatever he wants, and I will willingly follow like a lost puppy.

Not this time.

Banging my fists against his chest firmly, I try not to think about how muscular and strong he feels under his black T-shirt. "Seriously, Jake, you need to let me out."

He doesn't reply, just stares with such intensity any hope I had of keeping my cool begins to dissipate. I want to stay angry, but my body is having the opposite reaction. Needless to say, the breathing exercises I did were a complete waste.

Taking a small step towards me, he raises his hand. He shouldn't be worried, I'm already turning to a pile of mush he can do whatever he pleases with.

In the few minutes we've been locked in here together, I haven't worked up the courage to properly look him in the eye, scared of what I'll see there. Finally, I swallow and lift my eyes from the floor, trailing my gaze up his body, before settling on his face. It physically hurts being so close to him and all the old feelings and memories resurface, along with the pain I've tried so hard to work past, but Jake doesn't care. He doesn't care how painful this is,

113

being near him and not being able to touch him. He does whatever he wants and always will.

Rather than backing out of here like he should, he crouches down so we're at eye level and brushes a piece of hair carefully out of my eyes. "I'm sorry," he says.

"You know, you wouldn't have to keep saying sorry if you didn't always act like such a dick to me," I reply.

Any coldness that was lingering in his eyes disappears at my words and he smiles. His eyes crinkle at the sides, showing early signs of the years that have passed between us. I feel lost in those brown eyes. No matter how much time goes by, they always manage to draw me in.

He leans in towards me. He's so near I could kiss him. His smell fills my senses, overloading my already overwhelmed body. We're millimeters apart and all it would take is one of us to move forward, just slightly to remove the last bit of space between us.

"Jake?" I whisper, not knowing what's going through his head and where he's about to take this.

"You're mine Abby West. Don't forget that."

He turns and exits the small restroom, leaving me alone once again, to deal with the aftermath of his words.

***

We're headed to Hradec Kralove in the Czech Republic, where the next festival is being held. The bus ride feels excruciatingly long. Three days is a lot of time to be in such a confined space, even with rest stops. The whole experience is tiring and at times, the atmosphere is oppressive. There isn't much to do, apart from stare out the windows at the scenery as we pass by.

There's air conditioning, but it still feels stifling, which may have more to do with being around Jake twenty-four seven. After what happened in the restroom, I'm permanently a hot and sweaty mess. He's got me riled up, being so close to him without any relief. I try to avoid him at all costs which is almost impossible when we're stuck in a tin can together, my best bet proves to be faking sleep but there's only so long I can do that for. It's not just about avoiding his watching eyes that don't miss a move I make, it's also about avoiding Amanda, and wherever Jake is, she follows closely by.

When we finally arrive, Zoe darts off the bus screaming, "Freedom!" at the top of her lungs. Sooz and Sophie follow, while I finish up packing a bag with my camera kit, which I'd pulled out to catch up on some work for the last couple of hours.

"Meet us later."

I remove my gaze from my bag and find Jake sitting across the booth from me with a pleading look in his eyes. Oddly, Amanda is nowhere to be seen.

"Why should we? Don't you think it might be better if we just keep things professional?"

He sits and takes in what I've said. "Maybe we should, but when have we ever followed the rules? Come on, Abby. You and the girls should meet us out. We're gonna go to a bar and chill out. We have a couple of days before the serious work kicks in, so why not have some fun?"

With excellent timing, my cell flashes on the table, alerting me to a message from Dan. I watch Jake stare down at it, his brow furrowed, but I can't tell what it is he's thinking. Unsure whether it's because I actually really want to go—I just can't say no to Jake—or because of the guilt of being caught speaking with Dan, I find myself stupidly agreeing. "Ok, we'll come."

I get a nod in return and then he moves out of the booth and back to the band, leaving me sitting, questioning, not for the first time in our relationship, what I've just agreed to.

***

A few hours later I'm making my way through the streets en route to the bar with the girls. As we're all rather tired and quiet, Zoe takes it upon herself to offer some more of her insightful comments to Sooz, Sophie and myself.

"I feel like we're in *The Sound of Music*," she says.

"I think you're a bit off with that one," replies Sooz chuckling. "But I get what you're saying. Some of the European architecture is similar and very—"

"Fucking weird," says Zoe, cutting her off.

Sophie rolls her eyes before adding her own view, "You could also look at it with a completely fresh set of eyes and say it's beautiful, unlike anything you've ever seen before." She looks around dreamily.

Some of the places we're visiting are Sophie's idea of heaven. She's a sucker for a happily ever after and these places scream excitement and romance.

"I think I'll stick with weird," disagrees Zoe.

I know what she means, but secretly I'm also besotted with the place where we're staying for this leg of the tour.

We're making our way towards a large, busy square lined with tall buildings which are a mix of white and multicolored, topped with red roofs. Each is lit up against the slowly darkening summer night sky, creating a magical feel. The cobbled street full of people bustling around adds to the olde world feel.

"Where are we anyway?" asks Zoe, breaking up my daydreaming.

Sooz, who's been engrossed in another of her trusty tourist guides, looks up and answers, "We're apparently in the smoke district."

Zoe frowns. "It doesn't look very smokey to me."

"It gets its name from the bars. They're all shisha bars."

Sophie and Zoe's eyes light up in delight.

"Now we're talking!" shrieks Zoe, jumping on Sooz, giddy like a kid on Christmas morning.

"I thought you'd get excited by that." Sooz shakes her head. After the tense bus journey we've been through, she's ready to let go and enjoy herself as much as the rest of us surely. She directs us to a corner of the large square where there is a buzz of activity, and not very surprisingly, smoke. "The bar where the guys are should be just over here."

It takes a while for my eyes to adjust when I first enter the bar. The smoke district lives up to its name. The room is relatively large, with an arched roof, exposed brick walls and a bar lit up to one side. Rock music fills the room and an eclectic crowd sits at the tables, laughing, joking, drinking, and indulging in shishas. With the mix of alcohol and heat, there's a sexy atmosphere.

I wish Shaun were here. He'd love to see a place like this and get inspiration for Riffs, his bar back in Brooklyn, but he won't be with us until later in the tour. I opt for taking a few snaps on my cell, making a mental note to show him when he arrives.

"Where are the guys?" I ask close to Sooz's ear, so she can hear over the noise.

"They should be here somewhere. This is the place they texted to meet. Let's grab drinks first, we can find them after."

I couldn't agree more and the pull of a large, refreshing drink has never been stronger. We make it through the crowd, near to the bar where Zoe expertly pushes her way to the front. We should be concerned she's the one ordering, as her choices are always ones we regret the next day, but tonight none of us care. I need something strong to loosen the tension that has built up in the days following my encounter with Jake in the restroom.

After not too long, she comes towards us with a huge tray full of cocktails, beers and shots. As she approaches says, "And these, are all for us."

We all look at them nervously.

She has an evil glint in her eyes. "Bottoms up, ladies. There's no work tomorrow so let's make this a night to remember, or not ... if you catch my drift."

Sophie leads, grabbing a shot and knocking it back, then encourages Sooz and I to do the same. It burns my throat, and I can feel it make its way down to my stomach. Instantly it creates a warm buzz in every part of my body. We all grab the remaining drinks so Zoe can discard the tray, then make our way through the bar looking for the guys.

"Over here!" calls a familiar voice. We turn and find Sam waving, with the rest of the band in a corner, surrounded by a group of girls who are all tall, blonde, and leggy.

"Who are they?" groans Zoe, voicing what we must all be thinking.

"Who cares," says Sooz. "Girls' night, remember." She turns, raising her glass for us all to toast in defiance, then knocks back the larger one of her drinks.

If the night continues this way, it will only be an hour before one of us is being carried out, and for once, I have a feeling it won't be me doing the carrying.

"Slow down, Abby bear," says Sam. "We all know what you get like when you're on one."

I scowl at his comment to show I don't appreciate it, then reluctantly head over to greet him properly.

"Hardy har, Sam. Carry on and it will be you who gets my drunken wrath." He throws his head back laughing, before grabbing me and pulling me onto his lap.

I don't miss that Zach shakes his head with a small smile tugging at his lips. He knows this is the sort of thing that will rile Jake up the wrong way.

I look over and find him staring at us, his face devoid of all emotion. Rather than making a remark about Sam's behavior towards me, he grabs the first blonde within reach, tugging her down into his own lap, then begins whispering in her ear. All the while he never takes his eyes away from mine. Although I'm getting irritated at his behavior, I try to keep my face complacent, knowing it's a game and he's trying to provoke me.

"He bites every time," sniggers Sam, going in to nuzzle my neck playfully.

"You're doing this on purpose." I manage to pull my eyes away from Jake's and look at him properly.

"Somebody's got to have some fun around here. Plus, it does have its perks." He gives a cheeky wink which in turn earns him a gentle punch to the arm in warning.

"Be careful, Sam. There's having fun and then there's poking the bear with a stick."

"But what if deep down the bear likes being poked?"

I shake my head. "You're ridiculous sometimes, you know that?"

"And you wouldn't have me any other way. I've missed you, Abs."

"I missed you too, Sammy."

I snuggle into his side, loving how protected by him I feel. It's wrong for me to do it and all it will do is provoke a reaction from Jake, but he's playing his own games and right now, I just want to feel comforted by one of my best friends.

A couple of hours go by and we all carry on drinking, thankfully at a much slower pace. Still, the amount we consume is more than enough to create a good vibe, and even Jake seems to relax, something I didn't think would ever be possible. Zoe also gets her own way when the whole group indulges in a couple of shishas.

As the night carries on, the whole bar becomes alive, and a DJ sets up near a small dancefloor in the center of the room.

"We're dancing!" shouts Sophie, dragging me into the middle of the crowd that's quickly gathered.

The beat is slow and sensual, and soon we've unintentionally paired off with some random guys around us. I'd never normally do anything like this but what the hell, especially after how Jake has been acting with other women right in front of me.

As the music continues to pump and the alcohol courses through my veins, I sway close to my dance partner. It's not long before his hands inevitably wander up and down my body. I choose not to complain or push him away, too worked up from being around Jake. It feels good to be wanted and whoever he is, he's there to serve a purpose.

Just as I get lost in the moment, I'm hastily yanked out of it, when a strong pair of hands grab hold of my waist and tug me away from my dance partner. It all happens so quickly. I feel disorientated, and the room sways with the abrupt movement. The hands keep a firm grip. Their owner pushes me through the bar to a dark corridor. I should protest. I should refuse to go where they're taking me. This could be a stranger, but I know it's not. Deep down, this is the reaction I was subconsciously trying to provoke.

They curse as they move through a set of doors and then begin frantically rattling the handles of others, searching for one that will open. I continue swaying to the music which carries down the corridor where we're standing, in my own world.

Eventually a door opens, and I'm shoved into a small, dark space. A dim light flickers on overhead, creating a dull light, but enough that when I turn around, I'm able to make out Jake's features clearly.

My instinct was right.

"What the fuck are you doing, Abby?"

His stern words bring me out of my drunken haze, sobering me slightly.

I'm irritated by how he's speaking to me. "What do you mean?"

He shakes his head angrily. "You know what I mean, don't play dumb. Throwing yourself at every guy who comes within a two-foot radius. First Sam, then some random guy you don't know. Then coming back here when you didn't even know who it was with."

"It's called having fun, Jake. You should try it sometime. Oh, and FYI, I knew it was you."

"There's fun and then there's acting like a slut."

I'm fuming that he's insinuating this again. It's his go-to attack and I know it but it doesn't stop it hurting. I refuse to back down and cower at his feet, so I stand with my head raised defiantly.

"I can be as slutty as I like, Jake. I'm single remember?" I say, calling his bluff. "I can do whatever the hell I like, and I don't have to answer to anyone."

Thanks to the limited space, we're pressed up against each other and I can feel each rise and fall of his chest as he struggles to contain his anger.

"No, Abby. You can't."

I stare back, challenging him. "And why is that?"

"Because you're mine."

My brain doesn't get a chance to catch up. Suddenly he's everywhere, closing what little space there was left between us and pushing me back up against the wall behind, before his lips come crashing down on my own.

The kiss is frantic, and he devours every part of me. All I can do is sigh in return, savoring how good it feels to have his lips on mine. It's been two years since we've been together like this, but it feels like no time has passed at all, it feels so familiar and so right.

We don't need to say anything, we both know what it is we want. We're past pussy footing around each other which is why I don't protest when he lifts me in the air, pressing me against the wall where he anchors me with his hips, as his hands slide my dress up around my waist.

I moan in satisfaction as he carries on kissing me. Moving his lips down to my neck, he sucks gently,

122

and I thrust my hips into his. He groans back his own satisfaction. I can feel how much he wants me. He's rock hard. Full of pent-up frustration from us being so close to each other for the past couple of weeks, without being able to do anything about it. There's been no relief from any of it. I know how he's feeling because I feel the same. We're in sync, absorbed in each other's pain.

It's not long before the kiss is out of control. I continue moaning at how good it feels to be in his arms. I don't complain or protest when he manages to unzip his jeans and push my pants to the side. I also don't complain when he thrusts inside me at a relentless pace, tipping me over the edge faster than anyone ever has, following with his own release. I would never complain about anything with Jake, because he's everything I need, and he makes everything seem right.

It's different than the first time we had sex in Brooklyn. It's hard and fast, we don't have much time, whereas last time we had all the time in the world. Or so we thought.

Eventually, he pulls out and there's a tug in my gut at the loss of closeness and contact with him, even though the sexually charged energy still lingers in the room. I feel awkward. We've barely spoken on the tour and most certainly haven't spoken tonight apart from our blazing row. Yet here we are, literally screwing the frustration out of each other.

Jake pulls his pants back up. The noise of his zipper closing makes the reality of what we've done seem even harsher. At the same time, I pull my dress down, uncertain what to do or say next. I decide to look up into his beautiful, sweat-covered face. Wrong move.

It unsettles me and tugs at strings I don't want pulled when he smiles back. This was sex and nothing more. There is no room in my life for Jake, but if he keeps looking at me the way he is, then the walls that only he knows how to bring down will start to crumble. He's done it before and will do it again if I allow him.

I swallow and say, "So, that's what a hate fuck is like ..."

The words do exactly as I intended. The smile on his face disappears and his big brown eyes become cold and distant. I expect him to bite back and react in anger, but oddly he doesn't.

He simply replies, "It would never be a hate fuck with you, Abs, because I could never hate you."

I try to avoid all eye contact with him, looking back down at the ground. He places his hand under my chin and lifts it, so I look directly into his eyes. Guilt eats away as I remember Dan, the Rock God who's waiting to see me again. Yet here I am in another messy scenario, with the ex who just won't stay an ex.

I shake my head sadly and say, "We shouldn't have done this. I might have finally met someone, and here you are pushing your way back in. You don't get to do this, Jake. It's not fair. How am I supposed to move on with my life?"

"Maybe you're not meant to."

"Why?"

"Remember in Brooklyn when I told you it was always you ... I was wrong."

"How does that make this situation any clearer?"

"Because, Abs, it's not always you, it's always us. Remember that when you're with him. Remember how it feels to have me inside you, how good it feels just us being around each other. It doesn't matter how far or who you run to. It doesn't matter how much time passes. You will always be mine and I will always be yours. There will always be an us."

Stepping back, as if to prove a point, he unlocks the door and walks out of the room without saying another word. It takes a while for me to come back down to earth and eventually I find my way to the girls' restroom to clean away any evidence of what we just did.

His words constantly run through my mind and I can't help but wonder to myself, is he right? Will it always come back to me and him, no matter how hard I try? No matter where I search, is the answer always us?

Twelve

Jake

I've never known what I'm doing when it comes to Abby. She worked her way under my skin back in high school and I haven't been able to get her out since.

The first time she left, there was the odd girl and then Amanda, because I'm a guy and I've got needs. The second time she left, I went on a bit of a bender. Let's call it a fuck-Abby-West rebellion. In all honesty, things were sticky for a while there. I'm lucky I didn't wind up with a kid, and if I had, I'd stand even less of a chance winning her back than I do now.

Luckily, Sam and Zach convinced me to pull my head out of my ass and move on with my life, like she had. But that's the thing, I couldn't move on.

I went through the motions, put on a good show, but never committed to anything. I was just about managing to get by. Then one day, it was like a switch flicked and everything stopped working completely. I began missing practice sessions with the band, turned up late to meetings, refused to answer any calls from the guys outside of work and went back to spending each night in a different woman's bed. It was like I was living in a nightmare, one in which all I can do is focus on her, and how my life doesn't fit right without her.

It was around six months ago when Sam picked me up at Riffs, wasted beyond belief and gave me hard words. I never thought I'd be locked in someone's room for a week, but that's what he did. Cut off my alcohol supply and left me to go cold turkey. It was the wakeup call I needed and that's when my dry spell began. I've not been able to look at another woman since.

It's also where I came up with the plan to get her on the tour with us. I wanted the chance to mess with her, uproot her life like she did to me. I might have been a bit of a dick to her in the beginning, but it was nothing compared to what I originally had in mind. I should have known as soon as I saw her that all bets would be off. The plan, of what little there was, went out the window.

Watching her give love eyes to Dan White the other night set off a chain of events with an inevitable outcome, because when it comes to her, I have no control. So, what did I do? I forced my hand, because it will tear me apart if she falls for that guy. If she chooses him over me.

She's had it easy so far and been able to avoid me, so I made myself un-fucking-avoidable. I knew what I was doing when I rang the girl's boss, Ange, and played the fame card, demanding they had to be on the tour bus with us. I didn't want there to be any escape, I want to be there every single day until she faces up to how she feels about me, until she stops hiding from it. Sooz went nuclear when she found out what I'd done but promised she wouldn't tell Abby the truth.

I'm not the same sweet guy she met back in high school, the one who would do what people wanted. I'm not the people pleaser or the one who cowers to what his family wants. I make my own rules and play my own games and that includes anything involving Abby.

What I didn't expect in all of this, were my feelings to come back full force. That day in the restroom was like a sucker punch to the gut, being so close I could inhale her scent again. Watching her nervously bite down on those full pink lips, bat her eyelashes and stare at me with those giant blue eyes. I was a goner, but I'll be damned if she's the one in control, not this time.

This time I'm the one calling the shots and dictating how the game is played, not her. Forget nice, we've played nice in the past and it hasn't gotten us anywhere. Maybe that's why I did what I did. Last time I was a fool for everything she did and said. Naively I figured she was the same girl I loved as a teenager. Not a stronger, ruthless version, capable of pummeling the beating organ in my chest to a pulp.

Then there was tonight, which I didn't expect. Something took over me; I saw her dancing with that guy and lost it. Instinct took over and next thing I know, I'm pissing all over what's mine. I don't want to say I fucked her. With me and Abby, it would never just be fucking. It might make me sound like a pansy, but with her it's something more, something deeper. Hearing her describe it as a hate fuck made me feel nauseous and it makes me nervous how all this is going to pan out if that's the way she sees things between us.

Maybe I'm not ready to fully commit to how I'm feeling. I know she's not, she's the one cowering away. One thing is true though, and that's what I said to her in that little room tonight. There is always us. I walked away before I started rambling even more and blurted out in the moment that I'm still in love with her. It might be true, but it's not the right time to tell her yet, I'm not ready to put everything on the line when she's such a flight risk.

She needs one thing from me and maybe I can give it to her, but she needs to prove that risking everything with her is worth it. She needs to prove that this time, if she doesn't like what she hears, she isn't going to just up and walk away.

I know from firsthand experience it doesn't matter how far apart we are or for how long. It doesn't matter how much we deny it or try to get our fill in other people. Nothing will ever change that it is always us.

I just don't know how many times I can come back from losing her, and whether it's a chance I'm ready to take.

***

Abby

What on Earth is that God forsaken noise and why won't it stop? I don't remember setting my alarm last night, but whatever the offending noise is, it's not going away unless I pay it some attention. Finding the strength to roll over in what I'm praying is my own bed, I search for my cell. One hand fumbles around as both eyes stay firmly shut. Eventually I find it on the bedside table where I vaguely remember placing it when we got back last night. This brings hope that I am in fact, in my own designated bed after last night and not some stranger's, or even worse, Jake's.

With that snippet of hope, I open one eye, gradually taking in my surroundings and relief floods over me when my eyes land on the messy blonde lump sprawled out next to me that resembles some form of Sooz.

"What is that noise?" she whimpers, stirring slightly. "Please make it stop."

I still have to find out why my cell is making the awful noise and when I look at it, I see it's flashing with a reminder to take my birth control pill. On shaky legs, I make my way over to my bag, quickly managing to find and swallow it down. Now, my main agenda is getting back into bed because man does my head hurt.

"I feel like crap," mutters Sooz, having still not moved from her spot on the bed.

"You're not the only one," I reply.

The longer my eyes are open, the more my head pounds and the hangover from hell creeps in. I can already feel my stomach beginning to twist and turn, threatening to bring up the contents of what could possibly have been the entire bar I consumed last night.

There's a knock on the bedroom door and I groan at the thought of having to move again, before remembering we have adjoining rooms with Sophie and Zoe, so they can let themselves in without me having to move a muscle.

"Come in," my voice doesn't want to work but I manage to shout loud enough for them to hear.

The door opens and Zoe and Sophie bound in, bouncing on the bed, and disturbing Sooz while also making me feel even more nauseous.

"Did you guys not drink last night or something?" I moan with all the jostling.

"Of course, we did. You forget we're seasoned pros." Zoe smirks. "There has to be some perks to drinking like we do, and one of them is not suffering hangovers after a couple of measly drinks."

"Leave them be and let them suffer in silence," says Sophie smugly. She's loving seeing my pain and obviously remembering how I forced them around Berlin after their absinthe escapades. "Bad head, Abs? You look a little green."

I could slap them both as they collapse on the bed in heaps of giggles, but that would involve moving and I can barely manage to keep my eyes open.

"Please don't make so much noise," the request comes from Sooz who has yet to move.

Of all of us, she's the one who drinks the least and I'm guessing is suffering the worst. She enjoyed herself last night and let go of her uptight work attitude. I vaguely remember her dancing with a group of guys who looked like they were from the cast of *Jersey Shore*, before hopping on a table and shaking her ass for the whole bar to see. It was hilarious at the time, but she's paying for it now, and no doubt mortified.

"Anyway ..." Zoe sits up and looks at me with purpose. "You owe us one mighty big explanation."

"You said you'd give her at least ten minutes to come around," says Sophie sternly. "You promised."

"And you know I'm crap at keeping promises, especially when it involves gossip with our dear friend. Now, spill."

They both look over at me, waiting expectantly, but I don't know if I'm ready to give up the details of what happened between me and Jake so easily. And I don't know if my stomach can handle the task of talking.

I look around innocently, avoiding eye contact with either of them or they will be able to see the guilt in my eyes. "I don't know what you mean."

"Bull," says Sooz, randomly coming to life and joining in with the conversation. "You were gone for half an hour and conveniently so was Jake."

I can feel my cheeks redden as all three of them stare, waiting. I haven't even acknowledged myself what happened between the two of us and I don't know if I'm ready to tell them the truth. It felt like a dream, one in which I'm unsure whether the implications will be good or bad. However, the ache between my legs confirms that without a doubt, last night in that little dark room, I let Jake win. He pissed all over his territory as if to prove a point. Yes, it was fun, but the exchange we shared after was far too confusing.

I confess under my breath, "We had sex."

I place my head in my hands in embarrassment. They all sit in stunned silence, lost for words.

"Holy shit!" Zoe gasps. "I was expecting a kiss, but the full shebang? Seriously? Did he like rub himself in catnip or something? I thought it'd at least be a few more weeks—"

"Not what she needs to hear right now," Sophie cuts her off before she can make me feel any worse, then looks at me sympathetically.

"I fucked up, I know," I admit.

"That's one way of putting it," says Zoe bluntly.

Turning to Sooz, the implications of what Jake and I did last night begin to register. This wasn't just a case of having sex with my ex, we work together as well. What we did was beyond professional and muddies the waters. "Am I in trouble?"

"Not if you don't make it trouble." She tries to smile positively but knows our history isn't straightforward.

"Basically, I'm screwed." My hangover is one of the worst I've had, lump all this on top of it and it's beginning to feel like the end of the world.

"How did you leave things?" ask Sophie.

She's not prying, only trying to be helpful, but I don't know if I'm ready to part with the things Jake said to me afterwards. I feel like I need time to deal with it and what it might mean.

I opt for giving a vague version of the truth. "We left things ok. We didn't really say much. I told him it couldn't happen again, and Jake being Jake didn't respond, he just walked away. Whether he plans to stay away or not I have no idea."

"This is so good. I can't believe you guys hate fucked in a bar. It's so hot. You don't get shit like this on Netflix!" exclaims Zoe, while dramatically fanning herself.

"We didn't hate fuck," I echo the words Jake said to me when I described it that way.

She raises an eyebrow. "Then what would you call it?"

"Well, it certainly wasn't making love ..."

Zoe begins gagging before saying skeptically, "Yeah, because that exists."

"You just have to meet the right person," says Sophie. "Which you won't ever do when all you ever look for is a quick hookup."

"Yeah, yeah. Thanks, Mom," says Zoe and rolls her eyes. "Less about me, more about Abs."

"It wasn't really anything. Maybe we were just rehashing things for old times' sake?"

"That's a load of shit."

Sooz's response takes us all by surprise.

"I saw what you were like when you first moved to South Africa. There's no way you had sex with him without any feelings being involved. I don't care how wasted you might have been or how much you claim to hate him."

"Fine, it was amazing, life changing, and my head is totally messed up. Is that what you all want to hear?" I look around exasperated.

Zoe jumps in, "At least you're admitting it. Now that you're not living in denial, we can do something about it and actually help you."

"Whatever." My head is beginning to pound at an unbearable rate.

"Your main focus now needs to be Dan."

"If that's what she really wants," says Sophie, knowing I hate feeling like I'm being backed into a corner and not capable of making my own decisions.

"What do you mean, 'if that's what she wants?'" says Zoe at a pitch that makes my ears ring. "It's Dan freakin' White. How could she not want to focus on that?"

"Because she loves Jake and always will."

Hearing them go back and forth with the overwhelming scenario I'm faced with, paired with the hangover from hell becomes too much. "I'm gonna puke."

I race out of bed, making it to the toilet just in time before what feels like a day's worth of fluids makes its way up. It comes out of my nose and at one point feels like it makes its way out of my ears, but I may be being slightly dramatic there.

When I feel like there's nothing left to bring back up, I sheepishly make my way back into the room, collapsing on the bed.

"Gross, you smell like a sewer," complains Zoe, as I cuddle into her lap needing comfort from someone, anyone.

"Now you know how we all feel on a regular basis," I reply, before drifting off to sleep and leaving the girls to chat between themselves.

***

It takes two days to recover from my binge drinking with the girls. After emptying my stomach multiple times that morning, I vowed never to drink again, but I guess we will see how long that one lasts.

After two days of hiding from the world and wallowing in my own self-pity, Sooz forces me to drag myself out of bed. Really, I have no choice because it's the bands turn to perform at the festival and as much as I want to, there's no way I can avoid everyone, including Jake.

I make an extra effort with my appearance, going for a simple look which took over an hour to perfect, thanks to the toll the hangover has taken on my body. When I'm happy, I make my way down to the hotel lobby where we've been staying, with my camera kit hanging from one of my shoulders.

"You look hot," says Zoe. "Jake will hate it."

She winks and turns to get in the cab outside. I don't need any more reassurance. Her words have done the job they were intended to.

When we arrive at the festival, everyone settles into their roles quickly, bustling around and making sure everything is ready for when the band arrives. Today needs to run smoothly, without any hiccups. After the incident with Jake, this will set the precedent for the rest of the tour and we need to make it work.

My cell vibrates in my pocket. I pull it out to find a message from Dan which instantly brings a smile to my face. Our communication has been limited, but when I read the message which says, *10 days*, I can't ignore the excitement it stirs inside me. Maybe I'm not a lost cause after all.

"Must be someone special to make you smile like that."

I look up to find Jake, with what is becoming his signature frown. I shrug, not knowing what to say. Heat travels up my neck by just being near him and the memories of the other night invade my mind.

When I find the courage, I reply, "I guess you could say that."

He grimaces slightly. I know Jake, and I know he wanted me to welcome him with open arms, tell him there's no one else. But after everything that has happened between us, I can't lie. Every part of me screams to fall into his arms, but there is someone else beginning to give my heart a reason to beat. It's not something I can just walk away from, especially when I know how disastrous Jake and I can be together.

"Are we ok? You know, after the other night." He rubs the back of his neck and looks at me with those brown eyes in such a way that he seems years younger.

"Why wouldn't we be?"

"I know the other night was ... unexpected, and I haven't heard from you since. I didn't know if you were avoiding me."

"I've hardly been avoiding you." It's a little white lie which I'm not about to 'fess up to. "More like I had the hangover from hell. In case you couldn't tell, I was absolutely wasted."

I don't mean for it to come across so harsh and insinuate what it does, but by the way he frowns, I know he's read more into it than I meant him to.

"Well, in that case, I don't have to worry about you thinking just because we had sex there's still something between us. Thanks for clearing that up."

I flinch as he spins around and heads back towards the group with a face like thunder. Zach looks over with pity, understanding even from far away that the exchange hasn't gone well. I shake my head as a signal for him to leave it alone, praying to God this doesn't affect their set. I'll never be able to forgive myself.

"Trouble in paradise?"

It's been a blissful few days in which I haven't had to listen to her voice, but now, Amanda is here and very much in my personal space. She doesn't look happy.

"It's none of your business," I try to say it as politely as possible, but she's picked the wrong moment to piss me off.

"I told you he was mine." She's like a child claiming a toy.

"Does he know that?"

"You just can't keep your hands to yourself, can you?" she snaps. "One guy on the cards wasn't enough for you a couple of years ago and it still isn't. I knew the moment I met you that you were a whore."

It feels like I've been slapped. I'm stunned she has the balls to say exactly what she's thinking to my face. I stammer back, "E—excuse me?"

"What's the matter? Cat got your tongue? Or maybe you've been shoving it in too many places?"

I look around hopelessly, but everyone else has moved on to wardrobe to get the guys ready for their set, so lucky for me there's no one to intervene.

"I've told you once and I'll tell you again. Jake is mine. I made the mistake two years ago of underestimating you and I won't be doing it again. If you value your job and everything you've worked for, you need to back the fuck off." With that she throws her bleached blonde hair over her shoulder and barges past me, storming away and leaving me to wonder how I keep finding myself in one ridiculous scenario after another.

Thirteen

Abby

"She said what?" Zoe says.

"Shh," I say.

We're back to the joyous confines of the tour bus, en route to Denmark, so don't have the luxury of that little thing called privacy. We all peer around the booth and see that Amanda is further up the bus, too engaged in hanging all over Jake to be listening to what we're saying.

"Who does she think she is saying something like that to you?"

"I always thought she was nice, but maybe there's a side to her we didn't see," agrees Sophie.

"I sometimes got the vibe she wasn't quite as nice as she made herself out to be," I say. "Especially once Jake and I started to get closer."

"That's because you bitches turn crazy when it comes to the big D." We look up in surprise to find Sam standing in the walkway next to the booth.

"How much did you hear?" I ask, mortified.

139

He winks. "Enough, but don't worry your secret is safe with me. Your voices didn't quite carry all the way down the bus."

"Do you think I should tell Jake?" I ask uncertainly.

"Nah, I'd leave it. He knows what she's like. Let's just say when they broke up, she showed her true colors."

My eyes widen. "That bad, huh?"

"Worse." He laughs awkwardly and says, "Jakey must be good in the sack to keep you all hanging on so long. I might need to get some tips from him."

I shoot him an icy glare, hoping he gets the hint not to take the conversation any further. I'm not sure whether he knows what happened between me and Jake, but we need to keep the conversation away from sex in case he doesn't. Zoe and Sophie aren't exactly subtle, and I promised Sooz I would keep things professional, which won't be possible if the whole tour group knows about my sex life.

I make an effort to change the subject. Luckily, Sam's concentration span can be limited at times, so he doesn't realize what I'm doing. "When is Shaun joining us?"

"Back in Spain, then it's party time!" he hoots the last part loud enough for everyone to hear.

A "hell yeah" comes from somewhere else on the bus. I assume it's the other band member Ryan, who we have very little to do with. He just seems to be there in the background, loving life. Not that it's a problem. It's nice for there to be one person on this tour who does their own thing and minds their own business. I wish everyone else would take a leaf out of his book.

"It'll be nice to see him again." I smile.

I've missed Shaun. Along with Sam, when I spent time in Brooklyn, I got close with him again, thanks to working in his bar. He's so carefree and easy to get along with but has a deeper side that helped us connect on much more than a boss-and-employee level.

"Zoe's excited, aren't you, Zo?" Sam says and winks.

I don't miss that her cheeks go bright red, which is unusual as she never gets embarrassed by anything to do with guys. But then I remember how they were all over each other on more than one occasion when I was home. Usually when alcohol was involved, but it feels significant.

"Shut up," she snaps.

Sam catches the vibe and chooses to turn his attention to poor, unsuspecting Sophie. "Hey babe, how's it going?"

"Babe? Seriously? Get lost Sam." She shoves him hard in the side.

I laugh but don't miss that she looks flustered. What is wrong with my friends? They are both acting weird and not like themselves. I put it to the back of my mind, in a box for later, making a mental note to keep a close eye on them for the rest of this tour. I've been so absorbed in my own drama with Dan and Jake I may have neglected to see that my friends need something from me, which leaves me feeling like the worst friend in the world.

***

The drive to Denmark is straight forward and thankfully, for the sake of our sanity, we only have one overnight stop. We all need space from each other. There are far too many sexually charged

141

hormones flying around the bus for any of us to get comfortable. The only person who seems to be able to keep their head on straight is Sooz, which is to be expected as she's the one who has her shit together. She makes sure there isn't any shit to deal with.

The tour bus was scheduled to stop outside our hotel, so the girls and I could get unpacked and settled before any work that needed doing. But when it pulls up outside a tall building on the outskirts of Roskilde, it's clear that somewhere along the line, the plan changed.

"Everything ok?" I ask Sooz.

"Fine," she replies with a smile that doesn't suggest there's anything to be concerned about. "There's been a slight change with the schedule. Nothing we can't adapt to."

"What are we doing here then?"

"Photoshoot. The one that was scheduled for tomorrow has been pulled forward to today as some of the models can't make it otherwise. Something to do with being double booked. Not our fault, but we need to get this done. The guys could have done with a good night's sleep as they look like crap, but it's nothing a bit of makeup won't help. Maybe it will add to that rugged rocker image?"

"Maybe ..." I focus on the word models.

"You good?"

"Fine," I say quickly, managing to collect myself and make it seem like I am, when actually my stomach is twisting. The thought of the band being with models bothers me. Jake being with models in particular. Gorgeous, Danish models whom I could only dream of looking like.

As if he's in tune with what I'm thinking, Ryan shouts at the top of his voice, "Bring on the Danish pussy!"

Sooz swoops in on him instantly. "As your lead PR rep, I'm telling you now, you can't say things like that. Are you trying to have a lawsuit handed to your ass?" I've only seen this side of her a couple of times, she's like a panther. I wouldn't want to get on the wrong side of her.

I don't blame him when he cowers down and says, "Sorry ma'am."

After Ryan's outburst, the band and PR team gather their gear together and move off the bus and into the building where the photoshoot is to take place. Three floors and lots of panting later, we're in a lofty space where, thanks to the Danish summer weather, the heat is unbearable.

"Just what I want to be doing. Watching models strut around while I sweat my ass off," moans Amanda.

I look in her direction and see she looks as flustered as I am. She catches my eye and offers a small smile which takes me by surprise. She's been so cold since we first met on the tour and rightly so, but at this moment we share a common ground. We're both about to reluctantly watch our ex, who we both still have feelings for, have models draped all over him. Meanwhile we sweat like pigs, working our asses off. Maybe for this short time, we can form a united front. Either that, or when this is all done, we can find a dark corner to lick our wounds together.

In true model style, they're all late and we end up spending an extra forty minutes, unnecessarily, in the stifling heat. If we thought we looked bad before, it's nothing compared to what we look like now, as all the models waltz in looking effortlessly beautiful and completely unaffected by the temperature. Just to rub salt in the wound.

Sooz walks over to them and begins speaking in Danish, it doesn't come as a shock that she knows how to speak it. At each of the locations we've been to so far, she's known the local language. It's just another reason why she's so good at her job. People tend to underestimate her, seeing just a pretty face, working an easy job in an apparently easy industry. But I don't know anyone who speaks as many languages as she does, who can coordinate anything like she can.

It's hectic as we attempt to get everyone organized, in the right outfits and briefed on what we're looking for from the photoshoot. We all breathe a sigh of relief when we're done. It's a great room to work from and the lighting is perfect. The lofty feel creates a cool vibe for the test shots I begin taking, which is fitting with the band's image.

I start by taking photos of the group all together, which will work as great promo shots for new releases and generic media pieces about the band. According to Sooz there was a request from somewhere that the band's image needs to be a bit sexier, hence the Danish models.

The rest of the band is easy work. Sam and Ryan revel in having blondes lounging all over them, making the atmosphere that filters into the images: fun while still being suggestive, staying true to their characters. Zach takes the whole process a bit more seriously, but that's merely a reflection of his character and what I capture looks great.

Then there's Jake. He awkwardly asks, "Where would you like me?"

The other guys did whatever they wanted, and I followed their lead, giving direction if needed. They loved the freedom of making the shoot work for them. Hearing Jake sound uncertain catches me off guard.

I expected him to walk in and be all cocky. Seeing him so vulnerable tugs at my emotions and threatens to draw me in. Before I have a chance to reign in my feelings, my heart is hammering against my chest, aching at being near him and teased by a glimmer of the guy I fell in love with.

"Abs?" he asks quietly.

I snap out of my thoughts, embarrassed at being caught out losing my cool. "Erm, sorry. I'm not sure. What do you want to do?"

"You're the photographer, you tell me," he says, frowning, as if he expects me to come back with an answer right away.

My mind goes into overdrive. Think on your feet Abby, you're making yourself look like an idiot.

A velour armchair in the corner of the room catches my attention and I have an idea. The other guys all took standing shots with the girls, but for Jake, something different and edgy would fit who he is and the hidden depths he has no one gets to see.

I thought I might have been broken for a moment there, that I wouldn't be able to go through with the shoot. Thankfully, instinct takes over and I finally act professionally and show I'm capable of doing my job. Sooz lets out a sigh of relief from a corner of the room, I don't doubt she was apprehensive I would choke and mess it all up when it came to Jake.

When we manage to place the chair in the perfect position, I instruct him on how to sit, encouraging him to lounge back with one leg raised up over an arm. I turn away to inspect all the models, choosing the least attractive three, hoping no one will notice. When I shout for them to join us, they wander over smiling and I turn back to find Jake smirking. It hasn't gone unnoticed by him the reason I chose the models I did. Whatever. He'd do the same thing if he were in my shoes.

I would never admit it, but the whole thing kills me inside. I hate having to position the models and encourage them into the sexiest poses I can, watching as they drape themselves over him.

I direct him to place his hands on the two girls in closest reach, picking just the right places so the images will be sexy but not too provocative. When I'm happy with all of their positioning, I nod silent confirmation in his direction to let him know the photoshoot is about to begin. He's still smirking, knowing exactly what this whole situation is doing to me, but not saying a word, which irks me. When I grab my camera, he takes on a more professional aura, the smirk gone from his face as he stares, waiting.

I raise the camera and look through the lens, beginning to snap away from all different angles. The hard work comes when I need to get closer. So far, I've managed to avoid looking into his eyes, but now there is no hiding from them. I step nearer, not wanting to use the zoom as it can reduce the quality of the image.

I become breathless looking back through the lens and into his smoldering eyes. He might have his hands all over other women ... gorgeous, blonde, incredibly sexy women, but there's only one person he's interested in, and that's me. It doesn't matter that there is a lens in the way. The heat of his gaze is searing and my heart pounds erratically, sending the blood coursing through my veins. Every part of my body feels alive. It also doesn't matter that he made me come just a couple of days ago, I want him now, I need him. But we can't be together again like that, ever, so I carry on snapping, trying to keep my focus and cover up everything I'm feeling.

When I'm happy with the shots, I put the camera down and lightheartedly say, "All done." I'm determined to make it appear I've been unaffected by the moment we shared. One bonus of the heat is being able to use it as an excuse for any flush lingering on my cheeks.

I glance over and watch as Jake detaches himself from the models, barely giving them the time of day as he thanks them politely. He's completely oblivious and uncaring to the fact he's just had their bodies pressed all over his own.

"Holy cow, that was so hot," Zoe says quietly, standing to my side. For once she's managing to be discreet. "Did you see the looks he was giving you? He wants your ass again. I'm putting down bets that the other night was not a one-time thing."

"It was and there won't be another time," I say and start packing away my gear.

I turn at the same moment Jake does and he catches my eye, looking at me like I'm the only person in the world that matters. He constantly gives off hot and cold vibes and I don't have a clue what he wants from me but being near him is awakening the heart I've spent two years struggling to silence. I need to get out of here and stay as far away from him as I can.

Fourteen

Jake 1 Year Ago

*I*t would have probably made sense to go home after the performance. For the first time ever, I drank before and during a set and was well on my way to being wasted by the end. It's something I never do. I'm spiraling and there's nothing I can do to stop it. Zach tried to convince me this wasn't a good idea, but what can I say I'm in self-destruct mode.

The guys have gotten used to my benders, which are becoming more frequent with each week that goes by, and tonight has been the worst yet. They were reluctant and wanted to keep the night tame but changed their tune pretty quickly. Especially when I mentioned my plans to go to an escort club with a back-room VIP pass I'd managed to get thanks to the perks of making our way up the fame ladder. Ryan practically skipped out of the door, dragging us all behind him. Now, except Zach, they're all equally as wasted.

It all seemed like a good idea at the beginning of the night. It always does when the buzz is fresh. However, like with anything I do at the moment, it only lasts so long before it gets out of hand and I'm left feeling empty.

A group of women walk in. They're gorgeous, dressed only in lingerie. Sam and Ryan both groan beside me. They never can hide their love for women, and despite their protests of how I've been behaving recently, it's part of the fame game they love the most. They wouldn't be here otherwise. I know that deep down their intentions are the same as mine.

"Holy shit," slurs Sam. "I didn't know it was possible to look so damn good."

"Remind me why we can't touch them again," says Ryan, adjusting himself inside his pants.

Looking down at the joint in my hand, I try to piece together where it's come from but come up blank. I take a long drag, too long as I begin choking on the smoke I've inhaled, looking like an amateur. "If you value your balls and want to keep them where they belong, you won't touch any of these girls. It's against policy," I say.

I might be wasted, but even I'm not a big enough fool to break the rules. It's always the case with places like this, you can look but you can't touch. Even VIPs have to follow the rules. There are special places if you want to go further, but you're stepping over a line, going into a world much darker than even I'm willing to go, no matter how far down the rabbit hole I am.

Like the joint, out of nowhere, a tray of drinks appears on the table in front of where we're sitting and I lean forward, picking one up and downing half in one go. I'm gonna pay for this tomorrow, but for now I need to forget.

"Are you sure you want to keep drinking?" asks Zach.

Out of all of us, he's the one who kept his head on straight tonight. He's had the odd drink but I'm sure the only reason he came along was to make sure we all left at the end of the night in one piece.

"If you don't like what you see, you can leave," I snap.

I shouldn't speak to him like I am. He's one of my closest friends and only has my best interests at heart, but when I'm in self-destruct mode it means shitting all over the people who care about me the most in the process.

"Don't be a dick." He looks at me sadly and I know he gets why I'm being the way I am. He knows I'm hurting, because of her.

All it does is piss me off. I don't need his pity. I give him the one fingered salute, down the rest of my drink and pick up another, knocking this one back in one gulp.

He shakes his head. "You're going to regret this ... you know you are. Pushing your career down the gutter isn't the way forward. If you fuck everything up by losing yourself at the bottom of a bottle every night, then the reason she walked away will have been for nothing."

"You don't know what you're talking about." The room tilts dramatically from side to side as the two drinks I consumed begin to take effect.

"I'm right, you know I am. She would be disappointed in you if she saw the state you've got yourself into. She walked away for you, and what are you doing with that opportunity she gave you? Fucking it up, that's what."

It's gotten to that point of the night where the clubs' inhabitants are wasted, and there's only one *thing on everyone's mind: the women. The music amps up a notch, as if someone knows I need the relief from this conversation. It's so loud there's no way we can continue talking, thank God.*

What Zach said is too much for me to handle, so I do my best to focus on the beautiful women in front of me, all who begin dancing in a group.

"Let's get the party started, boys," I hoot. I sound like a grade-A dick. Sober me would cringe, but I'm so far gone I don't care. Standing, I fish out my wallet and throw down a huge stash of bills on the table and wink over at Sam and Ryan. "Extra services."

Ryan's eyes practically bug out of his head at the sight of all the money on the table. "Holy shit! Where did you get all that?"

"The old man left it behind. It's dirty money and it's what he would have done with it. Something worthless just like he was."

"Blowing away your inheritance now as well," shouts Zach over the noise, coming in for another round. "You're not proving anything by using the money he gave you like this. You just look like a fool. Maybe it would be a royal fuck you to him by doing something useful with it, something he hated. Like putting it into your music?"

He's right and what he's saying makes perfect sense, but I don't care, I'm too lost in myself.

"If you're going to keep bitching at me, you might as well leave." I gesture with my hands towards the door.

He doesn't take the hint. Instead, he shakes his head. "I'm your best friend. I'm not leaving you here when you're like this."

"Whatever."

Without realizing it, the girls had scooped up the money and began a sensual dance in front of us. There's one with long, coppery brown hair, dressed in some sort of silver sparkling underwear that catches my eye. Trying to focus, I raise my hand, staring directly at her. I wiggle my finger, beckoning her to come towards me.

She smiles seductively, making her way over. When she's closer, she pushes me back into the armchair I'm sitting in and straddles my lap.

Continuing her dance, she starts grinding down into my groin. Of course, I enjoy it. I'm a guy ... a heartbroken guy. Who wouldn't enjoy having a beautiful woman rubbing themselves all over their body?

"Tell me what you like," she whispers huskily into my ear.

"Anything, baby," I reply.

My palms are itching to touch her, but I can't or this night will be over and our asses will be tossed out on the sidewalk before we know what's happening. I close my eyes and lean my head back against the chair, relishing in the feeling of having a woman close. It's been a while and it feels good, even if I can only look.

A few minutes pass, and I can feel the last drinks I downed taking over. I'm beginning to lose all sense of reality as the room starts spinning at an unbearable rate. I'm past the point of return and nothing makes sense, but this is what I wanted, wasn't it? I wanted to come out, get wasted and forget about everything.

"Jake, you need to open your eyes." I hear Ryan's voice somewhere in the distance.

"They're open," I say. Maybe they are, maybe they aren't. I'm not sure anymore.

"Seriously man, I'm not messing. You can't fall asleep in here. You'll have us kicked out."

"That's what you wanted isn't it?" I say, with a slur. Some part of my brain is still able to function, and I open my eyes, only to have them lock on the woman dancing over me. At first, I don't believe what I'm seeing. It can't be happening, it's a dream come true as I stare into those bright blue eyes I know so well, her long brown hair draping over me. I feel like I've died and gone to heaven. How is it possible she's here? "Abby, baby. What are you doing here?"

"Jake. Abby isn't here," Zach's voice is closer.

I turn and find him crouched down next to me, his face worried.

"Shit. You're so far gone. I knew this was a stupid idea." Shaking his head, he stands, turns to the girl and says, "We're done here."

They all titter in disappointment at the fact they won't be getting any more money out of us tonight.

Zach shakes his head firmly, letting them know he means business. "We're done," he repeats more firmly.

They must see something written on his face, as they don't argue and begin leaving the room.

"What did you do that for?" moan Sam and Ryan in unison.

"Because Jake is beyond wasted. If we stand any chance of getting him out of here in one piece we need to go. Now."

They both look over, and mutter, "Fuck" under their breaths when they see the state I'm in. I'm a mess, I don't have to see myself to know it.

I don't know how I get home, I black out before we even leave the club. I've sunk to a new low.

There's a small part of me that knows how bad I've allowed things to get, now I'm even hallucinating she's here with me. It doesn't matter what I do, I can't get Abby West from my mind. It's been over a year since she walked away, and rather than helping my life become better like she claimed it would, I've spiraled out of control, to the point of no return.

This has to end. I can't keep going on like this or I'll destroy everything around me. Even in an unconscious state, I'm fitful, dreaming of the girl with the big blue eyes who walked away and took my heart with her.

She didn't help me. She broke me. Now, she haunts me.

***

Abby

I stuck with my gut instinct and even though we've been in Denmark for three days, I've managed to avoid any contact with Jake like the plague. It should have been easy considering the band's staying on the tour bus and the PR team in a hotel, but I'm beginning to learn that when Jake wants to be in my life, he will stop at nothing until it happens.

There's been the odd PR event which made it inevitable I was going to see him, but it's the other times that have been baffling. No matter where I go with the girls, conveniently he appears at the same place with the band. Each time I've made it clear I want nothing to do with him, turning back around and walking away. However, there's only so many times that's going to fly before he begins to push harder.

We're at the next festival, getting ready for the band's set. It doesn't come as a surprise when I turn around, after being standing for a good ten minutes organizing my kit, and slam straight into a strong chest. I don't need to look to know it's him. My body reacts instinctively.

His voice comes out gravelly, as he attempts to keep it low, so no one else can hear. There are press and bloggers swarming around the tent, and the last thing we need is them picking up on what he's going to say, as it would no doubt find its way right to the gossip pages.

"You've been avoiding me."

It makes it so much harder when I have to look in his eyes so I don't, but I can't stand staring at the floor, it's making this whole thing even more awkward. I raise my eyes and focus on his chin, it's a happy medium, and to the outside world I look like I'm engaging with him. Really, I'm avoiding the penetrating gaze of those brown eyes that make me do and agree to things I wouldn't normally.

"I haven't," I blatantly lie.

Not impressed, he snaps, "Yes, you have. I'm not an idiot, Abby."

"I know you're not, but I haven't been avoiding you. I've been busy."

"Oh really?" My eyes move up to his face despite my best efforts, to find he's looking at me with an amused expression. "What exactly have you been busy with?"

It's annoying that he thinks I just run about doing whatever. He knows how important my career is, and the fact he's belittling what I do riles me up.

"I'm here to work this summer, Jake. The purpose of me being here isn't just to chase you around."

Throwing his head back, he lets out a deep laugh. It's been a long time since I've seen this carefree side to him. The last time was back in Brooklyn, the morning we were in bed together. Blinking, I try to get my mind back on track, rather than reminiscing over the time we had together.

Recovering from his outburst, he replies, "Calm down, Abs. You're so easy to wind up."

I should have known he was doing it on purpose, trying to get a reaction. "Whatever."

Even though he was joking, I'm pissed. More so that he managed to get a reaction from me so easily. It shows I care what he thinks, and that's the last thing I want him to know.

"Have dinner with me."

Stunned into silence, it takes a moment to understand what he's just asked. "Excuse me?"

"You heard. Have dinner with me." His eyes have softened, urging me to say yes.

"You can't just order me around like that, and we can't mix work with pleasure. After last time when you said the help came with benefits, I'll end up with a reputation."

"I was being an asshole back then, and so far on this tour. Let me make it up to you."

It's playing out just like my time in Brooklyn. Angry, passion-filled meetings where we snipe at each other while secretly wanting more but not admitting it to ourselves or each other. The difference now being that neither of us is attached. So, what is there holding me back?

Dan springs to mind. We barely know each other in the grand scheme of things, so what does it really matter what I do? I'm hardly breaking his trust when we've yet to even go on a date. I can't deny the connection we shared the couple of times we met though, and it's that which has me hesitating.

Would he be happy if he knew I was running around with other guys? Most likely not. But can I trust him to be a saint himself? He's the singer of one of the biggest rock bands in the world and with that comes groupies and hordes of women throwing themselves his way for a chance to be with someone famous.

If I say yes, it feels like I'm giving up. Giving up on what my gut is telling me, that no matter how we both feel about each other, it's still not the right time. Something feels off and it doesn't feel like everything will slot into place like it needs to. If I say yes, the past two years of pain and heartbreak will have been for nothing, because we're in the exact same predicament we were back then, with the exact same battles awaiting us. Even if he finally told me the truth, Jake and I are both at pivotal points in our career, we would hold each other back.

My head's spinning, I'm so confused and at a loss as to what to do. Life's short though, and what have I got to lose, apart from my heart to Jake, again? It's when I look up and see the eager expression on his face, those giant, pleading brown eyes that undo me every time bearing into my soul. I know I'm a goner.

"Okay."

***

Trying to concentrate on photographing the band is proving more difficult than I thought after agreeing to go out with Jake afterwards. Attempting to keep my focus, I stand with my camera held up to my face, waiting for them to come on stage, wanting to capture the very first moments, the expressions on their faces when the enormity of the crowd registers for the first time.

It will be near impossible if I carry on daydreaming about tonight and the possibilities of what could happen. What do I wear? Is it a date? Does he expect something to happen? What does it mean for us if something does happen? Just a handful of the questions flooding my mind.

"You still love him, don't you?" Amanda is standing next to me, looking up at the stage also.

"I don't know what you're talking about," I lie through my teeth and look back through the lens.

The stage lights up and the crowd goes wild as S.C.A.R.A.B.'s opening riffs fill the night sky. I spend the next few moments in the zone, capturing as many pictures as I can and almost forget Amanda is there.

The loud music doesn't deter her from what she came to say. "He's not right for you."

This stops me in my tracks. "And you would know that how?"

"Surely you would be together after all these years if it were meant to be. Can't you see that it's not?"

Part of me agrees with what she's saying, it's like listening to the voices in my own head. Still, I refuse to back down despite the truth in her words. The same truth running through my mind over and over.

Breathing steadily through my nose, trying not to lose my temper, I reply, "It's none of your business why we are, or aren't, together."

I'm fuming and any hope I had from the day at the photoshoot, that maybe we could work past our issues and get along, are flushed away. One thing we both agree on is we don't want to see Jake with other women, model-like women. One thing we don't agree on, however, is that we each want Jake and who should have him.

"You made it my business when you went behind my back and took him from me. What was it? Five minutes after I left Coney Island before you jumped the gun?"

It stings how true her words are and make me sound like the world's biggest bitch. What she doesn't understand is that Jake was never hers. There's only one heart he's ever belonged to and that's mine.

I'm losing control of everything, allowing myself to think, feel, acknowledge things I've been working so hard not to. If I begin to go down this path, I may not find my way back. I look back at the stage and at Jake, who, even though he's performing in front of thousands of people, has his attention centered on me and the conversation I'm having.

He looks worried and I don't want to distract him anymore, so I move around, taking photos of the other band members. I see Sam glancing between me, Amanda and Jake with a worried expression. This isn't good. If we carry on like this, it's going to mess up their set and that's the last thing Amanda or I want.

I spin around and almost crash into her. I hadn't realized she'd been following so closely.

"Look. There's a time and a place to have a conversation like this, and this isn't one of them. I know you have beef with me but bringing it up in the middle of one of their biggest performances is not going to help anyone. You want to win Jake back? Then leave, now. Ruining his career is not going to make him fall back in love with you. Now go and do your job, so I can focus on doing mine."

She scowls knowing I'm right and turns to leave but there's one thing that doesn't sit right with me. The guilt from that summer. I quickly grab her arm and she looks at me bewildered that I have more to say after my little speech.

I swallow and say, "For the record, I'm sorry. I never meant to hurt you."

I return to photographing the set, and after a few minutes, in the corner of my vision, I see her turn and walk away, heading back into the VIP tent.

Letting out an aggravated breath, I try to give my attention one hundred percent back to the guys on stage. It's not for myself, but for the band and everything they've worked so hard for.

Fifteen

Abby

"That bitch just doesn't know when to leave it alone," says Zoe angrily. She's standing behind me, tugging at my hair as a vent for her frustration. She's supposed to be curling it as I'm getting ready to head out with Jake, but at the rate she's going there may not be anything left to curl.

"Ow, watch it!" I yelp when she waves the searing hot curling tongues incredibly close to my face.

"You need to see things from her perspective," says Sophie. "She's heartbroken."

Which is why I apologized. Not that I say this out loud.

Zoe lets out a shrill laugh. "Honestly, you guys and your heartbreak. You need to practice casual sex. There's none of this heartbroken shit. I mean come on. It has been over two years. How can she still be pining for him? She needs to get a grip."

"You could also be saying the same thing to me ..." Feeling disheartened, I look down into my lap my gut sinking at her words.

Realizing her mistake, she begins to backtrack, "You know what I mean. It's different with you guys, you have history—"

"But we weren't together near as long as he and Amanda were," I interrupt.

This shuts her up for a few minutes. She continues curling my hair into soft waves. I can see she's concentrating hard, figuring out how to respond. She's so lost in her own thoughts I'm worried she might end up burning my hair.

"I think what Zoe means is that Jake's always shown he's been interested in you. You keep going back to each other and the feelings are mutual," says Sooz, joining in the conversation even though she's trying to work from her laptop on the bed. "Jake wasn't interested in Amanda for a long time, and she needs to accept that at some point. I'm also assuming he hasn't given her any reason to believe he wants to be with her, especially as he's spent most of the tour staring in your direction."

"No, he hasn't." I shake my head dismissively which earns a hair tug from Zoe, along with a stern look, making me aware I need to sit still.

"Yes, he has," confirms Sophie.

Wide eyed I ask, "When?"

"All the time. You spend so much time trying to avoid him and any contact with him it's not surprising you've missed it."

I've noticed on the odd occasion that he was looking at me, but the rest of the time I've missed being stuck in my own little world of avoidance. "Has anyone else noticed?" I ask.

"Everyone has noticed." Nods Zoe. "We've got bets running on how long it will take for you two to fuck properly."

"You were actually being serious about that?" I say, my voice going up a level in volume.

If she didn't have half my hair in her grip, along with a dangerously hot object, I'd be doing more than raising my voice at her.

"Don't worry. We haven't told the others about what happened between the two of you. Your secret is safe, but it's pretty damn obvious. Why do you think Amanda chewed your ass tonight? She knows something is happening again and that she can't just sit back and wait. She's scared of losing him, so she's fighting for what she wants. Wasted energy if you ask me."

I never knew that everything happening between Jake and I was so obvious to everyone else, but I don't know why I'm surprised, in the past they've known things were happening before we even knew it ourselves.

"Do you think tonight is a bad idea?"

Sooz coughs awkwardly, making it clear what her response would be. She's all about work and staying professional, but knows when it comes to me and Jake, it's a very blurry line. Sophie just looks at me and gives a gentle nod of her head. No matter what I decide, she always supports me and if I'm ever looking for the answer I want to hear, she's the one I turn to.

Then there's Zoe ... "If I were in your position, I think my head would be as screwed as yours is."

"Nice."

"I mean that in the nicest possible way. I honestly wouldn't be able to do what you're doing, being around him like this and ignoring the feelings you have. It must be hard and must feel downright impossible at times." It's not often Zoe speaks about anything with such sincerity, so I relish in the words

163

coming out of her mouth. "But you need to be careful and you need to follow your gut instinct. A couple of summers ago it was a shock for us all when you packed up and left, but looking back now, I get why you did it. Seeing how the band took off, and your career. Your paths never would have aligned, and you would have made things harder for yourselves. At least by cutting things off like you did, you were able to focus on what was important rather than muddying the waters with a relationship that truthfully, was never going to make it."

It's refreshing to hear that someone understands why I did what I did. Often, it's not the case.

On a roll, she continues, "But, if it really wasn't meant to be, there wouldn't still be this pull between you both, which I guess you can't ignore. There aren't many people who can say that almost a decade down the line they still have the chemistry you guys have. That's not to say you should ignore this thing with Dan ... he's the first guy to have caught your eye in a couple of years and it would be a shame to see that go to waste. I think there's no harm in going on a date with both. You're not committed to either of them so don't let yourself feel guilty."

In the mirror I give her a nod of appreciation, to show how much her words mean and that she gets it. I never thought out of everyone, she would be the one who understands everything I'm going through.

"So, I should just enjoy tonight?" I ask.

"Hell, yeah enjoy it! Christ, you're not married to anyone so why shouldn't you? But if things start to become more serious with one of them, then you need to remember there are other people's feelings on the line, not just your own."

"I know. I don't want to hurt anyone."

Deciding it's time for Zoe to have a break from her speech, Sooz says, "They're big boys, Abby, and they work in an industry where affairs and cheating is rife. They're surrounded by it. I'm not saying you're doing either of those things. You haven't been on a date with either one of them yet, but they know what the real world is like and that it's not all sunshine and roses. Give yourself a break. You're never going to be able to choose between them if you don't give yourself an opportunity to be with the both of them. You'll never know which direction your heart wants to go in. It's just unfortunate they've both come at the same time."

"They're right," agrees Sophie. "You know I'm one hundred percent a supporter of being faithful to the partner you're with, but in this situation, you're doing absolutely nothing wrong. Just go with it and enjoy yourself for now."

With their words fresh in my mind, I feel a renewed sense of energy going into the night with Jake. Maybe I don't have to give it my absolute all and commit everything I have to either of them. All I have to do is enjoy myself. What harm is there in a bit of lighthearted fun?

I should have known though, when it comes to Jake, things are never quite as simple as being lighthearted.

***

It's late when I finally head out for our date, not that it makes any difference. When you're part of the festival world, the days are long and the nights are longer, merging into one. Time is unimportant as you become lost in the excitement of it all.

I got a message from Jake an hour ago confirming where to meet. I thought we'd stay near the hotel where I'm staying and where the tour bus is parked but was surprised when his message said to meet back at the festival entrance. I can't decide if I'm a little disappointed. I expected something more intimate for the evening, not where we spend our days working. Maybe this is a good thing. If it's not too romantic, it might help us to keep some distance.

For the first time since the tour began, I've made an extra effort with my appearance. Before, I've always been too frazzled by the drama and didn't see the point. Throw into the mix the ever-increasing humidity, and it seemed pointless spending hours on my makeup and hair, only to look exactly the same as when I started half an hour earlier.

Zoe used her expertise, dousing me in products that would make sure everything stayed put as it needed to, despite the stifling heat. Thanks to her best styling efforts, I know I look good. We might all laugh about her 'career' as an influencer, but there's no denying she's good when it comes to things related to fashion and beauty. Tonight, I'm a prime example of her talents.

I also chanced letting her help pick my outfit, something I would never normally allow. Deep down I know she wanted me to go for something more risqué, that would push me outside my comfort zone, so I was relieved when she pulled out a soft midi dress which flows lightly around my body. It's comfy but hugs my curves in all the right places.

"Wow."

I look up from the spot of grass I was staring at and my breath catches at the sight of Jake. He looks effortlessly cool in his usual band getup which has stayed the same since high school, and tonight is no different.

"Hey." My smile is uncertain. All our interactions have been so angsty it seems strange to not be at each other's throats straight away, to be doing something so normal.

"You look ..." he tails off, appearing unsure how to continue.

He glances into the distance and rubs the back of his neck. I can tell it's not just me who is nervous about tonight. It's like we're back in high school, dancing around each other, neither knowing how to move forward with the evening.

"Jake?" I prompt him to carry on, or at least direct us so we can move from the spot where we're standing awkwardly.

He looks back down, then takes a couple of steps forward so he's in my personal space. It should feel wrong, I should push him away after all the fighting we've been doing, but at the same time it feels so right, and I can't deny I've missed having him so close.

Finally, he finishes what he began saying, "You look beautiful."

Capturing a lock of my blowing around in the breeze, he tucks it behind my ear. It's such an intimate gesture, so gentle and a complete contrast to the last time we were alone together, when it was anything but sweet. Everything tingles and I close my eyes, taking a deep breath to try and gather myself together. I will never get over the effect he has on me, even after all the years that have passed. Without trying, he can render me, Abby West, the focused, career-driven photographer, completely useless.

Panicking that I can't quickly think of a cool way to respond, I say, "Thanks." Just as I think I've gotten

167

away without embarrassing myself, my mouth continues of its own accord, "You look beautiful too. I mean—" I stop myself babbling, trying to backtrack. Oh my God, did I seriously just say that? Cool Abby.

It's not a lie though, he is beautiful, there's no other way to describe him. His dark hair is swept back in the way I love, and I could get lost in those brown eyes which are glistening in the night light. He doesn't fit the typical rock band image. Normally they go for the starving artist look that's popular, either that or it's a result of too much sex and drugs. But not Jake. He's big, strong and just so God damn manly I could drool just looking at him. Seriously, I need to chill out. We haven't been together for five minutes and I've already lost the plot, struggling in the fight to stay away from him.

He echoes my reply with a chuckle. "Thanks."

Even though I'm mortified, I don't need to be. He knows the effect he has on me. He always has.

I try to move on from my blunder and ask, "So what are we doing? I thought you said dinner, but it doesn't exactly look like we can get anything to eat around here."

He's been staring at me so intently, that my question takes him by surprise. "Right, sorry."

"Are we going back into the festival?"

"Not quite, come with me." He grabs my hand and drags me behind him.

A small part of me wants to pull it back, keep it as my own and keep some distance between us, but who am I kidding? It feels too good to pull away. Even when I spent the summer back in Brooklyn, we were never together like this. We never had the chance to be a normal couple again and it feels right.

As we're walking, I warn myself to keep my head on straight, this is Jake after all. We can't really be together like this, it's merely a test run to see how things go. Then I tell myself not to forget about Dan. Guilt makes my stomach twist in a knot as I think about seeing him again in a few days, when the tour moves to France and we agreed we would meet up. I'm meeting Dan for a date but I'm here with Jake. I need to remember what the girls said. I'm not committed to anything, I'm a free agent and can do what I want.

Their words don't change that this thing with Jake feels different and always will. I don't know if Dan could ever truly compete with that. It doesn't matter how much time goes by, there's always something between us. It's as if the universe keeps throwing us together, our paths crossing unexpectedly. How else is it possible to explain this summer and how we wound up working together when we were based on opposite sides of the world? There is no way it's down to chance, it has to be fate.

Jake looks over his shoulder and down at me, with a frown, and I realize I'm dragging behind.

"Everything ok?" he asks.

"Fine," I squeak at being caught again, lost in my thoughts of him. I need to get my head together and enjoy tonight. That or I need to put an end to it now. But could I really walk away from him when I finally have him all to myself like this? No way.

We've been walking for a few minutes and I notice we've bypassed the festival where the band played. It's a relief because I'm getting my fill of the festival buzz just through work. The thought of being flung back into it tonight isn't appealing.

Eventually we arrive at a small carnival surrounded by a wooded area. It's big without being too big, maintaining an intimate feel. It's full of rides, food and game stalls as you'd expect, but the atmosphere is what makes it feel perfect for a date. In the background, music from the main stage at the festival can be heard. What steals my attention is the small stage set up to one side of the carnival, where a folk acoustic band is playing and adds a lighthearted and romantic vibe to what I see before me. And then there's the lighting. I've never seen anything like it before—thousands of lanterns and fairy lights hang above, twinkling against the almost darkened night sky. There's only one way to describe it: Magical.

Jake's face seems unsure, like he's regretting bringing me here. "You've gone quiet. Do you want to go back to the festival? Is this too much?"

I place a hand on his chest and his breathing steadily increases. I don't miss it. I don't miss anything.

"Jake, this is perfect. How did you know about it?"

"We've had a few days to ourselves and I was getting tired of the festival scene, even though that's all the guys want to do. I agreed to come with them a couple of days ago and this caught my eye when I went for a walk on my own. I saw it and thought you'd like it."

"Like it? I love it, it's amazing. Thank you for bringing me."

I realize my hand is still resting on his chest at the same time he does. Rather than holding my eye contact, he grimaces and looks away, as if having my hand on him is painful.

"Sorry." I snatch my hand back and look away to avoid any further embarrassment.

"It's not that." He places his hands on my face and turns me back to face him. "It's not that I don't like having your hands on me, believe me, I more than like it. It's hard that's all."

Holding my hands up, I twiddle my fingers at him playfully. "I get it, sorry. I promise no more hand action for the night."

"Well, I wouldn't say no to a bit of hand action." He winks and some of the tension between us lifts.

I look around. "What now?"

His expression changes to a playful one, and I try not to squirm in excitement. It almost feels like we're back to being the old Jake and Abby. Carefree, before everything went wrong.

"How about we have some fun?" he says.

We spend the next hour running around the carnival like kids, enjoying just being together. I don't know what else I thought tonight would be. When I first arrived, I may have been slightly disappointed we weren't spending time at some fancy restaurant in the city, but we could do that anywhere. I don't know why I expected anything different. This is just so Jake, so us.

We make our way around the different games and Jake attempts to win but fails miserably, which has me crying with laughter. Then we venture on a few rides, but I don't feel up to being thrown around. Eventually we decide to get some hot dogs and French fries—he did promise dinner after all—and sit on the grass watching the acoustic band on stage.

Sitting in an amicable silence, I feel content and have the urge to lean into Jake and snuggle. It takes everything in me not to, and I have to keep reminding myself that's not why we're here. Leading him on would be wrong when I don't know how I feel about Dan. It doesn't change how inviting the thought of cuddling into his warm chest and taking in his scent is though.

After a while of contemplating the best way to express how I'm feeling, without making it too big a deal, I decide to just be honest. "I'm happy we did this," I say.

"Does that mean you're glad I made you come?"

I arch an eyebrow. "You didn't make me do anything Jake, I'm a big girl and make my own decisions."

"Okay, you're glad I *encouraged* you to come?"

His attempt to turn his words around to something more appeasing makes me giggle.

"It's been a great night." I don't add the part on at the end that I wish it would never end, that I wish we could stay like this in our own little bubble forever.

"It's not over yet."

I don't know what he means, but don't have to wait long to find out. He jumps up and brushes crumbs away from his clothes, before grabbing our rubbish from the ground and stalking off.

"Jake, wait!" I shout, completely bewildered with what's come over him.

I quickly get to my feet and chase behind. It doesn't take long to figure out what he's up to, as I watch him stalk towards a large, illuminated Ferris wheel.

Glancing back over his shoulder with a mischievous glint in his eye, he shouts back to me, "Hurry up, slow poke."

Since it's getting late and the carnival is winding down, we don't have to stand in line. The families from earlier have left, and all that remains are groups of teenagers and couples, adding to the already romantic vibe. For the second time tonight, Jake grabs my hand and drags me into one of the passenger cars and takes a seat. The door closes behind us. My mind tries to catch up to what is happening and then figures out how close we're going to be for the next fifteen minutes. Maybe this isn't the best idea. But I don't have a choice in the matter as the Ferris wheel begins moving and we're rotated up through the sky.

We sit in silence for a while, moving slowly up through the air. It doesn't feel awkward or uncomfortable, still, I can't help wondering if Jake is unsure which direction to steer the rest of the night. I don't think it's a coincidence he's managed to get me alone to the point where I cannot physically run away. Being stuck about two hundred feet in the air, there's no escape.

All I'm aware of is how the side of his body presses against mine. He feels hot and everywhere his skin touches mine, it feels like electricity is sparking, causing goosebumps to erupt all over my body. Thanks to the strappy dress Zoe picked out for me, I can't hide the evidence of how my body is reacting physically to him. I can feel his eyes watching me, watching my body. I stay looking straight ahead but sense as they trail up and settle on my face.

"Are you cold?"

"No," I reply quietly.

I refuse to turn and look at him, because if I do, any resolve I have for us to keep this night purely on a friends-only basis will disappear. All it would take is one look into those deep brown eyes for me to give up and say fuck it.

Jake's never respected the walls I've put up. He's always smashed them down and pushed me out of my comfort zone, forced me to live and feel alive.

It catches me off guard when his tone changes and he firmly he says, "Look at me, Abby."

I swallow before mustering up the courage to raise my eyes and meet his. When they do, it only takes a fraction of a second before his lips come crashing down on mine.

He literally has me caged with nowhere to go, but would I really run away from this? Never. The tension that's been building since our night in that little dark room, comes pouring out as his hands tangle into my hair and pull my head back, trying to deepen the kiss.

Even though it feels urgent, it means so much more than the past couple of times we've let our guards down and been together. His lips are eager, yet gentle and hesitant at the same time. It's as if he's trying to pour everything into this moment, trying to make me feel everything he is. We've been unknowingly thrown into this summer together and somehow, we've made it to a point where we're together again.

The kiss feels like it lasts an eternity, but it could never last long enough. I don't know how long we stay, hanging in the sky along with the remnants of evening light, the sun settling in the horizon and the glow of the carnival below us.

The moment seems to come to an end, as Jake's movements slow and he pulls away slightly, pressing his forehead to mine with his eyes still closed. But whatever goes through his head, he ignores and lets out a deep groan before kissing me again, this time more urgently. I have no control over anything my body does, and it appears he is the same. His hands untangle from my hair and begin exploring my body over my dress.

Moving his kisses from my lips to my neck, it's the place where only he knows I'm most sensitive and my body shudders. I'm struggling to keep ahold of my last little piece of control.

"God, Abby, you feel so good. I've missed you," he whispers into my ear.

My heart warms, feeling like it could explode, so full of emotion from his confession. I let out a soft moan in response. "Jake ..."

That's all we manage as we become lost in our kisses again, both hungrily running our hands over each other's clothes, wishing they weren't there. If we were anywhere but in this cage, hanging in the sky, I have no doubt there would be no barriers between us.

When his kisses move to my chest, he sucks down gently, just above my cleavage and leans his body over mine. His weight forces me back onto the bench and he presses every part of himself against me. I can't stop myself squirming underneath him, needing some friction between us to ease the ache between my legs that signals how much I need him.

He's lost in himself and my body, as he continues kissing me everywhere, forgetting where we are. "God, if I'd have known forcing you to work with me was the way to get you back in my life, I would have done it sooner."

A second passes and then my blood runs cold.

Sensing my change in mood, he pulls away abruptly. "Is everything ok?" he pants, desire still swirling in his eyes.

I push him away and sit back up, adjusting my dress into the right position. "What do you mean you forced me to work with you?"

His face pales and he runs a hand over it.

I want to add, yes, ass-hat, you said that part out loud, but choose to try and keep my cool for now. "Jake?"

I notice we're still hanging at the top of the Ferris wheel even though it felt like time had sped up while we were kissing. But no time has passed at all and if my gut is anything to go by, I have a feeling we're going to want this thing to start moving soon, so we can get off and get away from each other.

"It was nothing. I was just caught up in the moment." He looks guilty and rubs the back of his neck, the nervous tell which gives him away, every single time.

I frown. "Like fuck you were."

"Always one for such delicate words." He attempts to lighten the mood by being playful, and reaches over to stroke my face, but I swat his hand away.

"Don't fuck with me, Jake. I'm being serious. I heard what you said loud and clear. What did you mean you forced me to work with you?"

"We're having this conversation then?"

"You bet we are. Tell me the truth now, or so help me God I will never speak to you again."

"You probably won't after this anyway, so what difference does it make?" He looks me in the eyes, and his own that were filled with so much lust, just a few seconds ago, are now filled with regret.

"Well?" I snap.

His voice drops low, as if he thinks that by speaking quietly, I won't be able to hear what he says next. "I requested you work on the tour with us?"

I shake my head. "I don't understand."

My stomach is in knots, waiting to hear the full story of what he's been up to, how he's been messing with my life.

"Maybe not requested, more like ordered. I pulled some strings with the record label and personally demanded you be part of the tour. Said I wouldn't do it unless you were working with us."

Suddenly it all makes sense, the randomness of the whole situation. Why the work is split between two PR teams, which seemed ridiculous all along, but

I figured it was fate playing her hand in our lives again.

Fate my ass. It was Jake fucking Ross.

"How dare you." My hands are twitching. Itching to slap him, punch him, pull him towards me and start kissing him again. I don't know what I'm feeling or what I want to do. Ultimately, I feel rage. "You had no right to tamper with my life."

"I know, I'm sorry." He looks guilty, but it's not enough.

"Why did you do it?"

"I don't know. I had no idea what I was doing and was blinded by this sudden need to see you with no idea why. I didn't expect this to happen between us, I swear. This wasn't just an attempt to get in your pants, I promise."

"Nice," I reply bluntly, at him belittling what's happened between us so far.

"Shit. I didn't mean it like that, Abs, I swear. You know it was more than that between us."

By some miracle, the Ferris wheel slowly begins moving, taking us steadily towards the ground. I cannot wait to get out of this cage and away from him. I feel like I can't breathe or think straight when he is still so close. I need space to properly comprehend the conversation we are having. I stare ahead, fuming, as we continue moving.

As soon as the attendee opens the door, I dart out without looking back at Jake.

"Abby, wait!"

He chases behind me and it doesn't take much for him to catch up, thanks to the huge height difference between us. He doesn't expect me to turn around as abruptly as I do, almost crashing into me before coming to a halt.

"Damn, sorry." Steadying himself with his hands on my exposed arms, I despise that even though I'm so angry with him, my body still tingles and responds to his touch.

My voice is quiet but my tone serious. "Get your hands off me. I hate you sometimes."

The hurt on his face is so strong it makes me feel sick, but I don't regret the words that have come out of my mouth, I'm too mad.

"You don't mean that," he says solemnly.

"Do you know how hard it was to walk away from you? I'd dreamed about us being together again for years, and I finally had you, but I had to give you up. I did it for you, for us. I know you think I didn't and that I just ran away scared. But I did what I had to, so we didn't hold each other back. You were so blinded by your own pride, you couldn't see what I was trying to do, how I was trying to help the both of us."

Just mentioning that night in Brooklyn, outside Riffs, causes his mood to change. "What a load of bull. You were scared. You say you weren't, but you were. You were scared to finally have what you wanted and let me back in again."

"You're wrong, I did it for us. It was you who was scared. You were the one who couldn't give me the one thing I needed: an explanation, closure." I don't need to explain that I don't trust him. His actions that have led to this point prove why.

"God, how many times do we need to have this conversation, Abby?" He runs his hands through his hair, tugging on the ends.

I know I'm pushing him hard, but he needs this. If there's any way anything will come of what's between us, he needs to start telling the truth rather than hiding and doing things behind my back.

I narrow my eyes and calmly say, "Everything always has to be on your terms, doesn't it? Why am I here this summer? Why are you making it so I can't move on from you?"

"Because I wanted you here, ok? Why? I don't know. At first I thought I wanted to mess with your head—"

I roll my eyes and look away. "Great."

"Will you let me finish? You want an explanation and I'm trying to give it to you. I requested personally that we have you on this tour because I *needed* you here. The guys, everyone, knew I was drowning. Sam told me to sort my shit out and this happened. And now? Maybe I want more than why I originally had you brought here."

Had me brought here ... it annoys me the way he's throwing his new power, fame and money around. He's flaunting it in my face and showing me how he can use it to get his own way. "I'm not a toy, Jake. You can't just have me when you want me and then throw me to the side when you don't. It was the same back in high school, one day you loved me, the next you didn't. Then you interfere with anyone who shows any interest in me because you can't decide what it is you really want."

"It wasn't *my* choice!" he roars.

I've never seen him lose control of his temper like this and the people around us begin to stare with unease. It doesn't help that the majority most likely don't speak the same language as us, so don't have a clue what is being said.

"What do you mean, it wasn't *your* choice?" I ask, bemused. "Of course, it was your choice. Who else's choice could it have been?"

He looks away and huffs. "Forget it, it doesn't matter."

"And once again we've done a full loop and we're back to where we started. This, Jake, is one of the main reasons I walked away. How could we have fully committed to each other, when I never knew why you really left me the first time? Why you threw me to the side like scraps you were ashamed to be seen with?"

"You believe that Abby. Believe whatever you want, but the night I told you I loved you, I meant it and you know I did, so fuck you if you don't believe it. It took everything in me to open up to you like that, when I didn't have a clue how you felt. Like I've said before, my feelings for you have never, ever changed. It's always been us."

"It's not enough Jake. I need more, I need answers. Until you give me them, whatever this was, is done. We can't keep pretending everything is ok and then when it gets to the end of the summer be in the exact same position we were back in Brooklyn. It's not fair. So, until you decide finally I'm worth the truth ... that you can trust me the way you expect me to trust you ... we're done."

I don't know at what point tears began streaming down my face, maybe they have been all along. As I walk away, I probably look as much of a mess as I feel. This was one of the most romantic nights I've ever had, and it was ruined because something always gets in the way of me and Jake. Maybe it's not fate—that sure became evident when I learned I wasn't here by accident. Maybe it hasn't always been us like he thinks. Maybe we need to let go and accept we're just not meant to be.

As I make my way through the exit of the carnival, leaving my night with Jake behind, my cell vibrates in the satchel bag hanging at my side.

Pulling it out, my frown softens just a little.

"Dan, hi."

Sixteen
Jake 8 Years Earlier

We've been talking for weeks but not met. She's cool to talk to, but damn she's shy. You know what they say, good things come to those who wait. She definitely seems like she'll be worth the wait. Her name's Abby. We don't go to the same high school, but our mutual friend Zoe introduced us, gave us each other's number and we've been speaking ever since.

Somehow, I feel this connection to her, and I can't explain it. I don't talk to the guys about how I've been feeling, or they'd label me a pussy because they can be assholes like that. There's just something about her. I'm not used to her type, I'm used to girls throwing themselves my way, so confident they believe I will want them. Their chat is boring though and often results in a quick hook up, that's it. It's all so superficial and there's no substance to it, but that's high school.

But not Abby. I don't have a clue what she wants from me. We talk about anything and everything;

we have conversations about real things. It's endearing. There's something between us I don't want to lose. What's even more appealing is that she isn't solely focused on the fact I'm in a band, and how this can boost her reputation. She's awakened something inside me. I wake up each day with something real to look forward to. It's something I didn't even realize I needed. A connection with someone, something deeper than what I look like or can offer them in the popularity stakes.

I've been looking forward to this day. It's taken a while to convince her it's a good idea, but finally, she's agreed to meet. It's in a group setting, but small steps seem to be the way forward with her, pushing her slowly out of her comfort zone, so she doesn't even realize it's happening.

I've been sitting with the guys in Central Park for over an hour. Luckily, it's early September so the days are still warm and we're not hanging around freezing our asses off. When Sam asks if I'm sure they're coming, I shrug. I have no clue. I spoke with her last night and she promised she would come with Zoe and Sophie, promised she wouldn't stand me up, yet here we are. I'm getting antsy, and I don't know what's wrong with me, I never get like this with girls. She's gotten under my skin without me realizing it and today means more than I care to admit.

Eventually, starving and fed-up, I tell the guys I'm heading to a store close by to pick up some supplies. I'm gone fifteen minutes, but when I return and can see the group from a distance, it's clear it's grown in size and added to it some female members.

I've only seen pictures of her, ones she sent, having vetoed the others, making sure I like what I see. But there was no need. I could tell I liked her,

182

even with how blurry the pictures on my cell were. There's nothing not to like about Abby West, with her dark brown hair, highlighted with bits of copper that catch the sun. Even from a distance she's mesmerizing.

Some would say she's plain, but they're not looking properly. She's anything but. She doesn't fit the stereotypical blonde bombshell mold most guys my age go for and that's where the appeal strikes. All it takes is one look to know there's something more, that this connection with her isn't just skin deep. She's not just a pump and dump, she's the real deal, the type who's in it for the long haul, the type you marry.

I don't know how long I stand in the distance, watching her like some crazy stalker, but it's long enough for Sam to look around trying to figure out where I've gotten to. Realizing I can't stand here forever, I make my way to the group, slowly, like a predator stalking its prey. The last thing I want is to startle her and scare her away, especially after I've worked so hard to get her here.

Everyone is still sitting on the grass where we congregated earlier, spread out and relaxed. She's laughing at something one of the girls says, lost in her own little world and completely oblivious to the fact I'm even there. The girl she's talking to, who I've never met, whispers in her ear while looking in my direction. I haven't been the focus of her attention yet, because it's clear now, I'd know if I had.

She turns her head, looking up into my face and a slight flush rises to her cheeks as she swallows. She's nervous and it makes her even more appealing. Finally, when those bright blue eyes lock on to mine, there's no doubt in my mind this girl is it for me. No one else will ever compare to Abby West.

We might only be at the start of our journey, but I know now my heart is hers and hers alone. I'm done for.

***

Abby

"I still can't believe he's the reason we're all here," moans Zoe from her seat on the bus.

It's been a couple of days since our huge blow up at the carnival, and I've spent that time simmering in my own pit of fury. It's taken me this long to calm down enough I'm able to open up to the girls about what's been wrong and why I've been so angry.

Sophie rolls her eyes at Zoe's comment. "It's not like you're hard done by. We're on a European tour …"

"Yes, but still …" All she wants to do is fight my corner.

We've picked a booth as far away as we can from the others so we can carry on our conversation. Being on a bus, even if it is a big fancy tour bus, we still need to keep our voices low as there isn't exactly much space between us and everyone else.

Sooz has been unusually quiet during our whole exchange. She's normally one to offer some sort of input, but not today.

I turn and ask, "You good?"

She doesn't reply, just mouths the word *no* at me.

"Are you feeling ok? You're not sick, are you?"

"I'm fine, apart from the guilt eating away at me." She bangs her head against the table dramatically.

"What on earth is wrong with you? You're never like this."

184

She takes a deep breath and says, "Abby, I have something to tell you."

"Right?" I still haven't a clue what's gotten into her, but whatever it is, it can't be as bad as she's making out.

"It's about Jake."

Of course, it is because everything is always about him. It's like he has to filter himself into every part of my life.

"It can't be that bad, can it?"

"I don't know. You've been pretty upset these past couple of days and now I know the reason why, I'm scared to tell you."

My behavior has been irrational, but it always is when it comes to him and I'm annoyed with myself that it's making one of my closest friends think they can't tell me something.

Sweetly, I say, "You know you can tell me anything, Sooz. I promise I won't go off on one."

"We'll see …"

Zoe and Sophie look eagerly between us, they're suckers for gossip, all they need now is a bowl of popcorn and they could be watching Netflix.

We wait expectantly, until Sooz continues, "I knew about what Jake did to get us here this summer."

The shock on my face must be obvious, because she flinches. I tell myself to relax and remember this is my friend and work colleague. I can't lose my temper like I did the other night with Jake.

"How did you know?" I ask.

I must be doing a good job keeping my emotions in check because she doesn't hesitate when she continues, "It just came so out of the blue. The email and then the workload. It didn't make sense. When we got back home, I started fishing around and finally got some answers. I found out there had been a

185

request put in that specifically asked for you to be on the tour. Just you. Ange must have put her foot down and said we were a package deal and that's how the work wound up being split between two firms, but I knew something wasn't right. I never got official confirmation, but I guessed what had happened."

For a moment there, I thought Sooz had some part to play in all this, so it's a huge relief to hear her explanation and know she's not actually responsible for us being here, just that she figured out the real reason why.

I nod, wanting her to keep going, wanting to know everything.

"Remember that first meeting you guys had in the VIP tent back in Nuremberg when I made him go change? I confronted him then about my suspicions and he confirmed it. I just didn't know what to do with the truth. I didn't want to upset you. I'm really sorry, Abby. I've wanted to tell you for so long, but I knew how upset you'd be and with things between the two of you being so volatile already—"

I cut her off, not needing any more of an explanation. "Sooz, it's fine. If it were the other way around, I would have done the same thing. I know I can come across as a crazy bitch when it comes to anything to do with Jake."

"Or maybe you're just a crazy bitch full stop," says a voice from behind us.

We all turn and find Amanda with an evil glint in her eyes.

"The only crazy bitch around here is the one chasing an ex who clearly doesn't want her," Zoe says. She's been itching for a fight with Amanda since day one and it looks like she's finally going to get it.

"You have no idea what you're talking about," Amanda snarls back. She's angry, but obviously hurt by the truth in Zoe's words, I can see it in her eyes.

It doesn't last long, and the bickering doesn't have chance a to go any further, as the bus suddenly lunges to a halt and Amanda goes flying down aisle, hitting her head against the wall.

"What the hell!" she cries out in pain.

"We're no way near Arras. What's going on?" asks Sooz to the rest of the bus, as if they would know any more than she does.

We don't need to wait long for our answer, as the doors open.

"Oh my God, some psycho killer is about to get on," squeals Zoe, before diving under the table.

"Really, Zo?" I look to where she's sitting by my feet, bemused at her cowering form. "The driver knows what he's doing. He's not just going to pull over for a stranger."

We all look at the door, as a tall figure skulks through the frame, struggling as it appears too small for them to fit through easily. When they make it up the steps and stretch to full height, a familiar face is revealed.

"Honey, I'm home!"

"Shaun!" We all shout in excitement, diving up from our seats to greet him.

Once the guys have said hello, I move forward sheepishly.

"Hey, Abby bear." Beaming down at me, he uses the same affectionate name as his brother. "Long time, no see."

"No hard feelings?" I ask.

The guys' reactions to seeing me again have been a mixed bag and I have no idea how Shaun feels about me leaving so abruptly, even after all this time.

"Abby, this is me you're talking to. Come here."

Before I know what's happening, I've been enveloped into a bear hug.

"I thought you weren't supposed to get here till we hit Benicassim?" I ask when I pull away.

"Like I could stay away from this shit show for that long."

I don't know why I didn't guess that he would know what's been going on, the guys have always been close and don't keep anything from each other.

I sigh. "You've heard then?"

He shrugs and says, "Sam's been keeping me updated. But I could have taken a guess at what's been going down."

"Are we so obvious?" I chuckle.

"Yes. I know you both and know what you're like when you're thrown together. Messy. Enough said."

"That's one way of putting it."

"Hey ..." He lifts my chin and winks. "You'll get through it, you always do."

I wish I could be as convinced by his words as he is.

"Maybe."

"Anyway, less about you. You don't always have to be the center of attention you know."

He glances around and his eyes have a mischievous glint to them. Looking over my shoulder, his eyes lock on Zoe. His expression changes to one of mischief. "Now there's the girl I've come for."

What. The. Hell?

Seventeen

Abby

"I've never been so happy to be off a bus." Leaning back in my chair I take in some of the hot afternoon sun, loving how it feels against my skin.

After Shaun got on the bus, the journey got a bit rowdy with him and the band. The girls and I spent the rest of the journey to Arras in France, trying to block out the sounds of Amanda's high-pitched squeals once again.

I'm looking forward to a break from all of this and don't know how much more of the rollercoaster summer with Jake I can take. Thankfully, we only have two more stops on the tour before we have a two-week break. I've yet to decide what I'm going to do with my time off, but what I do know is whatever it is, I'll be making sure Jake is nowhere nearby.

"I'm just happy to finally be somewhere that doesn't make me feel like I'm in the live version of the *Sound of Music*," mutters Zoe to herself.

"I see we're still throwing out the stereotypes." Shaun approaches from behind and shakes her gently, knowing it will piss her off. She hates unnecessary physical contact.

She flips him off in return. "I see you're still being an ass-hat."

"Loving as always, babe." He blows a kiss at her. "We'll see if you're this bitchy later tonight."

His tone and words are playful, but if you look close enough, there's something amiss in his expression. He's staring at her far too intently for it to be considered a joke. After what he said when he first got on the tour bus, I don't know what to think about the two of them anymore, it feels like there's more to their relationship than meets the eye. When he doesn't get the reaction he wants from her, he backs down and walks over to where the band are.

I pick up my coffee, wanting to move on from their little drama. The fresh aroma hits my nose, and it smells like heaven. Zoe is still squirming in her seat, and I watch her closely over the rim of my cup.

Eventually she looks up and snaps, "What?"

"Nothing," I reply with a musical ring to my tone.

"Bullshit. You've got that I-know-something-you-don't-know look on your face. Spill it, now."

"Sheesh, calm down will you? I just found it interesting how Shaun was being with you. It's not the first time he's acted a bit, strange. Plus, you're not exactly your normal self around him. Has something happened between the two of you?"

"No, and it won't either," her reply is far too quick.

"Some would call it sexual tension," contributes Sophie.

I snort when Zoe's face turns beet red.

"Leave it guys, seriously. There is nothing going on, I promise."

We sit in silence for a few minutes until Sooz comes bumbling over, a frantic sweaty mess.

"Oh Em Gee. I tried to get here as fast as I could. Hot rocker alert." I look at her confused. "God, you are so oblivious sometimes. Dan's heading this way. *Your* Dan."

I giggle. "He's not *my* Dan. We haven't even been on a date yet."

"Minor details, but what you're not listening to is what I'm actually saying. He's heading over here, like now. I bumped into him and he asked where you were. I couldn't not tell him."

It dawns on me what she's saying. My eyes widen. "Now? Holy cow, I look like crap. He can't see me like this!"

"Too late, he's already found you." Zoe straightens up and starts fluffing her hair.

Sophie sits twiddling her hands nervously.

Even from a distance I can see how gorgeous he is. Why does he have to look like *that* when I look like *this*. I'm regretting not taking the trip to the restroom with Zoe to freshen up, I was too focused on getting my first caffeine fix of the day.

Dan and his band quickly approach our table and he smiles in my direction. It's the kind of smile that reaches the eyes and makes them crinkle at the sides, showing someone is genuinely happy. The way my stomach churns at seeing him proves he's not the only one feeling this way.

I was apprehensive that I may have blown my feelings for him up into something bigger in my mind, that I'd built him up to be something he's not. It's been a couple of weeks since we've seen each other, but as he stands in front of me again, I feel like I need someone to pinch me to convince myself this is real. It's hard to believe this gorgeous, genuinely nice guy is interested in me, out of all the women he no doubt has throwing themselves at him.

"Abby West," he says.

"Hi Dan."

I feel awkward and unsure of myself even though I know I have no reason to as he's never done or said anything to make me feel this way. It helped the first time we met that I didn't have a clue who he was. The second time, I was so starstruck and overwhelmed the whole night became a blur.

"How've you been?" he asks.

His band and the girls are staring back and forth between us, making me feel embarrassed.

I don't appreciate having an audience, which is why, rather than answering his question I ask, "Want to go for a walk?"

He nods. "Sure."

When I stand, I notice Jake and his band in the distance also watching the exchange. I give them a small wave, letting them know they've been caught. To Dan and his friends, it will seem like I'm just being friendly with the people I'm working with, but to everyone else who knows what's going on, they know that the meaning behind the wave is a big *fuck you* to Jake. It's unbearable how he's staring as I move around the table to walk away with Dan. I know I'm going to pay for this later on.

I wait until we've made our way down the street and out of earshot of the others before I turn and say, "Sorry about that. It was getting a bit uncomfortable having an audience. What were you saying?"

He shrugs. "I didn't notice they were all there to be honest. I was only focused on one thing."

My heart begins racing at his words, and his English accent almost has me swooning like a character out of a romance novel. There's something about it that's just so sexy. I'm beginning to feel a bit hot and bothered.

"Abby?"

Embarrassingly, I've gone into a daydream. I'll be lucky if by the end of this exchange, he thinks I'm normal and even worthy of a date. "Sorry ... I ..."

God this is getting awkward, and I'd like to put it down to him being the hot shot singer of a world-famous band. It's not that though. There's something about him I didn't notice back in Barcelona. Now, seeing him here again, he's affecting me in a way only one other person has before, and to be frank it's freaking me out.

He looks at me warily and asks, "Are you sure everything is ok? We can head back to the group. I thought by the way things were in Barcelona, and the texts, that you'd be happy to see me. I've been looking forward to this, but if you're not feeling it and I've misinterpreted anything I really am sorry."

He's so polite and understanding I want to scream at myself for acting so ridiculously.

His blue eyes look uncertain. You'd never know he stands on stage and sings in front of thousands of people, that he has millions of adorning fans. Right now, he looks like a normal guy putting a bit of his heart on the line with a girl who has become a blundering wreck. The way he's looking at me makes me pull my act together.

I give myself a quick mental pep talk and finally find the courage to speak properly to him, "This is so awkward. It's been years since I've acted like this, but I promise, you haven't misread anything. I'm just a little bit ... shy?"

His face relaxes and his torn expression is replaced by a grin that lights up his face and is so infectious it has me beaming right back.

"Good to know," he says, a cockier tone is creeping in. It suits him, with his rock star image, but it doesn't put me off, not when I know there's a whole other side to him. It merely adds to his sex appeal.

Laughing awkwardly, I finally answer his original question, "So, how've I been? Hmm, want the perfect answer or the honest answer?"

"I'll go for the honest one. That's what I like about you."

"Things have been a bit crap is the honest one, but it's a long story. It doesn't matter anyway as they're suddenly looking up."

I glance up through my eyelashes and notice he's blushing slightly, meaning my words are affecting him in the same way he does me.

"And that would be because?"

My body hums at the fact he's flirting, even I can't misread this situation. I hope I'm not too forward and it doesn't put him off when I say, "Well, there's this really hot guy in a band who's been texting me. I think he might want to ask me on a date, which would be really fun."

"Is that right?"

He comes to stand closer, and that's when the butterflies take off and start fluttering away again, a reaction I'm starting to associate with him. He places a hand on my hip, taking me by surprise, as his move is more confident than I would expect, but I don't complain. Having his hands on me again is nice and reminds me of our almost kiss the first night we met in Barcelona.

"Well then Abby West, how would you like to go on a date with me?"

"I think—wait, I know—I'd really like that."

Any cockiness he was trying to portray before is gone, and he's back to being the Dan who is starting

194

to grow on me, which I prefer. It feels like we're a normal guy and a girl just having a normal romantic moment, without any pressure or history confusing things.

"When are you working?" he asks.

"The band have their set tomorrow afternoon and we have a few bits we need to do to get ready today. I'm free tomorrow night?"

"That would be cool." He backtracks, "What do I mean cool? I sound like some American douche. Shit. Not that being American means you're a douche." He groans.

This time it's his turn to do the blabbering and all I can do is laugh. At least I'm not alone in making a fool of myself today.

After taking a moment to consider properly what he's going to say, he continues, "What I mean is that would be great and I'm looking forward to it." He's more polite with his revised version, which is more fitting to him and how he is.

I can't hide the cheesy, over-the-top grin he's put on my face and don't try to hide my enthusiasm. "Great!"

"Great." He looks at me and my breath hitches.

I know he wants to kiss me, but I won't let him here. Not when Jake is close and could be watching. If I let him kiss me now it wouldn't be because I want him to, it would be revenge and a way of pissing Jake off. When Dan and I kiss, I want it to be all about us, so I really know how I feel about him.

I take a small step back to put some distance between us giving him a smile at the same time, so he knows it's nothing personal.

"Shall we head back?" I ask.

He pulls out his cell, which must have been ringing while we've been talking and reads a message.

"Actually, the guys have had to head back to our bus. We have some PR stuff in a little while, so I better get going. Will you be ok walking on your own?"

I love that even though he's strapped for time he's still concerned about me. I don't doubt if I said no, he would be late for his plans in order to make sure I was ok.

"I'm a big girl, Dan. I'll be fine."

"Great. Well, I'll text you tomorrow about meeting?"

"Sounds good."

He leans in, pulling me close and places his hands on the small of my back. Everything feels like it stops, it feels like he's about to try and kiss me again even though I attempted to make it clear only a few moments ago I didn't want that to happen.

I should have known that he's a nice guy and capable of picking up on my signals. He places a gentle kiss on my cheek and pulls away, letting out a ragged breath.

"You don't know what you do to me, Abby West." Walking backwards, he puts some much-needed distance between us before one of us ends up jumping the other. "There's something about you, I don't know what it is, but I have a good feeling about this."

"I know what you mean."

Normally I would avoid being so open and honest with a guy so early on, but like he said, there's something there and it makes me want to throw caution to the wind. As we both walk away heading to our destinations, I look back over my shoulder to get one last glance at him. When I catch him, the world-famous Rockstar doing the same thing, all I can think to myself is that I have a good feeling about this too.

***

A wolf whistle comes in my direction.

"Who's got you dressed up all fancy?" yells Sam, as we make our way into the VIP tent the next day.

When Dan messaged me with the only time he could book a table for food, it didn't leave any time to get back and ready after the band's set, so I resigned myself to the fact it would have to be before, which would give the game away. Now, I've been caught, but I don't care who knows I'm about to go on a date. I'm proud of it.

"It's none of your business." I fiddle with the strap to my bag of kit nervously.

"Yeah, yeah. Word on the street is a big shot is hedging his bets with you. Do I need to vet him?"

He's joking but there is also a seriousness to his expression. I know that even with a world-famous musician, he'd stand his ground to make sure I was safe and in good hands. It's a shame he can't do the same thing when it comes to his best friend.

"Are you really going on a date with Dan frickin' White?" asks Shaun eagerly.

"I might be," I reply quietly.

I'm not ashamed, but I know Jake is listening and as much as I'd love to rub it in his face, I can't bring myself to do it. Just being here, dressed like this and him knowing where I'm going is enough.

"Holy cow, Abs, you have well and truly upped your game." He doesn't mean anything by it, but we all flinch slightly. He notices our reaction and sheepishly turns to Jake. "Bit too much? Sorry man, I didn't mean anything by it, but you know I'm a massive fanboy of Dan White."

Jake doesn't reply, just walks off in the direction of the backstage.

Letting out a whistle Sam pulls up his brother's blunder. "Not cool, bro. If he fucks up on stage, it's your ass going in the grinder."

Shaun looks back at me.

"Sorry. I didn't mean anything by it and didn't mean to cause you any problems."

I shrug. "It's not your fault, you've not been here all summer so how would you know how things have been? It's been difficult."

"Understatement of the century," Zoe chuckles.

Shaun's eyes light up mischievously. "You, me, together watching this thing, now."

There's no room for her to protest, as he throws an arm around her and drags her away in the direction of the VIP zone which is located right behind the frontstage.

I notice Sophie is hanging back and haven't forgotten the conversation we had earlier in the summer. We don't have long to speak, but this snippet of time might be all we get alone thanks to the group living in each other's pockets.

"How are you doing? I haven't forgotten what you said at the beginning of the tour," I ask.

"I'm good, promise."

Her answer is too vague for me to believe. She normally goes into great detail about anything and everything, which is how I know she's not telling the truth.

"You still don't seem like yourself. You've been quiet."

"I'm just ready for change. I feel like I'm at a time in my life where I need to make some decisions, start thinking for myself. There's only so long you can live off Mommy and Daddy's money."

She looks lost and it tears me apart that I can't help her.

"Are you sure it's just that? I haven't seen you try to hook up with any guys either?"

She sighs. "I'm just over the whole dating game. I know *we're* not old, but *it's* getting old if you get me. I'm tired of chasing guys, only to pushed aside for a better piece of ass, as if I'm second best. I want someone to finally see me for me."

I get what she's saying and it's true. I've found being single these past couple of years a shock to the system after I was with Michael for so long. The couple of times I did try and dip my toe in the dating pool was a daunting experience, one I really don't want to repeat. I can't imagine having to go through that for years on end like Sophie has.

Before I have time to say anything else, Sam pivots from where he was standing, obviously having listened in on our conversation. He says, "I see you, Soph."

I stand blinking, not sure what to make of what he's just said. Is he implying what I think he is? I never knew there was anything even remotely like that between them, but I've been gone a couple of years and a lot can change.

It doesn't appear to affect Sophie. All she does is laugh. "Whatever, Sam. I know you see me, but I mean *really* see me. Not just like a friend."

Something flashes across his face. I can't tell if it's hurt or disappointment, but what I do know is there's something going on with both of the Riley brothers and they're up to no good. The guys' set is about to start and there's no time to go into it, so I let them know I need to get ready and walk in the direction of the frontstage.

My stomach flips as I get set up, anticipating the night ahead with Dan. It's refreshing that for once all of these things I'm feeling aren't related to Jake, and that something positive is happening in my life which isn't solely focused around him.

Most of the guys' performance runs smoothly and for once it feels effortless photographing them. It's one of the first sets I haven't had to resist the urge to storm on stage and tear Jake's head off. It gives hope for the rest of the summer.

I should have known things are never straight forward, and it was naïve to think Jake would go down without a fight. He'd been unusually quiet after our argument in Denmark, but I thought he'd taken on board what I'd said and accepted that if he wasn't going to give me the truth, he would have to back off.

Oh, how wrong I was.

There's only one song left and then I'm a free agent. I'm taken by surprise when a throat clears over the mic. I'd been so centered on getting a shot of Zach that it jolts me away from what I was doing, and I pull my camera away. I look properly up at the stage and realize the person who cleared their throat was Jake.

What the hell?

The crowd remains rowdy, so he clears his throat again, which does the job as thousands of people behind me begin to settle, intent on hearing what he has to say. It's then that his attention becomes fixated on me. His eyes zone in on mine and my stomach feels like it plummets to the ground.

Whatever he's about to do, it can't be anything good.

"I don't do this very often," he says awkwardly, and some of the females in the crowd giggle and titter. "But this song is for someone special. It seemed only fitting, as I was the one who wrote it, that I did the dedication. Abs, this one's for us, because it will always be us."

A resounding "Aaawe" rings out from the crowd behind me, and I can feel myself blushing furiously. I'm not sure if it's out of anger or embarrassment.

"Mother fucker," I fume.

This wasn't the romantic gesture everyone thinks. He knows exactly what he's doing and knows it will get back to Dan. I can only hope that somehow it gets overlooked and he doesn't hear about it, at least not before our date, so I can broach the Jake subject myself.

I'm too angry to care about the last song and refuse to stay and photograph him after what he's done. Spinning around to make my way back into the VIP tent, I stop dead in my tracks. Standing to the side where I didn't notice him is Dan, with a small bunch of flowers hanging at his side. So much for broaching the subject in my own time.

I approach him nervously and give him an awkward smile, hoping I can brush it all off. A fleeting thought passes through my mind, I try to be optimistic and reason that maybe he wasn't here the whole time and missed what Jake just said. However, his face is unusually cold, showing he heard every word.

There's no more room for doubt when he asks, "Is there something you haven't told me?"

Eighteen

Abby

I've spent the past couple of weeks dreaming about how romantic our first date could be. For the first time in years, there was a chance I might have a connection with someone and feelings that resembled what I've had with Jake on some level.

I should have guessed when I watched the way he fumed walking off in the VIP tent that he wouldn't just leave what Shaun said alone. But I never thought he'd go as far as sabotaging my date in front of thousands of strangers. I should have known better after he dragged me halfway around the world, just because he wanted to.

Who knows what he's capable of anymore?

It tore me to pieces seeing Dan's expression when I approached him. He wouldn't look at me the same, and it seemed like he was contemplating whether to call it a night. Clearly, he thinks more of me than I gave him credit for, as I somehow managed to convince him I had an explanation and to at least give our date a chance so we could talk.

After a quick cab ride from the festival, we're back in the center of Arras and luckily not far from the hotel if the night bombs. It's a short walk to a small restaurant located along one of the winding streets off the main square. Under normal circumstances it would be incredibly romantic, as music drifts in the air from street performers in the distance. The smell of delicious food reaches my nose, and the sound of laughter rings out into the night. It's perfect. At least it would be if it weren't for the now awkward atmosphere the two of us are attempting to navigate.

It's disappointing how strained things are and doesn't fit the mold of how Dan and I have been with each other from the moment we met. We may have only met a few times, but sometimes you just know, and with him it genuinely felt like we had some sort of connection. Everything seemed so easy, but not anymore.

We sit down at an outdoor table and I begin playing with my napkin as Dan places an order for a bottle of red wine with the waiter.

"Is that good with you?"

I'm so absorbed twiddling with my napkin, I don't notice he's talking to me until he clears his throat.

"Abby?"

"Sorry, what?"

"I asked if you're ok with the wine I ordered?"

I look at the waiter and confirm the order is fine so he can leave.

Finally losing my patience with the whole night, I look at Dan and say more coldly than I intended, "Sorry, I didn't realize you were suddenly speaking to me again. I thought we were going to spend the whole time not talking and you being angry with me."

I don't know where the confidence to pull him up on his behavior comes from. It's most likely residual anger from the situation with Jake, or that I'm tired of guys thinking they can be so hot and cold. Dan stares back blankly, looking stunned and then it hits me what I've said and who I've said it to.

I slap a hand over my mouth. I'm mortified and wish the ground would swallow me up. "Could this night get any worse?" I mutter under my breath.

Another minute passes and I'm about ready to stand up and leave, when Dan throws his head back and begins howling with laughter. People look at us bemused, and I shrink down into my seat with embarrassment. I'm not sure which is worse, dealing with his anger towards me or having him laugh in my face.

It takes a while for him to calm down. When he does, he says, "I don't know what happened there. Tonight, isn't exactly going to plan, is it?"

Not wanting him to see the tears threatening to pour from my eyes, I look away and pretend to focus my attention on something further up the street. He doesn't miss it, reaching over to grab my hand. The warmth of his skin against mine is soothing and gives me the confidence to sit up a little straighter.

"I owe you an apology."

I blink. "Say that again?"

"I've been a bit of an idiot and I'm sorry for that. I had big plans for tonight. I thought it would be romantic and I wanted it to go perfectly..."

I frown, trying not to let my mind wander back to Jake and what he did earlier. I don't want him to ruin this moment.

"You're not the only one," I reply.

"I like you, Abby, I'm not going to try and hide it. That's why hearing that guy up on stage declaring you as his made me angry. I acted irrationally and once again, I'm sorry. I should have heard your side to the story before acting the way I have."

It's not the fact he's admitted he was in the wrong for making assumptions, but the humble way he did it, which lights something inside me and fills a hole I didn't know was there. It's such a contrast to the constant fighting with Jake, where we both battle to be the one to have the last word. This feels different. It's like we're forming a partnership and value what the other person has to say. It's refreshing.

"It's not every day something like that happens, there's no need to explain. You had every right to respond the way you did. I get it, I would have done the same."

With perfect timing, the waiter brings over our bottle of wine.

Dan pauses the conversation and asks, "Do you want to stay with me on this date?"

I love that he hasn't assumed my answer would be yes, which is why I don't need to think about my response.

"There's nowhere else I'd rather be."

And truthfully, there isn't.

When the waiter has poured our drinks, we become lost in our own world as I fill Dan in on my history with Jake. He sits and listens, nodding and encouraging me to keep talking. It's as if he understands, that somewhere in the conversation, it stopped being about telling him the truth, and became more about me getting everything off my chest.

We've been talking for over an hour and broken into our second bottle of wine when my stomach begins growling. I haven't made it the full way through the story of how Jake and I wound up on tour together, or what else has happened between us, but Dan stops me.

"We should think about ordering some food or I won't be held responsible for my actions later on."

He winks and my blood warms. At the same time, my stomach grumbles loudly, but he ignores it and simply signals for the waiter to come over, saving me from any embarrassment. After placing our food orders, we settle back into a comfortable silence.

The copious amounts of wine flowing through my veins makes me bolder than normal and gives me the confidence to speak to how I'm feeling rather than trying to play it cool.

"I like being here with you. I'm glad you gave tonight a second chance."

"Me too."

His stare is full of hidden meaning and I suddenly wish there wasn't a table between us, that I could crawl into his lap, kiss him and show him exactly how glad I am.

It scares me how extreme my reactions to him are. I've never felt this comfortable or attracted to someone at the same time. It's always one, the other or neither. Apart from with Jake. It's reassuring to know I'm not in fact broken and can feel this way about someone else other than him.

"You're not completely put off by the drama with Jake?"

He doesn't wait before replying, "Everyone has history, Abby. We're all human. But is that what it is, history?"

How do I even answer that question? I have no idea. Is it history between me and Jake? Has it all been left behind? This summer would prove otherwise but shows we constantly go around in circles and never move forward from the past. I can't honestly say everything between us is done, not after what happened. What's worse, I can't say nothing will happen again.

What I do know, is that when I'm with Dan things feel different and the pull towards Jake isn't as intense. I also know we won't be able to see where things could go, as long as I allow Jake to constantly be a roadblock in moving forward. If I allow him to influence the decisions I make, I'll never get the opportunity to try something new.

That's why, despite an element of it being a lie, I answer, "It is." Because it could be history, if I finally give myself the chance to make it that way.

He lets out a sigh of relief, and I refuse to acknowledge the guilt creeping in which could have me changing my mind and spilling my secrets. It's for the best.

After all the shit Jake has pulled this summer, I'm done, once and for all. I can finally see myself moving forward with a genuinely nice guy and I won't let him ruin that.

"Well then," continues Dan, raising a freshly filled glass of wine in the air. "To fresh starts."

"To fresh starts," I repeat, clinking my own glass against his.

By the time we've finished our food and consumed the rest of the wine, every part of me feels content in a way I didn't think would be possible at the beginning of this evening. The night might have gotten off to a rocky start but thankfully it hasn't continued that way. It's been as close to perfect as it could get.

Eventually, we agree it's time to leave. It feels bittersweet, I don't want the night to end, and I know it's one I won't forget any time soon. As we make our way slowly back through the winding streets of Arras, night has fully set in. The restaurants are beginning to mellow out for the night and their lights give our path a cozy glow.

When we start to make our way through the main square, one of the most incredible voices I've ever heard reaches my ears.

"Where's that coming from?"

"Over here I think."

Taking hold of my hand, Dan directs us to where a street performer is sitting on the ground, singing his heart out with an acoustic guitar. We stand to the side, so as not to attract any attention to ourselves, he's drawn in quite a crowd and the last thing we want is to take the attention away from him with Dan's fame. I love how humble he is. The whole evening he's been nothing short of polite to anyone he's spoken with. At no point has he thrown his fame around in order to get what he wants.

When we settle in place to watch the performer, rather than standing next to me, he moves himself behind and gently places his hands on my waist. His body presses up against mine but not in a sexually charged way. It's comforting and protective, making me feel safe and fuzzy inside. And just when I think the night can't get any more perfect, he begins singing the words to the song in my ear, creating a beautiful harmony only I can hear. We stand, lost in the music and each other.

The song eventually comes to an end and he places a small kiss on my neck, beneath my ear, which awakens all my senses immediately. The contrast in reactions he causes in me is crazy. One moment I feel calm, the next I'm fired up ready to rip his clothes off. I try to keep my cool, not wanting to read the situation wrong, as he's been nothing, but a

208

gentleman and I don't want my raging hormones to ruin things.

Maybe it's the amount of alcohol we've consumed which makes me more confident, but suddenly I'm tired of waiting for him to kiss me, so I don't. I lean my head to the side, gazing up into his eyes, which stare back with a mischievous twinkle. It's the signal I need to know he's feeling and wants the exact same thing I do.

After weeks of waiting, he leans in and his lips meet mine.

At first, they're soft and hesitant which fits him perfectly. It wouldn't feel right, with how things have been so far, for our first kiss to be fueled by passion from the get-go. But then his lips become firmer and before I know what's happening, he spins me around, so I'm pressed up against his chest as he deepens the kiss. It's the kind of kiss that makes your toes curl with lust and he gives the perfect amount of pressure. His hands explore a little, hinting he wants me as much as I want him.

Eventually, he pulls away, letting out a shuddered breath. "Abby West, you're going to break my heart."

Before I get a chance to reply and ask him what he means, a series of bright flashes fill my vision.

I hear the words, "Holy shit it's Dan White," ring out around us. I guess that means our night's over.

***

Being the gentleman he is, we spent forty-five minutes with fans chatting, taking photos, and signing autographs. Finally, he held his hands up, informing everyone he was done for the night and politely asked them to respect his privacy, explaining he had a lovely lady to walk home. We were subject to a round of "Ahhh," sighs, and of course some jealous stares, but the crowd we had drawn in respected him enough to let us leave in peace.

The walk back to the hotel was slow and steady, neither of us wanted the night to end and when we stood outside the entrance, he leaned in for another kiss. As it was heating up, he pulled away panting and said, "There is no doubting how much I want you, but I want to take this slow."

Seriously, you couldn't make this shit up, I felt like I'd walked into a romance movie.

When I get back to the room, I'm on cloud nine, but startled back to reality when I see the lights still on and Sooz sitting in bed with her laptop working.

She raises an eyebrow at the stupid grin taking over my face. "Good night?"

"Perfect." I sigh, collapsing down on my bed and kicking my legs with a squeal.

"You deserve to be happy, Abby. I'm glad you've found Dan and I hope it works out."

"Me too. Honestly, Sooz, it was the most amazing night."

"He wasn't too mad about Jake then?"

"A little at first, but then he apologized. Sooz, *he* apologized! For once it wasn't me putting in all the groundwork."

"And that's the way it should be."

"I know, but—"

"The famous *but*," she interrupts. "Go on."

I sigh. "He asked if Jake and I were history."

"Ah," she replies knowingly.

"Yeah, ah."

"What did you say?"

"I told him most of the story. But then I may have told a white lie."

"How much of a white lie?"

"I may have neglected to tell him the bit about my recent escapades with Jake."

"Hmm," she replies, looking contemplative. "I guess it's not really any of his business what happened between you guys. You hadn't even been on a date when it happened."

"Is it bad that I've already lied to him though?"

"Some would say yes, some would say no. I'm choosing to stay indifferent. I think you deserve to be happy, and I think Jake muddies the waters a lot, and often on purpose, which isn't fair to you. You deserve a chance with Dan. Maybe if he'd come a bit sooner, things with Jake wouldn't have happened. I guess you could put it down to bad timing?"

Her words are encouraging, but there's one minor detail she's missing.

"That's all well and good as long as Jake chooses to stay quiet."

I don't need to say anymore, Sooz finishes off my line of thought.

"And that is where the problem lies. If tonight is anything to go by, Jake isn't going down without a fight."

What she means is, I'm screwed.

Nineteen

Abby

A combination of heat and the journey on the bus has me feeling unsettled and nauseous. It's been a long ride from Arras to Benicassim in Spain, where the last tour date is before a much-needed break. So far, the bus journeys haven't affected me, but this one has left me feeling God awful. It's most likely down to the excessive amount of wine Dan and I drank.

"You don't look too great," says Zach as he makes his way over to where I've been standing for the past few minutes.

The bus finally pulled in to where we're staying and as soon as it stopped, I darted up to the small kitchenette to grab a glass of water.

I just about manage to reply, as I fight to keep the nausea at bay. "I'm fine, just a bit of motion sickness. That or too much alcohol."

"That's what you get for partying with a rock star," sings Sam from behind.

He's oblivious to how sick I look and swings an arm around my shoulders, pulling me in closer and playfully rubbing at my hair.

"I probably wouldn't do that," says Zach. "She's looking a little green."

He pulls away to take a proper look at me before he understands what Zach is talking about. "Man, Abby. You could give the Hulk a run for his money. What's up?"

"I'm fine," I grumble, becoming annoyed with all the attention. All I want to do is curl up in a ball and be left alone. "Too much alcohol and a bouncy bus ride don't mix."

"Too right. We need to have a word with Ray. You're not alone, that drive almost had me making my way down to vom town."

I watch in amusement as he makes his way off the bus to meet the others. When I spin back around, Amanda is there watching me with suspicious eyes.

"Can I help you?" I ask.

She smiles. "No. I'm just enjoying watching you suffer."

"How kind."

With that I grab my bag and storm off the bus. Being annoyed is now on the long list of things making me feel like crap. It doesn't help that when I step out, the heat hits me like a ton of bricks.

"*Fuuuuck!*" I complain. This day just keeps getting worse.

Zoe laughs. "You've spent more of this summer hungover than I have. Looks like you're taking over my waster role for the tour."

The others chuckle which pisses me off even more.

"Leave her alone," says Sophie, looking at me sympathetically. A cold beer appears out of nowhere

213

and she places it in my hands. "Here, I know it's not what you think you want, but it should help."

Taking it from her, I pop the ring pull and it fizzes with a satisfactory noise. When I take the first swig relief floods over me as it quenches a thirst I didn't know was there. Impulsively, I guzzle most of the can in one go. It creates a buzz as it travels down and thankfully the nausea begins to dissolve.

"Steady, you don't want to wind up wasted," warns Jake.

It's the first time we've properly spoken since Denmark. For a moment there, I almost thought we wouldn't speak again for the rest of the summer after the way we left things. Maybe that wouldn't have been a bad thing.

I'm still pissed with the stunt he pulled on stage. "I'm a big girl."

"I know you are," he says softly.

I think he's going to say something more, but a fuss is created to the side of us by Zoe.

"What do you mean camping?" she barks at Sooz. "As in sleeping on the ground?"

Sooz rolls her eyes. "Yes, Zoe. That is what camping involves. Or is it different where you come from?"

"There's no way I'm sleeping on the ground. There are like bugs and snakes and shit."

"There are hardly going to be any snakes in a rowdy campsite full of thousands of people. You don't have a choice. Hotels around here are booked out the year before the festival so there was no way we could have gotten a room at such late notice. You're welcome to sleep on the bus which will be about a mile trek away."

Zoe scoffs. "Fuck no. I'm not spending any more time in that tin can than I have to."

"Right, then stop complaining," Sooz says dismissively, then walks away before Zoe can argue with her anymore.

Shaun saunters over, acting as if he might be able to diffuse Zoe's foul mood. "Come on, Zo. Where's your sense of adventure? You used to be so carefree."

All this does is piss her off more. "I am carefree ... unless I have to sleep on the floor."

"You'll be so wasted later it won't make any difference," he smirks.

Huffily she says, "Actually, I've turned over a new leaf."

"Oh really?" He raises his eyebrows. "I'll believe that when I see it."

She looks like she's about to blow a fuse but is stopped in her tracks.

"Anyway guys!" Sam shouts. "Believe it or not, there's one thing we haven't done yet this summer ..." He gains the attention of the whole group and we turn to listen to what he has to say. "Can you believe we've yet to actually be 'festival goers?' Five weeks we've been at this. You know what they say, all work no play ..."

Thanks to the beer I downed, my judgement is hazy. Before I know what I'm doing, I agree enthusiastically, "He's right you know. We should totally get our festival on!"

Zoe glares at me. "Get our festival on? Do you think you're part of the *High School Musical* gang or something?"

"Pack it in, Zoe." Sam appears to have had enough of her snarky mood for one day. "Get a few drinks down your neck and you'll be loving life with the rest of us. Now, how about we all go set up the tents and then let's chill out? There's been far too much working and bitching at each other for my liking this summer. Who'd have thought you could all be so boring?"

Sooz and Sophie laugh, leading the group to pick up the tents and pitch information. Once we've hauled our stuff off the bus, it's a long walk in the stifling heat.

We got lost for an hour before we finally found where we were meant to be setting up which didn't help improve Zoe's mood. Watching her try to figure out the instructions and get the tent up is something I hope I'll never forget. We all sit drinking, watching her cuss like a sailor. It's taken her so long we wind up wasted and are now past the point of being able to help.

Attempting to be the hero, Sam jumps into her rescue. "Don't worry, Zoe baby. There's room in my tent for you."

"Not happening," she snaps. "Will someone please hand me a drink before I die of dehydration."

We spend the rest of the late afternoon and early evening drinking and generally being happy which makes a refreshing change to the animosity bubbling away. Even Amanda and her team manage to join in without any drama. The sense of unity between us is well overdue. The tour has been rather angsty and we're all ready to have some fun.

As we're closing up the tents, ready to head off and watch some bands, my cell vibrates in my pocket. Pulling it out, I find a message from Dan, which has me smiling to myself. Opening it, I read the text:

Missing you, counting down the days x

When I look up, of course Jake is watching.

216

"Can I help you?"

"Is that him?"

His expression is torn and the hurt in his eyes is crystal clear. I hate that I'm the one who's put it there, but he's not innocent in all of this and has played his own part in hurting me over the years.

Not knowing how to handle the whole situation, I reply, "It's none of your business."

He moves closer. "Of course, it's my business, Abby. What's going on between you two?" his voice is firm, but he attempts to keep the volume down, careful not to alert the others to the fact we're arguing, again.

"It's nothing you need to worry about."

"But I do, Abby, because I worry about what's mine."

"Jake, how many times are we going to have this conversation? I am not yours. I haven't been for a long time. You gave up on us and until you tell me why, I won't be yours, ever."

I walk off to catch up with the girls. If they can tell I'm upset, they don't let on, determined not to let the night be ruined. We spend the next few hours drinking and enjoying every part of the festival. It's exciting to be out, living the life we've been working but not experiencing.

One of our favorite bands is headlining, and we all decide together it's a great place to end the night. We make our way as close to the stage as we can, which isn't very close considering the thousands of people tightly packed around us. It doesn't change how amazing it all is, and we all become lost in the show, letting loose for the final time. Thankfully, Jake and I have managed to avoid each other at all costs so there have been no more arguments. He's kept himself at such a distance, I barely noticed he was still with us.

It's not far from the end of the performance when the crowd begins to get rowdy. We close our ranks in an attempt to keep away outsiders, but we've all had so much to drink it proves difficult.

A guy from the group in front who has gotten wasted falls back into me, knocking my drink out of my hands while covering me in his own.

"Hey asshole!" I yell, wanting to let him know I'm annoyed.

Annoyed and sticky. He spins around and leers at me drunkenly. "Hey, beautiful," he slurs.

"I wasn't coming on to you. You spilled my drink and covered me in yours."

He looks down to where my top has become see through and his gaze changes from drunken to seedy. "Here, I can help with that."

He approaches but I back away abruptly.

"You're ok, I can sort myself out. Just watch what you're doing next time."

I wish I'd left it and not gained his attention, the situation doesn't feel right, and I start to feel apprehensive.

Swaying drunkenly on his feet, it takes a while for him to understand what I've said, then he grabs one of his friends and whispers something in their ear.

His friend spins around with the same leer on his face and offers his own drink. "Peace offering," he says.

Everything begins to feel familiar, but I attempt to swallow down the nerves and how uncomfortable I'm feeling. I need to keep my head together and my wits about me with these guys.

I shake my head and reply, "It's fine, thank you. I don't need it."

The guy's expression changes and is replaced with rage. "I said take it!"

He grabs my wrist, causing pain to shoot up my arm as he attempts to force his drink in my hand. I feel like I'm stuck in that night back in Brooklyn when I lost all control. Everything begins to look and feel the same, faces blur and I lose all sense of what is a flashback and what is reality.

Panicking, I try to find words, try to choke them out and make the others aware I'm in distress but fail as my throat closes up. I struggle to breathe, and everything begins to go black. When I feel like giving in to my own despair, like no one is going to help, a fist comes flying out of nowhere, and then another, smashing into the faces of the guys in front of me.

I vaguely register when Jake and Sam dive on top of the two guys, their faces contorted with anger like I've never seen before.

And then all hell breaks loose.

***

Jake 2 Years Earlier

I should have known something was wrong as soon as we met with the girls. She wasn't right—I knew she wasn't and instead I let her carry on, for what, ten minutes? Ten valuable minutes that could be the difference in her fighting for her life.

The doctors said she was lucky and had a near miss. It could have been so much worse, what they used was strong and she was lucky we were there.

Their words and concerns keep ringing through my mind on a continuous loop I can't get out of my head.

God, she was so close to being ... being ... I can't bring myself to even think it, it's unbearable. I can't get it out of my head, the way she tumbled to the ground, lost all control. The way her body became lifeless. Sophie and Zoe are beside themselves and so they fucking should be. I don't know how many times we've warned them, and now it's Abby suffering for the mistakes they make time and time again.

I don't know how long we've been in the hospital, when eventually the doctors give the go ahead to take her home. On and off she keeps regaining consciousness, but they said she won't be fully with it for a few days and most likely won't remember the times when she's been awake.

All I care about is getting her somewhere comfortable and safe. Her parents can't get back in time to bring her home and she needs to rest, so they agreed, for now, to let her come to my place. I promised I wouldn't let her out of my sight, and they know I'll stay true to my word.

John West knows how much his daughter means to me.

I've spent hours watching over her, days even. I can't remember the last time I slept more than a half hour at a time, but there's no way I'm letting her out of my sight again. Not a chance in hell. Not until she's awake and resembles the Abby I know.

There's one positive that's come from all this though, it's solidified how I feel about her. The girl lying in front of me, I can't live without. I love her and I'd do anything for her. Cross an ocean, do anything she asked of me.

I just hope she feels the same.

***

Jake Present

I saw red tonight. There's no way around it. I completely and utterly lost my mind. I'd been keeping an eye on her all night long, I always do. Particularly when there's alcohol involved, especially after that night.

The crowd had been getting raucous and it made me nervous not being able to get close to her and keep her safe, so I moved myself into such a position I could watch what was going on. When I saw that dick lay his hands on her, I lost the plot and no one on Earth could have stopped me.

It doesn't matter how much time goes by, how much of a fight she puts up or how many times she says it's done. I will always be there watching over her, making sure she's ok and fighting her corner. I walked away once, and it was the worst thing I ever did. I promised myself I would never, do it again.

Watching, I knew what the guy was doing would affect her on a level no one else could comprehend. How could I forget the sleepless nights, watching over her as she tossed and turned and succumbed to the nightmares? She'll never admit it, but she suffered with PTSD after the night she had her drink spiked and it's clear now that she still does.

Two years ago, I watched as she powered on, pretended like everything was ok. No one would have blamed her for being how she was, she needed help to get through it but never reached out. But that shit doesn't just disappear, it lies dormant and festers, rears its head when you least expect it, like tonight.

Tonight, I saw the sheer terror on her face, she was going down a dark hole she wouldn't be able to crawl back out of.

I wanted to make her feel better. I wanted to make myself feel better. There's no excuse, but maybe that's why later, I did what I did. I shouldn't have pushed it. I know deep down she wanted to try and put her feelings towards me to bed. But tonight, seeing her like that, I couldn't just stand by and let that happen.

Twenty

Abby

"**A**re you sure I can't get you anything?"

"Yes. For the millionth time, I'm fine," I say, taking a large swig of the ridiculously strong drink Zoe handed me.

"Seriously, I've never seen you like that before," says Sooz, still looking pale from the events of earlier.

"It's called a panic attack, and I'm fine, or at least I will be once I've had a few more of these." Raising my glass, I knock the rest of it back in one. The beer from the afternoon is proving to have been good practice.

"I know I'm not one to talk, but maybe you should take it a little easier. You've been drinking all day and just been through something traumatic."

The worry on Zoe's face has me pausing before I reach for another drink.

"I'm with Zoe," says Sophie, making it official that each of the girls think I should stop drowning my sorrows in alcohol.

Never gonna happen.

"Let me get this straight. It's ok for the two of you to constantly get wasted but when anyone else wants to get drunk it's an issue?"

"It's not the same and you know it," Zoe says calmly, even though I'm pushing for an argument, anything that will help as an outlet to my feelings.

Folding my arms across my chest, I push harder. "Enlighten me."

She holds her hands up and says, "Look, do whatever you want, but you've already been sick once today. Do you want to make it twice?"

She has a point, but there's no way I'm listening to anyone. I'm too busy wallowing in my own self-pity, which is why I grab the bottle of vodka from her hands and make my way into my tent. I don't like how I'm acting, and I know they'll think I'm acting like a spoiled child, but I need this time to let off steam.

If they're all going to sit there judging me, I'll do it on my own.

I lose all sense of time as I sit and attempt to block out the memories of the night with each sip I take from the bottle. None of them understand, but I wouldn't expect them to. There's only one person who saw how I truly fell apart after what happened that night in Brooklyn, and how it really affected me.

That's why it doesn't faze me when I hear the zip of my tent go up and Jake's head pops through.

"Can I join in with the pity party?"

Before I get a chance to answer he's climbing into the tent regardless.

"Was there any point in asking?" a slight slur creeps into my voice.

"You sound like you've had more than enough already."

He goes to take the bottle from me, but I move it out of his reach.

"Jake, if you're going to come in here and start telling me off like the others, then you might as well make your way back out because I don't want to hear it."

"Fine, what's the saying? If you can't beat them, join them."

I shrug, not caring, and finally hand the bottle to him. He takes a gulp without flinching, then another. A part of me wonders if he does it so there's less left for me.

"I know what you're doing ..."

"I'm enjoying a drink, yes."

"Whatever," I reply, too tired to get into anything.

We sit in silence for a while, passing the bottle between us. In my slightly drunken haze, my eyes wander, and I find myself observing Jake's face as he lays back and closes his eyes.

He looks so beautiful and peaceful.

He also seems content, as if he wouldn't want to be anywhere else, maybe he doesn't. If his actions over the past few weeks are anything to go by, there is absolutely no place he would rather be, than here with me. I don't know what to do or how to feel. All I know is I find myself mesmerized by him being here.

I blame it on the alcohol for what I do next.

Reaching out, I run my hand up his chest, loving how his muscles feel underneath his shirt. His body feels familiar, but at the same time is a distant memory. He doesn't move or respond to me creepily touching him while he's laid with his eyes closed. I'm almost convinced he's fallen asleep, when suddenly he grabs my hand, stopping my exploration in its tracks.

His eyes flash open and his gaze burns into mine, silently questioning what I'm doing.

I'm saved from the embarrassment of having to explain myself, as somewhere in the distance, Zoe begins screaming at the top of her lungs. We both stumble out of the tent, to find her flapping her arms around hysterically, still screeching.

"What's wrong? You almost gave me heart failure!" shrieks Sophie, equally distressed.

"I was attacked!"

We all turn to Shaun for answers, as they'd been sitting together, but attempting to get any information from him is useless, as he literally rolls around on the floor laughing.

"What do you mean you were attacked?" Jake looks alarmed.

Maybe her choice of words could have been better, considering the events of the night, but she continues flapping her arms around frantically.

When Shaun manages to gather himself together and stands, wiping at his eyes, he finally explains, "It was a moth."

"You're joking, right?" I ask in disbelief.

"It wasn't *just* a moth." Zoe zeroes in on him angrily. "It was as big as a person."

"You're overreacting," Shaun's tone turns blunt showing he's beginning to get bored with the whole scenario.

Zoe looks to us and asks, "Have you ever seen *The Mothman Prophecies*?"

We all shrug, not a clue what she's talking about.

"It was worse than that. I swear it had a body like a person and everything. I'm never going to be able to sleep again."

Not missing a beat, Shaun seizes the opportunity to stake his claim. "That's a shame. I can think of other things we can do instead."

Unlucky for him, she doesn't take the bait. "Get over yourself."

Without another word, she climbs into the tent she is now reluctantly sharing with Shaun, after giving up on constructing her own hours ago.

"Looks like I'm in for a fun night." He sighs, before following in after her.

Sophie moves to go back in her own tent, and I ask, "You're not on your own, are you?"

"No, Sooz is with me."

She smiles between me and Jake before leaving us alone.

Some of my alcohol buzz has already begun to fade and I look at him awkwardly. "You don't have to stay with me. I promise I won't drink anymore."

"You think I'm going to leave you here in a tent on your own?" he replies.

"I'll be fine."

"No, you won't. I saw the state of you back there. Plus, it's not safe. You don't know who's around here and everyone is wasted. I'm not chancing you being on your own and having a random visitor, no way."

"Jake—"

He cuts me off before I have a chance to say anything else, "Get in the tent, Abby, or I'll carry you in."

Maybe it's the alcohol affecting my judgement, or maybe it's the fact that deep down I don't want to say no which is why I don't put up any more of a fight. I shouldn't be feeling this way though, I should be focusing on Dan—perfect Dan, who gave me a perfect night. I told myself I wouldn't do this, and I should know better than to allow myself to be alone with Jake, nothing good ever comes from it.

I climb into the tent and Jake follows closely behind. Thanks to the lack of space, I, not very gracefully, collapse on the floor on top of my sleeping bag, before attempting to explain my odd behavior earlier.

"Jake—"

Before I get a chance to say any more, I'm cut off, not with words, but with his lips as they meet with my own.

I should stop it. It's not fair and we can't keep doing this, going around in circles. Thanks to the alcohol and leftover adrenaline from earlier, all rational behavior goes out the window and rather than fighting it, I let his lips carry on kissing me and let his hands explore.

Doubts creep in with memories of the night before: Dan's lips on mine; the unsaid promises we made to each other ... Then I remember how I told him wholeheartedly that everything with Jake was done when that is obviously not the case.

He must sense my hesitation, as he pulls away, panting. "Sorry. I don't know what I'm doing any more."

It's the first time I've heard him be so honest and let himself appear vulnerable and out of control.

I shouldn't care about how he's feeling, I should push him out of the tent and tell him to leave me alone, but I can't find the strength in me. I don't know if I'll ever be able to just walk away, not when he looks so broken.

"What do you mean?" I ask.

"I feel lost without you, Abby. Watching you with him is tearing me apart. I can't keep doing this, pretending I don't feel the way I do."

"But you've never told me how you feel."

"I shouldn't have to, I thought it was pretty obvious. You knew what I wanted, and you walked away." He throws his hands up annoyed. "Do you think I brought you here this summer for no reason, just to have a quick catch up? I told you, you were mine and I meant it. I'm tired of these games."

I blink and swallow nervously. I've never heard him speak like this. It has me squirming, itching to touch him and feel him inside me. But I can't, I promised myself I wouldn't do this again.

"I'm with Dan."

"Bullshit. You barely know the guy. You've been on one date and suddenly he's everything?"

"It's more than that, he makes me feel different." Which is the truth.

With Dan, things are simpler: we click and get along without all the drama. There's no emotional rollercoaster like there is with Jake and I'm not scared he'll rip apart my heart.

"He might make you feel different, Abby, but he will never make you feel like this."

Before I get a chance to object, his lips are back on mine, more urgently this time. He kisses me everywhere, and even though I'm riddled with guilt, my body is overwhelmed by all things Jake, refusing to stop this. Pushing me gently, back down to the ground, he lays me out on top of my sleeping bag and begins removing my clothes.

He leaves nothing to chance.

He's not asking any more, he's taking what he's repeatedly told me he wants ... me.

When he's naked and hovering above me, all I can do is moan in satisfaction. He leans down, slowly kissing up the inside of my thigh, making me squirm as he moves higher.

"Don't move," he says then unleashes weeks of pent-up frustration.

His mouth on me feels too good, and I can't hold back the moans that fall from my lips. When he thrusts inside me, I feel like I've died and gone to heaven. Two years ago, I never thought I'd get the chance to feel like this again.

I thought we were done.

It's not the same as the last time, in that small dark room. He takes his time, pulling in and out slowly, building me up, teasing and frustrating me in ways no other guy has ever been able to. It feels so wrong, but so right at the same time. Any hope I had of feeling anything like this for anyone else is well and truly obliterated.

He spends the night making love to me, whispering in my ear, telling me how much he needs me and how I'm his, only his.

Twenty-One

Abby

How many times am I going to wake up on this tour feeling like this? The world is spinning, and it needs to stop, right now. I don't remember much else after getting back to where we were camping. Nausea builds and it passes through my mind that getting drunk last night probably wasn't the best idea.

My next thought is that it's really hot in here, like incredibly hot, unbearably hot. Rolling over onto my side, I soon find the answer why.

Shit.

I'd recognize that back anywhere, although there are a few new tattoos since the last time I spent the morning memorizing it. God, what have I done?

As if subconsciously, he knows I'm awake, Jake rolls over and it's a sight to behold thanks to the fact we're laying on top of my sleeping bag rather than in it. My eyes greedily take in every naked inch of him. His eyes remain closed and I'm unsure whether he's asleep but can't help gawping. I could never get bored of watching him like this.

I'm more hungover than I have been in a long time, and the sick feeling is building at an alarming rate, not helped by the guilt tugging me backward and pushing me forward. In case I wasn't overwhelmed enough, I hear my cell vibrating from somewhere in the tent, alerting me to a new message I know will be from Dan, because fate is kind like that.

Finally, Jake opens his eyes.

"Hey, you," his voice has that sexy, gruff, early morning sound to it, which I'm trying not to let affect me. I can tell from how bleary eyed he is he's as hungover as I am.

"What have we done?" I ask, mortified.

"What we should have been doing every day for the past two years?"

He looks amused and it pisses me off.

"I'm being serious, Jake," I croak out. "We shouldn't have done this, again."

I want to scramble and get my clothes on, but my body has other ideas. It's officially broken, and no quick movements will be happening any time soon.

"You weren't complaining last night," he looks at me like this is all a game.

Even though I'm annoyed, I can feel myself becoming flustered as his eyes trail hungrily over my naked body. Why does he have to be so sexy, even hungover. Surely that's not normal?

"It was the alcohol." I'm clutching at straws, but I know he isn't going to let me get away with it that easily.

Some of his playfulness disappears as he begins to get annoyed. "You wanted it as much as I did, and alcohol had no part to play."

"Jake, I told you. I'm trying to make a go of things with Dan. This shouldn't have happened, and it can't happen again."

"You've had one date with him, Abby. We have years of history and you're going to brush that aside for someone you met a couple of weeks ago? Someone you've spent what? A few hours with max?"

"There's something there and I want to give it a chance."

It feels like we've had this conversation before and there's no doubt in my mind that it was last night when we were wasted, I just can't remember clearly enough.

"I didn't take you for a fame seeker because that's what this is, isn't it? He's *sooo* sexy and cool because he's world famous?"

I narrow my eyes at how childish he's acting. "That's not it and you know it. You know I'm not like that."

"I don't know what to think anymore, Abby. I thought you'd never walk away from me and you did. I never figured you'd fuck me twice and shove me to the side, yet here we are."

His words are degrading and make my actions sound slutty.

"How can you say those things to me?" I say quietly. I'm almost in tears, but I don't want to let him see how much he's hurting me.

"How can I not? Put yourself in my shoes. How do you think I feel being treated like this? Having to watch you with him?"

"I don't know what to say, Jake. We can't keep doing this, it's too much. Each time we break each other a little more."

"I told you, Abby. I'm not going down without a fight. You might not want to admit it to yourself, but you're mine. I'll let you have your fun for now, but don't forget everything that's happened between us."

He stands up as best he can in the small tent and begins pulling on his clothes. Before I get a chance to reply, he storms out without another word. When I'm certain he's gone, I fall back, covering my face with my hands and allow the tears I'd managed to hold in fall.

How could I have done this to Dan? We're only at the start of whatever this is between us and already I've been unfaithful. He asked me if Jake and I were history and I blatantly lied, to give us a small bit of hope at starting something, only to do the complete opposite the next day.

There's no way I *can't* tell him about this, but how will he take it? He doesn't strike me as the jealous or angry type, but this would be too much for anyone. Especially after what happened before our date. He had his doubts but put them aside, and what little faith he had in making something work between us, I walked all over.

I don't know how much longer I can keep doing this dance with Jake before it breaks me. Luckily, I don't have to for much longer. We have a two-week break coming up after the guys' performance later today and then I can get some much-needed space from him. Then there's one more tour date to make it through.

I can do this. I hope.

***

The rest of the day is awkward. We all spend our time wallowing in our hangovers, which isn't pretty. Whoever's idea it was to go out drinking the night before a performance needs to be put down. Painful doesn't begin to cover it.

Sooz is eager to get things done though, raging at herself for letting us all go wild like we did. It's a half hour before the guys are due on stage, and I watch as she paces back and forth in the VIP tent, becoming more and more frazzled as the minutes tick by.

"Where are they?" she growls.

"Who knows?" I shrug.

My mind is in other places, but for the benefit of the guys, I should also be worried about where they are. They should be here by now, ready and getting amped to go on stage. But we've heard nothing.

A few minutes later noise comes from the entrance to the tent, and when we look, the band walks through in good spirits. They look considerably better than they did earlier this morning, and are followed by Amanda, who looks smugger than smug, and her team.

"I hate her sometimes," says Zoe under her breath.

"You're not the only one," I agree.

Sooz ignores us both and zones in on the group.

"Where the fuck have you all been?" Her choice of language shows she's not her usual diplomatic self.

"Well ..." Sam's tone is playful. "Our wonderful lead PR rep let us go out and get wasted last night. We've spent as long as we can resting and making sure we're ready for our set. Luckily, we had Amanda close by to think on her feet and she brought all the gear we needed."

She preens next to him at his words. The way I'm feeling, I've never been so close to bitch slapping another woman, she's pushed me to the edge too many times this summer, and to be frank, she'd deserve it.

Sam has misread the situation entirely though and doesn't understand that when it comes to anything work related, Sooz doesn't have a sense of humor. She grabs him by the scruff of the neck and drags him through to where they need to be sorting their instruments, while muttering under her breath that she doesn't get paid enough for the shit she has to deal with.

I don't look at Jake, I can't.

What happened last night has been drip fed into my conscious as the day has gone on, like a slow form of torture. My body can't decide whether it needs to be angry, repulsed or turned on, and I'm not sure how much longer I can hold it together in my fragile state. Without a word to anyone, I turn and make my way to the frontstage with my kit.

All I need to do is make it through the next hour. I keep telling myself I can do this. I didn't expect it to be so painful though. Wherever I move with the camera, trying to capture the performance, I can feel Jake's eyes on me, burning into my skin. Each time I look up, his eyes are narrowed, and his expression is angry, causing my heart to race with anxiety.

At the rate I'm going, the images are going to be awful. I have no idea how I'm going to explain his expression to the record label, so I do what I can to capture him in the images without actually focusing on his face. I pay more attention to the rest of the band.

Maybe, just maybe we will all get away with this, without being in serious trouble.

***

Hours later, we all collapse at a long table in a restaurant on the seafront. The late evening sun is setting and has a calming effect on us all. It's been six weeks since we were all thrown together in this crazy scenario, and weirdly, I think we each feel a bit emotional at the idea of being away from each other.

We spend the first part of the evening drinking and eating, and finally recover from our hangovers from the night before. When we're all fit to explode, we relax and become peaceful.

Shaun stands to do a bar run with the guys. Before he goes, he leans down into Zoe and rubs her back affectionately as he whispers something in her ear which makes her smile.

I watch as he leaves before unleashing my wrath on her. "You slept with him, didn't you?"

Sophie gasps and Sooz looks elsewhere, not wanting to get involved. Amanda and her cronies sit watching closely, refusing to miss out on any of the gossip.

When she doesn't reply, I try to persuade her and say, "Zoe, talk to us."

Sophie leans in nodding and encouraging her to open up.

"I don't know what happened." She places her head in her hands.

I've never pushed what I've seen happening between her and Shaun. I didn't want to interfere. We're past that point now, so I don't try to hide that I've figured out something has been going on between them. "Maybe this has been coming for a while?" I say.

"How so?" She looks confused, maybe she's more oblivious than I thought.

"It's not the first time I've seen you guys flirting with each other. I thought there might have been something going on when I was back in Brooklyn, but

I didn't want to pry. It wasn't quite as obvious as it is now."

"Hmm." She looks away.

"You can't deny you have a thing for him," agrees Sophie. "I mean come on, he's gorgeous. No one would blame you."

Zoe shakes her head. "It's too close to home."

I understand what she means. She's seen how a relationship within the group can affect everyone and has watched as the whole group has suffered at times because of things between me and Jake. That's why I say, "Don't let me and Jake put you off trying something with him. We're not the best example to go by."

"There's nothing to try."

"How can you say that? This is Shaun we're talking about. I've seen the way you look at him."

"It was nothing." I know she's just angry and annoyed with herself for letting her guard down because she's scared.

She sleeps around and has one-night stands to avoid any sort of commitment, the same way she won't commit to anything in her career. She's scared that failing will hurt, so it's easier to not risk it. It makes sense.

"If it was nothing, then nothing would have happened." Sophie looks upset by how in denial Zoe is being.

"I said it was nothing and I mean it," her voice is firmer this time and increases in volume. "We fucked and that was it. It meant nothing."

"Nice, Zo."

Shit.

It doesn't take a genius to work out that the guys have returned with perfect timing without us realizing, and that Shaun is standing directly behind us and has heard every word.

Zoe's face pales and I watch as her eyes begin to glisten with tears. She will never admit it, but this has meant more to her than she's letting on, and she clearly regrets what she just said, especially that he's heard.

She goes to stand and as she's walking, she says, "Shaun, I'm sorry, I—"

He slams his drink down before he storms out of the restaurant without a word.

Something dawns on me as I watch his reaction. I remember the conversation we had one night back home when he told me he had met The One. Only now do I understand it's Zoe.

The reason he came here, the reason he's so upset, is because he's been in love with her and has been waiting all along. And the moment he finally got to be with her, she's stomped all over his feelings and shoved them back in his face.

I feel awful for them both. Shaun, because I know his heart will be breaking, and Zoe, because fate, the fucker, has once again intervened in a nasty way. She hasn't been given the chance to process what happened between them and what she's really feeling. Now it might be too late.

Zoe looks at me in despair.

"Go after him," I whisper, attempting to keep the moment private. "Try and explain, it's all you can do."

She nods solemnly and runs out of the restaurant after him, as fast as she can. I hope this can be sorted.

"Well, that was interesting." Sam takes the seat next to me. "How are you feeling?"

"I've been better. Seeing two of my best friends having their hearts broken by each other isn't the nicest thing to witness."

He chuckles lightly, pulling me in for a side hug. "Now you know how the rest of us feel."

After the explosion, the night is done. We don't even finish our drinks before deciding it's time to make our way back to the bus. I hang towards the back of the group as we walk, not wanting to be too close to Jake and chance having to speak again about what happened last night. I haven't told any of the girls yet and I'd be happier pretending it didn't happen at all.

"I saw him leaving your tent this morning."

Lost in my own thoughts, I failed to notice Amanda appear at my side.

"He was making sure I was alright after what happened," I reply.

"All night long? My tent was on the other side of yours. I heard everything. The two of you weren't exactly quiet."

It's dark so she can't see how I turn red with embarrassment.

"Can we just leave it, Amanda? It's been a long day and I'd rather not talk about it."

"No. You can't keep leading him on like this."

"You don't know what you're talking about."

"Yes, I do. I've stood by and watched it for the past few years. I lost him, because of you. Remember?"

I do remember, every day. There isn't a time I don't feel guilty and a horrible person for what happened, but I don't say that out loud, I've already apologized once.

"Look," she continues. "I don't want to fight with you anymore. In fact, I've never wanted things to be the way they are between us."

My brows furrow at the irony of what she's saying. This summer she's been the one to provoke arguments. "You could have fooled me."

"Give me time. Being thrown into this scenario hasn't been easy and watching the two of you together has been hell."

"I'm sorry."

"I know you are, and I know you didn't mean to do the things you have. But at some point, you can't keep stringing him along like you're doing."

"I'm not doing it on purpose."

"But that doesn't change the fact you are. I know you've tried to avoid him, but I also know the pull he has. You need to decide what it is you want."

It makes me sound ridiculous when I admit, "I want it all to be easy, and so far, it's been anything but."

"Relationships aren't easy, Abby. No matter how in love you are and how much passion there is, they still take work, and they can still be messy. You should know that."

"I do know that." At least I think I do. Have ever been in a relationship I've had to work around loving someone the way I do Jake and everything it entails? Never.

"Then why are you giving up on him so easily?" she asks.

"He won't give me what I need."

"Are you giving him what he needs? Are you helping him?"

This girl is speaking in riddles and it feels like my hangover from earlier is starting to return.

"I'm not following," I say confused.

"Come on, Abby, think about it. You finally got back together and as soon as there was any sign of hard work involved, of things not going the way you wanted, you walked away. That wouldn't exactly fill a person with confidence when you're asking them to open up and put their heart on the line."

"How do you know all this?"

"Jake and I have moved past everything and managed to become friends over the past couple of years. He told me bits of what happened, and it makes sense to me why he's holding back.

"You're demanding something from him he knows will test the both of you. Each time, as soon as he shows any resilience you walk away. It's like you have no faith in him that when he's ready and the time is right, he will tell you. You just need to give him time."

What she's saying makes sense. All along, maybe it hasn't been Jake who's been the problem. Maybe it's been me. I'm the one constantly throwing everything he says back in his face, won't hear him out.

I finally resign myself to the truth of what she's saying. "I've been a spoiled bitch, haven't I?"

"We all have our moments, don't think you're something special."

For the first time since we met, it feels like she gives me a genuine smile.

"I just want to see him happy, and he can't move on as long as you're there, and this thing keeps happening between the two of you."

"I know you're right, but I don't know what to do. I'm trying so hard to walk away, but each time I do, there's this pull between us, bringing us back together."

"Does that not tell you something? Perhaps you should stop walking away and finally give him a real chance. Let him come to you with everything else in his own time."

"And what about Dan?"

"Ah, lovely Dan." She looks dreamily into the distance. "That's where things get tricky. I see the appeal, I do. But do you know him enough to sacrifice

242

everything with Jake, once and for all? Is he worth it?"

I swallow. "I'm not sure."

"Only you can make the choice, Abby. I wish I could help, but I can't. This is all on you."

"Great." I roll my eyes.

Amanda laughs. "I hope one day we can maybe be friendlier towards each other. I know what happened between the two of you was inevitable, I see that now. I see that I never stood a chance. I honestly hope you figure out what it is you really want."

Satisfied that we've overcome some sort of hurdle between the two of us, and that maybe the rest of the summer could be somewhat bearable, I nod back to her, signaling we're done with the conversation.

But what is it I really want? Her words keep ringing over and over in my mind. Until I decide, there's only one place I will get any sort of clarity.

Twenty-Two

Abby

There are penises everywhere, literally everywhere I turn. It's overwhelming and I don't know where to look. What else would I expect sitting in my mom's office, she is a sex columnist after all. I've been waiting over half an hour, as she's been stuck in a meeting. That's what happens when you turn up to surprise someone: things don't always go to plan.

"Are you sure I can't get you anything, Abby?" Her secretary stands at the office door, asking me for the fifth time since I arrived.

I shake my head, the same as I did the other four times she asked. "Honestly, I'm fine."

The flight had some nasty turbulence that unsettled me, and my stomach's seen better days. The thought of coffee or anything else for that matter, is a no go.

It's been a long time since I've been home, having allowed Jake to drive me out of the city for a second time. But where else do you go when your life feels like it's spinning out of control? I wanted the visit to be a surprise, and thanks to Mom linking all our digital calendars together in the hope one day I would return, I knew neither of my parents were working outside of the city.

Slouching into my chair, I pre-empt that it's going to be a while before she gets here, so I shut my eyes to catch up on some of the sleep I missed. How people manage to sleep on flights is beyond me, they're ridiculously uncomfortable. Throw the events of the summer into the mix making my mind whirl for the whole journey, and any hope of sleep was long gone. It doesn't take long to drift into a deep slumber. With the soft whir of the air conditioning in the background, it's bliss.

I have no idea how long I've been out, when someone begins gently shaking me and a voice stirs me from my sleep.

"Abby, baby, it's me. Wake up."

It takes a while, but I manage to wake up, and find myself looking into the familiar eyes of my mom. I still feel groggy, but it doesn't stop me leaping out of my seat, throwing my arms around her and drinking in every part of the moment. I didn't realize how much I missed and needed her until now.

We eventually part and she puts some space between us, heading over to her coffee machine and making us both a cup. She hands me one and sits behind her desk. I wrinkle my nose at the cup, my stomach still not settled from the flight.

"To what do I owe this pleasure?" she says sarcastically.

"Really, Mom?"

"It's been a long time since you've been home. I'm guessing it's not a coincidence it happens to coincide with a certain someone not being in the country."

"Sorry." I look down at my lap guiltily.

"You never have to apologize, baby. Just promise me you're looking after yourself. You look like shit. Are you eating?"

"Thanks for that. There was turbulence on the plane, so I've seen better days."

She hums to herself before taking a sip of coffee.

"What's with all the, uh ... penises?"

"Annual awards for best of the bunch. They're samples that have been sent out," she says.

Being a sex columnist means being surrounded by penises, so it doesn't faze her. There have been moments it's been embarrassing, but my friends have always thought it's the coolest and funniest thing. She might be a bit off the wall sometimes, but she's an amazing mom who I can talk to about anything.

"It's good being home," I say.

"It's good having you home, and a very welcome surprise. I don't want to come across as abrupt, but why are you here?"

"Do you even need to ask?"

"Jake?"

"Always, Jake."

I gaze out of her window at the New York skyline. It's an unusually overcast and foggy day, for the middle of the summer, but it's fitting with my mood.

"How about I finish up here early and we get home? You can rest and then we can deal with whatever is wrong when your father is home?"

"That would be nice."

I exhale slowly, allowing some of the anxiety that has built over the summer seep away.

***

Nothing beats being in your childhood bed. A three-hour nap later and I feel considerably fresher than when I first arrived back in New York. Walking downstairs into the kitchen, my stomach grumbles when I inhale the aromas of my mom's cooking. I can't remember the last time I had a home cooked meal and I'm salivating at the thought.

She spins around and smiles. "Your father's just freshening up before dinner. How about we all eat before we take on the world?"

Chuckling, I reply, "It's hardly taking on the world, Mom."

"It might not be in a literal sense, but sometimes it can feel that way. Don't belittle your woes, Abby. What have I told you about internalizing things? It always comes back to bite you in the ass."

We don't get a chance to take the conversation any further as my dad enters the room, beaming with open arms.

"Here she is!"

"Daddy!" I squeal, running to him and engulfing him in a hug.

"How are you doing my little Abby bear?"

"Dad, I'm not little anymore."

"Humor me." He winks, and I see a few tears in his eyes. It's been too long.

Responding to his original question, I say, "I'm okay."

I give him a small smile I hope is convincing, before looking greedily at the food Mom has laid out on the table.

He follows my eyes. "By the look on your face, you're also hungry. Eat first, talk later."

It doesn't take long for me to devour everything in sight.

"Have you not eaten this summer?" Dad asks, amused.

"Not on the plane. Turbulence." I must look a sight as I reply with a mouth full of food, some of which spills back out on to my plate. I'm glad it's only my parents here to witness this. "Sorry," I say which causes more food to fall out of my mouth.

Mom shakes her head. "It's good to see you've perked up." She looks over to my dad and explains, "She looked like shit earlier."

"Mom!"

"Well, you did. There's no point beating around the bush. Speaking of. Why are you here, Abby?"

Both my parents stare at me with serious expressions on their faces.

"You know why." Wiping my mouth with a napkin, I lean back in my chair content.

"Jake?" Dad asks, not needing a prompt.

"Am I so obvious?"

"You only tend to appear where he isn't. And as he isn't in the city at the moment, and you've run away from where he was, I'm assuming it has something to do with him."

Not able to hold in the other key piece of information they're missing, I blurt out, "I met someone this summer."

"Really? You did?" Mom's expression is ecstatic.

She doesn't hate Jake, but she isn't the biggest fan of the two of us together, not after witnessing everything I've been through over the years thanks to him. If I really want them to give me some solid advice, they need to know all the details.

"Jake and I may also have rekindled things on more than one occasion ..."

"Oh." She takes a sip of her wine, clearly waiting for me to expand on this tidbit of information.

I pick up my own glass, staring at the crisp white liquid, hoping it might somehow fix all my problems. "Yeah, oh. I don't have a clue what I'm doing anymore."

"Who is the new guy?" Dad asks. His tone is authoritative and protective at the same time, after all, I'm still his little Abby bear.

"Dan White ..." I almost whisper.

Many parents wouldn't have a clue who he is, but Dad being an exec. in the music industry will no doubt know all about him.

Not surprisingly, his eyebrows shoot up as he instantly recognizes the name. "From Six Seconds to Barcelona?"

"The one and only."

"Wow." It takes a lot to shock him.

"You don't have to sound so surprised," I try to keep the annoyance out of my voice and look him in the eye. It's clear he's trying to figure out why a huge rock star would be with me.

"It's not that. You know you're worthy of anyone, more than worthy. But he's a big deal, a really big deal."

"You think I don't know that? It's part of what's making all of this so much harder." I want to slam my head against the table in Zoe fashion, but I know Mom would tell me to get it together and stop acting like a drama queen.

"How did the two of you meet?" Mom has a starry look in her eyes. I can tell her mind is in overdrive thinking up all sorts of picture-perfect scenarios of my first meeting with Dan.

She's a sucker for romance.

"We actually met in Barcelona," I say.

She frowns as she puts the dates together. "But that was weeks ago? Why are you only just telling us about him?"

"We didn't go on a date for a while, we were both busy working. Plus, I didn't want to jinx it. Especially with Jake lurking around every corner, doing whatever he could to make sure we didn't get together."

Mom asks the obvious, "So, he's not taking it well?"

"That's one way of putting it," I say bitterly.

Dad scowls and I know he's drawing up his own conclusions to what's really been going on. "He's been treating you well though?" he asks.

I shrug. "As well as can be, considering the circumstances."

He doesn't need to know exactly what's happened this summer. It's important I remember they work together. My father has had a crucial part to play in the band's success as he's the one who signed them to the record label. If he catches wind of some of the things Jake's been up to, it could jeopardize their reputation and everything they've worked for. Revealing too much, for the sake of needing to vent, isn't worth the risk.

"What exactly does that mean?" He knows I'm skirting around the subject and not giving the full truth.

"He's been fine, Dad. You don't need to worry."

"Do I need to kick his ass?"

"No!" I say, alarmed. He's not taking this well at all. "No asses will be kicked. Promise me?"

He grumbles to himself, then picks up his own glass of wine, finishing it in one go then instantly refilling the glass, full to the brim.

When I can see he's calmed a little and is ready to take on more information, I continue, "He just won't leave it."

Mom chooses to take over the questioning, "Leave what?"

"Us. He keeps saying I'm *his*. That we're not done."

"And how do you feel about that?" her question comes out cautiously. She wants to urge me to continue and to know all the details, but she also knows I have a bad habit of shutting down when it comes to anything related to Jake.

I take a moment to decide on an answer and realize I can't sum up how I'm feeling with just one word, so I spew it out all in one go, "I'm a mess. I feel confused, angry, frustrated, upset. The full shazam."

"A bit all over the place then?"

"That's one way of putting it." I let out a breath and continue, needing to voice how I'm really feeling after holding it in for weeks, "I've spent two years trying to move on from him again. It took everything in me to walk away and here he is ... again. He thinks he can just waltz back into my life and demand whatever he wants, acts like it wasn't hard for me to walk away. He doesn't get that I did it for the both of us, to help us."

"Maybe it's a sign he's finally fighting for you. Doing what he should have done a long time ago, and proving he's the one for you?"

It irks me how much truth there is to her words. I want it to be that Jake is just acting like a possessive asshole, but deep down I know that's not the case.

"He knows what I need, and he still won't give it to me, Mom. We just keep dancing around in circles having the same argument over and over."

"What is it that you need from him?"

"The truth! That's all I've ever asked for, is the truth," I exclaim. "Eight years it's been, and I still don't know why he walked away after telling me he loved me. How can I commit to someone when I can't trust them? How can I hand him my heart again after he stomped all over it?"

After remaining silent throughout my outburst, my dad finally speaks up, "If you get the truth, will it make any difference?"

"I don't understand what you're asking me?"

"When all this is said and done, will knowing the truth change how you feel? Will it really make that much of a difference?"

"Yes." I don't know why he thinks my answer would be anything else.

"So, you're telling us, if Jake turned around and told you the truth, told you what happened back then, you would drop everything for him. You would give up everything to be with him?"

I automatically go to say yes, but then stop in my tracks. "I ..." Nobody has ever asked me that. I haven't even asked myself. I've gotten so used to Jake refusing to tell me what happened over the years I've resigned myself to it never happening, never thought what would happen when he finally does.

"It seems to me this is all an excuse to avoid facing up to how you really feel."

"Dad, really?"

He's hit the nail on the head and the stubborn part of me refuses to admit he's right.

"I know you, Abby. I know you're scared, and I know you're using this as a reason to not have to deal with things and make a decision. But at some point, you're going to have to. It's not fair to Jake and it's not fair to you. How do you ever expect to move on and live your life if you're always living in the past?"

"Mom?" I look to her for help.

All I get is a solemn shake of the head. "Your father has said it all. You need to make a choice, Abby. With or without the truth. I agree with your father though. I don't believe having the truth will make your decision any easier. It won't change the fact he still walked away. He hurt you and it still makes you angry, so what does the truth really matter? What matters is whether you can move past it all, whatever the reason may have been, and whether your feelings for him are worth putting your heart on the line again. You need to decide if you can trust him."

Later that night, I lay in bed, mulling over the conversation with my parents. For so long I've been solely focused on getting the truth from Jake I never contemplated whether I would feel any different once I had it. After everything that's happened between us, the real question is, does it really matter anymore, and will it have any impact on the decision I finally make?

As I toss and turn all night long, dreaming of both Dan and Jake, I realize that no, it probably doesn't matter.

But am I ready to choose between my head and my heart?

***

My time back home doesn't seem to last anywhere near long enough, and I couldn't leave Brooklyn without making one final stop to someone who needs help as much as I do.

I hum with excitement as I step through the doors of Riffs. It's exactly how I remember from when I worked here a couple of summers ago. As expected, I find Shaun standing behind the bar, surrounded by a gaggle of women.

He looks up as I enter, startled to see me. Immediately, he says goodbye to the disappointed women, who turn to stare me down for interrupting their time with him.

"Abby, what are you doing here?" He envelopes me in a friendly hug.

"I was in town, passing by."

"All the way from Europe? It's hardly a cab ride away."

"I actually was in town. You're not the only one who had to get away that last night in Benicassim."

Sadness passes over his face at the mention of that night, then he asks, "Drink?"

"Please." I nod, before grabbing a table and getting myself comfortable, while he gathers supplies.

He returns with a tray full of drinks and snacks.

I shoot him a look and say, "Planning a party?"

"I assume I'm not the only one with a broken heart at the moment."

"True. However, mine's never *not* been broken, and everyone knows that. You, my friend, have some explaining to do."

He looks uncomfortable and takes a long drink. "There's not much to tell. Zoe summed it up rather graciously. We fucked, that's all it was."

I take a large gulp of my drink and sit for a few seconds, contemplating what to do next. I decide we've always had the sort of friendship where we haven't held things back and now isn't the time to start.

"I know she's The One," I confirm.

"What are you talking about?" He tries to feign not knowing what I'm referring to.

I don't let him off the hook easily. "The summer I came home. I remember having a conversation with you. You told me how you'd found The One, but you wouldn't tell me who it was. I also remember a couple of occasions I saw you looking at Zoe and thought there's something going on there. It's her isn't it? Zoe. She's The One."

He doesn't reply right away, just sits playing with a pot of peanuts which I make a mental note not to eat after he spends so long fingering them. I can tell by his face he's trying to decide whether to let me in and tell me how he's really feeling.

"Shaun, you can trust me," I say, prompting him.

It's ironic that I'm so invested in getting him to speak out about how he's feeling, when I myself do anything but.

Defeated, he says, "I love her, Abby."

I don't give anything away in my expression, I don't even blink.

"Does she know?"

"She hasn't got a clue. I think us sleeping together was the first time she's ever considered I might be remotely interested. You heard the way she described it. It was just a quick fuck to her."

Seeing how torn he looks makes me feel like my heart could break all over again. I want to make things better between them, but I don't know if I can, it's not my problem to fix.

"I'm assuming it wasn't just that to you?"

"Of course, it wasn't. I'm not sure how it happened, but she means so much more to me than that. She's so lost in herself though, in showing the world she doesn't give a shit about anything, that she's stopped seeing things for what they really are. It's like she's pretended she doesn't care for so long she's actually stopped. Unless it's to do with you or Soph."

I don't know why I do, but I apologize, "Sorry."

"There's nothing to be sorry about. At least she cares about something, otherwise I'd be really worried. I don't know what to do. There's only so long you can wait around hoping the other person sees the light. You get how that feels, right?"

Out of nowhere, my eyes start to water. I'm overcome with emotion. What he's said has touched a nerve. "I get you. More than you know."

He grimaces when he sees the sadness written all over my face. "Jake won't walk away. He won't go down without a fight."

"I know and that's what scares the shit out of me."

"Why? He loves you."

"Does he though?"

"He's pined over you for eight years, Abby. Eight, goddamn years. If that doesn't prove something to you, I don't know what will. What will it take for him to show you how much he cares?"

It's only later, at home in my bed, that I think to myself, is it possible that all along it's never been about why Jake did it, but the fact he did?

It comes down to trust.

No matter what the reasoning, it still happened.

He didn't trust me with his heart ... so how can I trust him with mine?

Twenty-Three

Jake

I should never have walked away that morning in the tent. I should have stood my ground and pushed harder to get her to listen to what I was saying, made her believe how much I needed her. I left instead, letting my anger and frustration get to me, and now it feels like she's slipping away.

True Abby style, she hopped on a plane, straight back to Brooklyn, to somewhere she knew I wouldn't be. Meanwhile, I'm left here wondering what the hell is going on and what we're going to do. She can't deny the pull between us.

It scares her. I know it.

I also know that deep down, this has never been about knowing the real reason why I walked away back in high school. It all comes down to the simple fact that I did. She hates that I left her heartbroken after telling her I loved her. Now, it's about earning her trust and making her believe what we have is worth risking everything for, even after everything that's happened.

When my cell rings, I'm surprised by the name flashing on the screen. I wonder whether I should answer and how much crap I'm in for him to call me at the same time his daughter has returned home.

"Mr. West ..."

"You know you don't have to call me that, son."

Hearing him say that brings up too many feelings, calling me son. One day I want him to call me it and for it to be true.

"Sorry, it's a habit."

He goes for small talk to begin, "Tour going well?"

"Better than expected. We're living the dream over here."

The conversation is more strained than usual and evidence he didn't just call to catch up.

"That's good to hear. But it's not why I called."

"Enlighten me." I chuckle.

"Abby ..."

"Should I have expected anything else?"

He lets out a deep laugh and some of the tension eases. Over time, we've built up an open relationship, and occasionally manage to talk about Abby despite being linked in a work capacity, without it complicating things.

My ears prickle at his next words.

"She's a mess." She must be bad for him to be so brutally honest and not cover things up to make light of the situation.

Immediately my mind jumps to worst case scenarios. They flash through my mind at an alarming rate and I begin to panic. "Is she ok? Is she hurt?"

"If you count a long-standing broken heart as being hurt, then yes, she is."

I groan. "I'm trying my best. I don't know what else I can do."

258

He doesn't need to know the exact lengths I've gone to in order to try and win over his daughter, I hope my word is enough.

"It's time to tell her the truth."

Thanks to John West's position at the record label and the social circles he's part of back in New York, he's had an inkling of what happened back in high school, but I never confirmed it.

Especially not when he warned me off his daughter two years ago, when I was ready for chasing her down at JFK before she got on a flight to Cape Town.

He echoed Abby's words: "You'll hold each other back."

It wasn't time for our happy ending, sometimes it feels like it never will be the right time.

I sigh. "It won't make any difference. She still won't trust me."

"Telling her gives her one less excuse to clutch at."

It makes sense and I understand what he's getting at. Without the past haunting us, Abby will have to face up to reality and live in the present. She won't be able to use the past as a reason not to commit to us. For her, the issue isn't the reason why I left, but the fact I left at all. I did it once and she's protecting her heart from me doing it again, she just doesn't realize what it is she's doing.

"I'm trying my best," I reply.

This summer has been hard, especially watching her fall for another guy, seeing my chance slipping away right in front of me. I don't know how much more of her pushing me away I can take, and I don't know how much more I have left to give to someone who doesn't want to see or hear how hard I'm fighting for them.

"I shouldn't have stopped you from following her. I know that now and I'm sorry. Whatever this is between you and Abby, it's as real as it gets, and it's messy, because love is." I hear him exhale down the line. "Fight with everything you have left, and when you're done, if you really love my daughter, fight some more."

The line goes dead.

***

Abby

The final part of my trip home went by in a blur. Spending as much time with my parents as I could and making up for lost time was cathartic. The rest of the time I spent resting and wandering the streets of Brooklyn and Manhattan with my camera. After my conversation with Shaun, I had some serious soul searching to do.

As I made my way onto the plane to return back to Europe for the final part of the band's tour, I would have loved to say I had a clearer head over the decisions I needed to make. But things didn't feel clearer in any way, if anything, I felt more confused than ever.

I keep trying to stem the panic inside, the feeling that I'm running out of time and will be forced to make a decision I'm not ready to make, but it's hard to keep it all in. All that keeps ringing through my head is the one question my parents and Shaun put at the forefront of my mind. Does the truth really matter?

I've spent the past two years hung up on the idea that if Jake gave me this snippet of information, things would suddenly seem clearer that I would be

260

able to make a decision, but in the grand scheme of things it would change absolutely nothing. I realize now that it was never about getting the truth. I gave him everything, gave up my heart and told him I loved him, and he left.

The real question is, do I have it in me to give him everything again, knowing what he can do when he has my heart in his hands?

We've been on the tour bus for a few hours, and I haven't said much to anyone. I know I need to get out of my funk and stop acting like such a bitch to everyone. We only have this last tour date left and I need to count my blessings and make the most of it.

"I can't believe we're in England!" Zoe throws her arms around Sophie, bouncing up and down in her seat, unable to contain her excitement. "I have *always* wanted to come here. I also can't believe it's sunny. I thought it always rained?"

You'd think over the trip she'd open her eyes more to the world around her, alas no.

"Again, with the stereotyping. You shouldn't always believe what you see on the TV," I say.

"Netflix has a lot to answer for. It's where I get most of my knowledge," she says smugly, as if it's something to be proud of.

"I can tell." I leave it at that, deciding not to take my bad mood out on her.

She ignores my underhand comment and moves the conversation on, "Where are we going?"

"I think Sooz said it was called Leeds Fest?" replies Sophie.

Attempting her best English accent, Zoe says, "Sounds a hoot. Is that what the English say? Hoot?"

"Seriously Zoe, you need to take it down a notch. What's gotten into you lately?" says Sophie.

She looks far too annoyed for just a few comments, which leaves me wondering whether during the time I've been home in Brooklyn things have been challenging between the two of them.

"Is she okay?" I lean in and ask Sophie when Zoe is preoccupied with something else.

She shakes her head. "I'm not sure. She's been over the top like this since that night with Shaun. I think she's trying to make us believe she's fine, when really she's not."

"Sounds familiar."

"Anyway, are you alright? Did being home help?"

"Yes and no." I look down the bus to where I know Jake is sitting. We've seen each other briefly, but all I could manage was a small nod of acknowledgement. I'm still not ready to talk to him.

"At least you had a break. Maybe it's done you more good than you realize."

"I hope so."

I don't tell her about the sleepless nights, tossing and turning in bed, wracked with guilt over the Jake/Dan scenario. I know she suspects there are things I'm not telling her, but she doesn't push it any further, for which I'm thankful.

"Have you spoken to Dan? Will he be here?"

"No and yes," I say.

"You haven't spoken to him?" She looks shocked by my answer.

"No. Is that bad?"

"Kind of. I thought you guys hit it off. You seemed deliriously happy after your date so I thought you might have at least spoken to him a couple of times."

"I've tried, but I just can't face it." I look away. I know I'm fighting a losing battle and I'm going to have to tell them what happened between me and Jake.

As if she reads my mind, Zoe returns to the conversation, "Is there something you're not telling us?"

"Uh ..." My hesitation is a dead giveaway.

Zoe narrows her eyes. "Abby don't fuck with us. We know when you're lying."

They both sit waiting, clearly not going to back down until I tell them what happened back in Spain.

"Jake and I slept together," I say looking down at the table briefly.

"That's a nice way of putting it, but you've already told us that," Zoe says misunderstanding what it is I'm trying to tell them. "I think last time you described it as 'he fucked you against a wall.'"

"No, you don't understand. This time we slept together ... When we were at Benicassim, in the tent," the words coming out of my mouth are humiliating. I've spent all my time telling everyone how angry I am with him, how I don't want him. Yet, as soon as the opportunity arises, I do the complete opposite. Even to my own ears I sound pathetic.

Zoe gawps. "Holy cow, but what about Dan? It seemed like he was really good for you."

"He was, I mean he is. I just don't know any more. My head is so screwed."

"It makes sense now why you ran back to Brooklyn," says Sophie, a look of understanding on her face.

"I just needed some space."

"Are you going to see Dan again? You can't just leave him like you have," Zoe says.

"I know. He wants to go out on another date later today. I haven't given him an answer."

"That's a good thing." The optimism on Sophie's face has me feeling the same, almost. "You've only had one date with him. How do you expect to make

263

such a huge decision based on that one night? I think you need to spend more time with him and get to know him a bit better. Then things might seem a little clearer."

"You're right. I'm just getting fed up with all the back and forth with the two of them. All I do is go around in circles."

"That's a sign it's time to make a choice. Have the date with Dan, enjoy it and see how you feel after. Let yourself have some fun and live a little, Abby. Don't overthink it, just see it for what it is, a date. If things don't seem clearer, that's fine too. No one is forcing you to decide. It's only you putting that pressure on yourself."

"I'll try." And I will.

But knowing myself and my own mind, I know it's going to be tough to allow myself to relax. Especially when guilt is constantly playing with my mind.

"Not try," says Zoe firmly. "You will, or you're going to drive yourself mad. Not everything has to be all or nothing. Jesus, we're only twenty-six!"

"I just feel that with Jake, my time's up. I don't think he's going to be able to take much more."

"If he won't wait and give you the time you need, then he isn't the one for you like he claims to be." It's unusual for Zoe to be so insightful, and what she's saying makes sense.

I've been pushing myself because Jake keeps pushing, but what's the rush? Why do I need to make a decision now, just because he's decided he's fed up with waiting? He should have thought about that when he kicked my ass aside all those years ago.

After our conversation, I feel refreshed and ready to see things with a fresh pair of eyes. It's time to take things into my own hands and make choices for myself, when I want to, not when other people think I should.

***

Zoe looks around at the thousands of female festival goers, with a bemused expression on her face. "Can someone please tell me why they're all wearing rubber boots? And why do they have such big hair? I didn't know back-combing was still a thing."

We're standing to the side of a large open area, taking in the scene around us. It's a little overwhelming and I'm feeling a bit disorientated.

Zoe continues to ramble on, "I thought England was so small they wouldn't have the space for a big festival. This is huge, like the biggest one yet."

"You're unbelievable sometimes, you know that?" I say.

Although she does have a point. I don't think any of us would have put this down to be the band's biggest performance.

"This isn't *one of* the biggest festivals," says Sooz. "It's *the* biggest festival. It's also where the guys' biggest market is and a really big deal. We've got our work cut out and there's so much PR stuff we have to do. We all need to be in top form."

"We'll get through it," I try to make my voice sound more convincing than I feel. "You're the best for a reason and everything is going to go without a hitch. Don't fret."

"It's not me I'm worried about." She looks at the three of us making it apparent she sees us more as a hindrance than a help.

"I'm going to pretend you don't mean anything by that," I laugh.

She walks off, leaving us to scurry behind, and shouts over her shoulder, "Of course I didn't."

A few hours, interviews, and photoshoots later, I'm starting to understand what Sooz meant. This is the biggest workload we've had by far and we're only a few hours in. Thankfully, Amanda and I resolved some of our issues back in Spain, as we've been working closely together. I don't think we would have managed quite as well if there had been the same level of animosity between us.

"I'm beat," I groan. "Like seriously, this is breaking me. Why is this so hard?"

"Are you coming down with something?" Sooz pales as she takes in my appearance. I must look like crap and the last thing she needs when we're this busy is to be a pair of hands down.

I try to brush her concern away. "It's just all the travel and emotional stress finally taking its toll."

"Is it just that? You've been looking a bit peaky recently. I guess life on the road isn't the healthiest. Maybe you're deficient in something? We'll have to get you booked in with a doctor when we get back to Cape Town."

When I think about it, she's right, I have been feeling off for the past couple of weeks. It probably has something to do with all the heavy drinking we've been doing. I have no idea how Sophie and Zoe have managed to keep going like this for years. How their livers are still functioning with the amount of partying they do is beyond me.

"I'll be fine, we just need to get today finished with and I can call it a night."

If only.

It was wishful thinking on my part that I'd be able to get through the afternoon and then be able to rest. Just as we're rounding things up for the day, I bump into Dan in the VIP tent. I want to be happy to see him, but I'm just too exhausted.

"Abby, hi," he sounds awkward and I don't blame him. He's sent multiple messages since our date, and I've replied to none. I'm surprised he's even giving me the time of day.

He still manages to bring a smile to my face. "Dan ..." that's all I manage, suddenly unable to muster the energy to say anything more.

"You don't look too great."

Under normal circumstances I would be embarrassed, but I don't care about anything other than finding somewhere I can be horizontal and undisturbed for the night. I reply wearily, "I've had better days."

"We can postpone tonight if it's too much?"

Even though I haven't replied, he's assuming we're going to have a date, but I'm too focused on my need to crawl into bed.

"I've been trying to call you for the past couple of hours, but I kept getting voicemail, the signal is crap out here. Are you sure you're not sick? You could have picked something up on the plane because you really don't look good."

"I don't feel it either."

He stands, with concern on his face, contemplating what to do. "Come with me."

He grabs me gently by the elbow and attempts to keep me steady on my feet as he steers me out of the VIP tent and away from the hustle and bustle of the main festival area.

When we've been walking for a while, I figure out he's taking me to where the tour buses are parked. Rather than heading in the direction of the one I've become familiar with over the summer, we detour to his. It's bigger than Jake's, and seriously sleek. I stop

267

and stand in awe when we enter, taking in the sheer luxury around me.

Steering me to a set of huge couches, he gently pushes me down with little effort. My body hits the huge squashy cushions and I sigh with relief, feeling like I'm floating on a cloud.

"Sit and don't move. You need food."

I expect a private chef to pop up out of nowhere and begin cooking up a gastro storm but am pleasantly surprised when Dan grabs an apron off the side of a small kitchenette and starts to cook.

"You cook?" I try to hide the amusement in my voice, not wanting to offend him in any way.

"There's a lot about me I hope you'll get to know."

I could become addicted to the smile he gives me. There's a twinkle in those blue eyes which are staring and making me feel things I don't want to. Things that make this whole mess even more confusing. Reminding myself of what Sophie and Zoe said, I shake the thoughts away and try to enjoy myself and getting to know him, rather than placing so much emphasis on making a huge decision with someone I barely know.

I sit back, get myself comfy and watch as Dan dances around, humming and cooking, filling the bus with the most delicious smells. However, not even the greatest meal in the world could keep me awake. I'm so bone achingly tired that before I notice and have a chance to stop myself, I give into sleep.

Twenty-Four

Abby

"Abby, you need to wake up."

"Huh?" I grumble at being awoken from a deep slumber, something that feels like it's becoming a regular thing.

It's official, this summer has beaten me.

I open my eyes and am greeted with the most beautiful sight. Dan leaning over me, all mussed up and sleepy himself. Looking around, I see it's no longer light out.

"Shit! I fell asleep? How long have I been out for?" I ask.

"Hours," he states, looking amused. "I was cooking, turned around and you were gone. You looked so peaceful ... I didn't have the heart to wake you. I must have fallen asleep myself, but luckily set an alarm."

Panic floods me. "I need to tell the girls where I am. They'll kill me for disappearing and not letting them know where I am."

He looks unsure as he says, "I hope you don't mind. I figured that would be your reaction, so I got our PA to find a charger for your phone. I texted ... Zoe, is it? Let her know you were with me and you were ok. I told her she could come check on you, but she said she trusted me and gave me the directions to your bus. We can make our way back whenever you're ready."

He's so thoughtful and confident in everything he's saying, I feel myself swoon.

"You really are the perfect gentleman, aren't you?"

He smiles. "I try to be. Not all famous people live up to their reputation."

"I could get used to this, waking up to you." I don't know where the words come from. I blush furiously at how open I've been with my feelings to one of the most gorgeous and famous rock stars in the world. "Oh my God. I can't believe I've just said that out loud." I face plant the chair and all I want is to escape and not have to face Dan's reaction.

"Hey," he says soothingly, dragging me up into his lap.

My heartrate increases at the feeling of being so close to him. We might have kissed, but we've never been so close physically and we've never been alone quite like this. It's making me nervous and every part of me begins to feel alive.

"You don't ever have to be embarrassed around me, Abby. I can guarantee, whatever it is you're feeling, I can double it."

I love his honesty. I never thought a rock star would be so open and humble.

"Why?" I stammer, my voice barely audible.

"Honestly, I don't know. I've said it before, there's something about you. I was drawn to you that night in the ice cream shop and have been ever since. I've

270

not felt this way in a long time, and I'll be damned if now I've found you, I'm going to fight it. I'm feeling all the feels. Is that how you Americans say it?"

I let out an embarrassing snort at how ridiculous he is, wishing I could bottle up the memory and never forget how easy and uncomplicated everything feels in this moment. When I manage to regain my composure, his expression changes, and for the first time I see lust swirling in his eyes. It seems like he doesn't want to hold back how he's feeling and what he wants, not now we're here alone together.

His lips meet mine and at first, he's tentative. I don't want to chance the kiss ending too soon, so I push back and give him more, trying to show him with my lips that I'm not as fragile as I look. I'm not sure how long we sit there, losing ourselves in each other, but it doesn't feel like long enough.

I don't want the kiss to end but Dan pulls away gently. "Believe me, Abby. There is nothing I want more than to carry on kissing you like this, but if I do, I can't guarantee I'll be able to stop myself taking things further."

"Would that be such a bad thing?"

I move in steadily, attempting to pick up where we left off, but he places one finger firmly against my lips, stopping me in my tracks.

"You still look exhausted, and you haven't eaten. Let me reheat what I made earlier."

Gently lifting me from his lap, he places me back on the couch before heading to the kitchen and putting a plate in the microwave. He turns and bursts out laughing.

"What?" I ask, sulking. I'm annoyed I haven't been able to continue kissing him and my body is still humming in response making me all kinds of frustrated.

Confirming exactly what I thought, he replies, "If you could see your face ... Chill, there will be plenty of opportunities for *that*. But when we do, I want to make sure you enjoy it. I don't just want it to be a quick shag."

His words warm my blood, and a steady ache begins to build in between my legs. Getting myself worked up is the last thing I need, especially when Dan has confirmed, one hundred percent he will not be going *there* with me tonight. I try to distract myself and think of something else but fail miserably, there is only one thing on my mind.

A few minutes pass and he returns with plates of food. My mouth waters and before he has a chance to even sit down, I attack my plate like a ravenous beast. He watches quietly with an amused expression.

When I eventually come up for air, he says, "Water?"

I nod my head eagerly, unable to respond thanks to my mouth still being full of food. He passes me a glass full, which I guzzle down, the cool liquid satisfying my thirst and it takes only a matter of minutes to clear my plate of food, which was big enough to fill a linebacker. If Dan weren't here watching, I definitely would have licked the plate clean.

"Just when I thought I couldn't like you more, you put on a performance like *that*."

I grin. "Attractive, huh?"

He winks. "One for the wank bank."

"Excuse me?" I scoff.

I'm not used to hearing him talk like this, but I like it. It shows another side to him I didn't know was there, but also proves the girls right. We've only had one date and barely know anything about each other. There are so many things we have yet to learn and we're only just starting our journey. That's if I'm willing to jump on board for the ride.

The girls said to give myself time, but it's unfair to string along a guy as great as Dan. Two guys in fact. Thanks to the anxiety caused by thinking about the decision I need to make, nausea threatens once more as my gut churns with guilt.

Dan seems to notices and stands. "We should get you back to your bus before it gets too late. You need to rest."

"I could always stay here?" I wiggle my eyebrows suggestively, in one last ditched attempt to change his mind.

"Not a chance. I won't be able to keep my hands off you, and that's not what you need right now."

Grabbing a jacket from the side, it's his signal that it's time to leave and I have no choice in the matter. As disappointing as it is, I get that it's not because he wants me to leave, but because it's what's right.

The journey back to my own bus is quicker than expected. Walking hand in hand, as we get closer to the doors, he stops and turns so he's facing me. Leaning down he gives me the gentlest, sweetest kiss I've ever had.

"Come see me play tomorrow. I want to know you're there watching me. We're on the headliner stage; it will be huge, but I can wangle VIP passes for you and your friends."

"That would be nice." Standing on my tiptoes, I give him another kiss.

He pulls away and I can't tell if it's my eyes playing tricks on me or if he just shivered even though the heat is unbearable. "I wish I didn't have to say goodnight."

"I wish you didn't have to either." I struggle to keep my emotions at bay because as much as I'm

273

fighting this, and as much as I feel guilty for hiding things that have happened between me and Jake, I can't contain the feelings for him developing at a rapid rate. It's overwhelming.

He lets out a sigh and takes a step back. "I'm going to leave now, while I still have it in me to walk away. Goodbye, beautiful."

I stand and watch his retreating form, swooning at his words and everything about him. It doesn't take long for the doors of the bus to open and I'm pulled in by Zoe's eager hands. She drags me to the back, shoving me down into a couch, where Sooz and Sophie are also sitting, with excited expressions on their faces.

"Spill!"

I smile to myself, getting lost in the memories of the evening. "There's nothing to spill."

"He said you were sleeping. Did you guys, you know ..." Zoe looks at me, expecting me to reveal some sordid tale, but she's about to be disappointed.

"No. I was exhausted and embarrassingly, fell asleep while he was cooking for me."

"I'm calling bull."

"I'm telling the truth. You saw how tired I was."

"Well, that's boring." She huffs.

"Sorry to disappoint. But he did ask us to come watch his set tomorrow. He said he'd get us all VIP passes."

Sooz and Sophie squeal with delight.

Sam wanders over, looking amused. "What are you girls making a fuss about?"

"Dan's giving us all VIP passes to his performance tomorrow," I reply.

"Great." He begins backtracking with a frown on his face. "I'll catch you guys later."

Quickly, he walks down the bus and I catch a glimpse of him sharing hushed words with Jake, who glances over in our direction with a pissed off look.

"What was that about?" asks Sophie, not missing the animosity in the air.

"Beats me." I shake my head and my shoulders slump as some of the happiness from my night with Dan disappears. It doesn't matter which direction I turn, there's always someone there, going against the choices I make. "Anyway, I'm still beat, so I'm going to call it a night."

I make my way to one of the bunk beds and settle in quickly even with the noise of the others around me. I may have been out cold all afternoon, but I succumb to sleep quicker than I ever have before.

***

God, I'm a hot sweaty mess. Coming to, I see it's dark and quiet on the bus, so I guess it must either still be night, or the early hours of the morning. Kicking off the covers, I hope it will give me some relief, but it does nothing. I'm hit by a huge wave of sickness. I can't figure out what's wrong with me, clearly this summer has been stressful and affected me in ways I didn't think it would.

I roll over and pray for the nausea to pass, but wave after wave hits, with such a force I break out in a cold sweat and it becomes unbearable. Racing to the restroom, I only just make it before emptying the contents of my stomach. When it feels like it's passed, I sit back against the cool wall, trying to catch my breath.

It's not long before another wave hits and I'm back where I started, with my head in the toilet, praying for it to end soon

A knock at the door startles me. I can't even puke in private, I'm so over this summer. "Go away," I croak.

I wish I'd locked the door, but in my haste, it was the last thing on my mind. All I can manage is a whimper when it opens, and someone makes their way quietly into the small room.

"What's wrong?" asks Amanda.

"What do you care?"

I shouldn't be bitchy, she's only being caring, but I feel so ill and she's the last person I want seeing me in this state. She chooses to ignore me and stands with her arms folded, waiting for me to reply more reasonably.

"I've seen better days," I reply more calmly.

"Do you need to see a doctor?"

"Have you never had a bug before?" I chuckle and then moan as it unsettles my stomach, another wave of nausea beginning to build.

"Yes, I have. But not one that goes on for weeks."

I blink at her. "This hasn't been going on for weeks."

"Are you really that dumb?"

"If you're going to start being a bitch you can leave," I snap.

"Sorry, it's a habit. As I was saying, you've been sick a lot recently ..."

"I think you're being a bit dramatic. We've been drinking loads and I'm constantly hungover."

"You've also looked like crap for half the tour."

"Jeez, thanks." If I had the energy, I would force her to leave, but I don't, so all I can do is sit and take what she's saying.

"I'm being serious, Abby. How many times have we all said you look exhausted? In fact, how many times have you complained you've been exhausted, and it's only getting worse. Now the nausea too ..."

I sigh. "It's a classic sign of anxiety. It's been a rocky summer."

"Hmm," she murmurs to herself.

I close my eyes as a few moments of silence pass between us and embrace the relief as another wave of sickness passes. When Amanda clears her throat, I look into her eyes and see her expression has changed. She almost looks sick herself.

"Abby ..."

"Yes, Amanda?"

"When was the last time you got your period?"

Honestly, this girl needs to get a grip. It's the middle of the night and now we're talking about my menstrual cycle. "The other week, why?"

"Give me an exact date," she demands.

"I don't know," I shrug. "I've lost track with the tour, but it was recently."

"Are you sure about that?"

"Of course, I'm sure." I raise one brow, beginning to get annoyed. "What are you suggesting?"

"Hear me out. You've been tired, particularly bratty, even for you, had spells of sickness that are getting worse ..." she trails off. "And I haven't seen you once have to go to a drug store, to you know, buy *supplies*." She uses her fingers to make air quotes during that last word.

"Jesus, are you watching my every move now?"

"Come on. I'm being serious."

"So am I."

"I need you to really think about it. All of us have been caught off guard at least once on this trip and had to borrow supplies from someone, but not you. Think hard. When was the last time you had a period?"

A feeling of doom begins to creep in. It dawns on me that what she's asking makes sense. I haven't the faintest idea when I last had a period and I begin to understand where her thought process is taking her.

I swallow hard. "It's not possible."

I must have said that part out loud because Amanda replies quietly, "It is possible, Abby."

"But I'm on birth control?"

"Did you ever listen in sex ed? You're not one hundred percent covered. Are you sure you've been taking it right?"

Oh no. "There was the night after ..." I stop awkwardly, not wanting to instill the details of Jake and I having sex on her.

She's too focused on getting to the bottom of all this. "I'm a big girl. I can take it."

"Well, I was sick the next day." It all comes flooding back to me, the reason my alarm had gone off that morning, being the most hungover I think I've ever been in my life. Puking my guts up not long after taking my birth control pill. "Shit!"

Amanda looks confused. "Do you really think you could be?"

"I don't know, maybe? But it was one time." Panic begins to set in, and I can feel myself starting to hyperventilate as it all becomes overwhelming.

"Abby, try and calm down," Amanda says soothingly, but all it does is irritate me more.

"You fucking calm down," I snap.

"Seriously," she hisses. "You could wake everyone up and then they're gonna demand to know why we're in here. Do you want that, before you even know what the answer is?"

"No."

"Then get it together."

The more I sit and think, the more it all makes sense. It would explain why I've been so up and down the last few weeks, the fatigue and the mood swings. I put my head in my hands. "Oh God, what am I going to do?"

"We can't do anything now, it's the middle of the night."

"No shit, Sherlock."

"You need to get a test as soon as you can. Maybe hold off on the birth control for the next few days, you know, in case you are."

She's so cool and calm, I would be too if I weren't the one thinking I was: Pregnant.

"Fuck, fuck, fuck."

She looks at me bewildered. "You really need to chill out. We don't even know for sure yet."

"Not that," I squeal, diving headfirst into the toilet and emptying my stomach for what is possibly the hundredth time.

What I least expect happens next.

The person who should hate me the most and who should be doing anything except helping me through this scenario, the one who should be licking her wounds and mending the pieces of her own broken heart, bends over, and spends the next hour holding back my hair, nursing me, until finally it passes and I'm able to settle again.

***

Making our way to Dan's performance, I'm a mess. I woke up after the few hours of sleep I managed to get, once Amanda had tucked me in, with dread consuming every part of me. My mind has been running at a thousand miles an hour, and my hand keeps instinctively moving to my stomach, rubbing it

279

soothingly. When I realized what I'm doing, I tell myself to pack it in before someone catches me and thinks I'm trying to rub one off.

Shakily, I got myself ready and managed to stomach a small bowl of cereal, but the nausea has been creeping back in gradually as the day has gone on. When I thought I was a goner, like an angel, Amanda appeared at my side with a bottle of sparkling water and some crackers, knowing exactly what I needed.

It was as if she could read my mind when she handed over some pain relief. When no one was close by, I quietly asked if it was safe. She shrugged and murmured that we didn't know for certain, so I should take it rather than suffering. Who would have guessed I'd be seeking comfort from someone who's caused so much aggravation over the summer?

Zoe keeps staring at me concerned, as we make our way into the VIP area near the stage, after she tried to buy me a drink and I refused. My stomach is still so unsettled I don't want to chance making it worse. It's one thing covering it up in the black of night, but now in daylight, it's all beginning to feel incredibly real.

It's not long before Dan and his band begin their set and the crowd goes wild. I look behind, in awe at the thousands of people standing and cheering, consumed by the music and his breathtaking voice. It still baffles me that someone as famous and talented as him would be interested in me. I have no idea what it is he sees in me, but it makes me happy in a way I haven't experienced in a long time.

Out of the corner of my eye, I catch Jake watching me, taking in my every move as my gaze moves back and forth between the crowd and Dan. I should try and hide the feelings I'm beginning to develop, at least attempt not to rub his face in it, but I don't have the energy to cover it up any longer.

"Did you take a test?" whispers Amanda in my ear.

I'm furious she would bring it up here, in front of the whole group, where any of them could hear us and figure out what we're talking about. "Where the hell would I magically get one? The pregnancy test fairy?"

"Abby, you need to find out, soon. You need to make sure you're both healthy."

I flinch at the way she says both. "Please Amanda, just leave it. When we're done here, I promise I will find out, but what am I supposed to do when we're in the middle of a festival?"

"Fine," she says. "Tomorrow we're going somewhere and getting one. You need to know for sure and then you need to tell him."

"Tell him what?" asks Jake, looking between the two of us. "I wasn't aware the two of you had suddenly become so friendly."

"It's none of your business, Jake." I push past him, choosing to move forward and drink in Dan's voice as he sings.

When he looks down into the VIP area, somehow his eyes find mine and it feels like everything around me disappears.

All I see is him.

Twenty-Five
Jake 8 Years Earlier

It's been four days since the shit show with Abby at my house. The night keeps playing on a constant loop in my head from the moment I open my eyes and keeps me awake at night. I can't get over it. I've been blatantly ignoring her, but what is there to say? Guys, we don't get embarrassed easily, but even I'll admit I'm humiliated by what happened. Being caught by your mom, about to take your girlfriend's virginity ... there's no coming back from that.

I've wanted to speak to her since the moment I watched her walk out the door, but I can't get the image of mortification on her face from my mind. Each time I go to call her, I hang up. My behavior is unjustified. I know I don't need to react like this, because Abby isn't like all the other girls and that's what I've grown to love about her.

Yes, love. What I said wasn't a half-assed attempt to get into her pants. I knew from the moment I first saw her she was going to be trouble. There's *something that draws me in, and I stopped trying to fight it a long time ago. Any other girl, and the effort it would have taken to break through those walls would have put me off, it wouldn't have been worth it. With Abby it's different, the chemistry between us is there constantly simmering away. But damn, if my balls don't feel like they're going to explode just being near her. The restraint it takes sometimes to hold back and keep going at her pace is physically painful.*

She's worth it though, the effort, the patience. The other night I got a snippet of what it could be like and now I want more. I had her so close, got to taste her, hear her moan my name. I now know there's nothing better than the feeling of her under me, in my hands. It's been the main focus of my fantasies which have more than doubled since that night. I'm lucky I don't have friction burn. I could have it all. But first I need to stop acting like a pussy and call her.

Finally, I work up the courage and decide I've messed around enough. Pulling my cell from my pocket, I get her name up on the screen ready to call and settle things. She might be a little hurt that I haven't been in touch, but we can get past it. She's not the type to hold a grudge, she was right there with me and experienced each humiliating second. I know I'm not the only one embarrassed.

Looking at the picture of us together I've saved for her caller ID makes me smile like an idiot. God, she's so beautiful, it takes my breath away. Shaking my head, I try to get myself together. I'm beginning to sound like some pansy chick novel, but this is what she does to me. The cool Jake I try to make everyone see goes out the window when it comes to her.

I'm about to hit call when a throat clears, the sound coming from my doorway. I look up from where I'm sitting at my desk and find my Grandpa, filling the doorway with a stern look on his face.

Here we go.

It wasn't enough that Mom spent the past four days chewing my ass over and over, about how irresponsible I'm being with my future, but now the old man is back in town and I get to go through another few rounds with him too. Great.

"Can I help, or are you just going to stand there all day?" I ask.

I attempt to stare him down, hoping if I can make him back away, then he will realize he can't push me around anymore. But he's relentless. My mom didn't get it from nowhere.

"Your mother had an interesting story to tell when I got back last night," he says.

The only saving grace of this whole scenario was that he was out of town working when shit went down. Even though he should be retired, the old grump still wants to keep earning money, keep pushing his social status, because between him and my mom, they can never have enough. The two of them together are a force to be reckoned with and the only person I ever got any peace with was my grandma, but she died years ago.

There might be some truth in thinking they put all their grieving and energy into me when she was gone. It's ironic and makes me bitter, because she wouldn't care what I did with my life as long as I was happy. She'd have made it well known that how hard they've pushed me over the past couple of years, into a life I don't want any part of, was wrong.

"Are you listening to me?"

284

I zoned out. "Yeah, I'm listening," I reply.

"So, you've found yourself a girl, a band ... you're becoming quite the little rock star." He's smirking, but his eyes are cold as ice. He's not done with me yet and this isn't going to work in my favor, I know him too well.

"It was a mistake. I've already said sorry to Mom."

"But if it hadn't been here, it would have been somewhere else. You're a teenage boy, of course you're not going to be able to keep your dick in your pants."

His harsh words take me by surprise. He can be hard sometimes, but this feels different. How he's speaking, it's detached and can't be a good thing, it means the worst is yet to come.

"She's my girlfriend, we've been together for a while ... I love her." I hesitate at telling him the last part. We've never had the sort of relationship where we talk about happy things and feelings. I'm hoping that by opening up to him like this, he might back down and give me some room to breathe.

"She's your girl, how sweet," his tone is sarcastic.

Any hope I had that being open about my feelings with him might change his mind with whatever punishment he has in store goes out the window.

"Will she be your girl this time next year when you're away at college? Long distance romances don't last, don't be naïve and think yours will be the exception. It won't. Just because she was going to let you pop her cherry, doesn't mean she won't open her legs to the next guy who looks her way."

I knew he could be a cold-hearted bastard, but this is a side to him I've never seen before. How can someone who held you as a baby and raised you as their own, speak to you this way? If I ever need an

285

example of the parent I don't want to be when I'm older, all I need to do is look at this miserable old fuck.

"There's a letter downstairs for you ..." he continues. He doesn't need a response or reaction. He knows what his words are doing. He also doesn't want my opinion because he's going to stand here and tell me how shit is going to fly.

Once again, I have to sit and listen to what's expected of me, then I have to follow in line, the way I have done my whole life.

"It's an acceptance letter to Columbia," he confirms.

Dread fills me. I don't want to go to any of the colleges they made me apply for. Truthfully, I don't want to go to college at all. I want to carry on with my music, but they would never accept that. Sometimes at night I lay awake, wondering if there is a way around it all, that maybe they will see the light and see my happiness matters more than going to an Ivy League school. Yeah. Right. Things can't get any worse, so I may as well try and put up some sort of fight to get what I want out of my life.

"I don't want to go to college," the words come out quietly, almost shaky. I feel like a pussy, but I've never defied him in this way, never answered back or stood my ground. I've always conformed. I have no idea what his reaction will be.

"Speak up boy. I can't hear what you're saying."

"I said, I don't want to go to college," this time when I speak, I stand up from my bed and square my shoulders, attempting to appear strong.

He narrows his eyes, processing, clearly unable to believe what he's hearing. "Excuse me?"

"You heard me. I. Don't. Want. To. Go. To. College," I speak slower and louder, making my point clear as day.

"I heard you the first time. You don't have to speak to me like that. I'm old, not senile."

"Well, you said excuse me," I grumble under my breath.

Why does he always have to be such an asshole? Most people's grandparents are loveable old men, but not him. Even knowing what he can be like, I don't expect the conversation to take the turn it does.

"What I meant was: excuse me, who do you think you are, telling me what you will be doing, like you have a say?"

In case he wasn't cold enough towards me, at the moment when he's about to rip my world from under my feet, he laughs in my face.

I swallow, answering back, my voice sounding braver than I feel, "Because it's not like college should be my choice, right?"

"No, it shouldn't. This family has decades, generations of standards to maintain and if you think pissing about in a band is going to fly, you've got another think coming."

"Most families would be supportive with what I want ..."

"We're not most families. We're one of the most prestigious families in Manhattan. That doesn't come without making some sacrifices."

"Some? You're asking me to give up everything. You want me to ignore what I want to do with my life, what I'm passionate about and love ... for what you want."

"I'm not asking you to do that."

His words give me a glimmer of hope, but when I look up at his face, the expression there tells me what he's about to say, I'm not going to like.

"I'm not asking you because I'm telling you. Who do you think would fund this little dream you have? Me. Will I do it? No. You will follow what I say and do what all of the men in our family have done before you."

"Right ..." If he thinks I'm giving up the band he's got another thing coming. I'll do what I've always done and go behind his back. It's surprising what you can fit into your day without your parents knowing.

"On to more pressing matters. It seems as if your focus has been even more compromised as of late."

I didn't think it was possible, but his eyes get a degree colder. Chills run down my spine and I hope he's not about to go with the conversation where I think he is.

"So, there's a girl?"

Of course, he's going there, he's ruthless, why wouldn't he?

I swallow. "She's special ..."

"Special enough for you to fuck her under my roof, where anyone could walk in on you?"

"It wasn't like that," I mumble, a slight flush creeping up my neck as I try not to remember the other night, how mortified she looked.

He narrows his eyes. "Humor me. What was it like?"

"I love her," my voice breaks and I know it makes me look weak, but I hate speaking about Abby with him. I want to protect her from this world my mom and grandpa are insistent I be part of. Kind, gentle Abby doesn't need to be part of all this. Nobody knows the deceit and the lies that go on behind closed doors. To the outside world, everything seems so perfect. It's a life most would dream to be part of. 'The elite.'

What they don't know is that it's an empty life, lonely. It's a dog-eat-dog world and Abby is too kind to have any part in that.

He scoffs at my words. "You're too young to know what love is."

"I'm not a child. I'm almost eighteen and in the eyes of the law I'll be a grownup."

"Then start fucking acting like one," he roars.

I'm shocked the windows don't rattle with how loud and angry his voice is.

He shows his true colors when he practically spits the next words at me, "You will end things with her. I've turned a blind eye to all this band stuff or whatever you want to call it, but this, is too much. You need to stay focused for the last part of the year and make sure you keep your grades up to get into college. We've worked too hard to get you this far and I won't have you giving it up now."

"What do you mean 'we?' From where I'm standing there's only one person who's worked their ass off in school, and that's me."

"Grow up. Your grades are average at best."

This is a lie, he knows it. My grades are exceptional and above all my classmates', but it's a minor detail in this argument.

"Do you think you'd be where you are and have gotten into one of the greatest colleges in this country if it weren't for the strings I pulled and the connections I have? Who do you think it is funding this little music daydream you've been acting out? Me. And who can take it all away in an instant? Me."

I swallow hard again, knowing he's right. For the first time in years, he takes a step into my room, but it's not for a sincere grandfatherly moment.

It's so he can get in my face and intimidate me with the next words that come out of his mouth, "You will end things with the girl."

I finally find my voice, "Or what?" If there's anything worth fighting for even more than the band, it's Abby. I'm not going to go down without fighting for our relationship.

"Or I will file a case against you for the attempted rape of a minor."

A faint ringing begins in my ears and the room feels like it starts to spin.

This time, it's me who says, "Excuse me," at a complete loss.

"You're both underage. Your mom walked in and saw you attempting to rape the poor girl. The people in our social circles know what a wild card you are and wouldn't put it past you. I also have my foot in the door with the police ..."

"But why?" I stammer. "I'm your grandson, your blood. How could you do that to me, to her?"

"As I've said, we have generations of standards to maintain. You've pushed and pushed, tested and this is how far we've come. Now, it's time I put my foot down. I told you that you will fall in line and you will. You will fulfill this family's expectations of you, or you will be pushed out. I don't want to do it, but I have done it before and will do it again."

He's calling my bluff, but I don't dare defy him. Nobody speaks about my aunt who was kicked out at sixteen because she wound up pregnant. Grams told me about her, how Grandpa refused to let her see her. I know that when it comes to this shit, he means business and won't back down for anyone.

"Think about it, you're a smart boy deep down and I know you will make the right choice."

He places a reassuring hand on my shoulder and gives me a warm smile as if I've just had a normal conversation with my grandpa.

Manipulative fucker.

As he leaves, I see my mother's shadow in the hall, where she's obviously been listening to the whole thing. Listening to her own father treat her son this way, ripping his future away from him. I should have known better. Known she'd never fight for me because then I wouldn't feel as disappointed as I do, but she's my mother and I thought she'd at least try.

I was wrong.

I don't acknowledge that she's there, instead I slam the door with every bit of strength I have. It's lucky it doesn't come off the hinges it slams so hard. Falling back on my bed, I stare up at the ceiling wondering what I'm going to do. But really, what can I do?

They've got me backed into a corner and they know it.

Every part of me wants to fight for Abby because I love her. But what choice do I have? Either way we're screwed. If I walk away, she will never want to speak to or see me again. If I stay, we will never get to be together. My grandpa will make sure I'm kicked out of Brooklyn and put my ass is in juvenile jail. If that happens, even in the future, I could never be with her. Her family would never allow it, not if they believed the lies, he told.

No matter which way I turn, we're screwed, and I don't know what to do. None of the paths I choose lead to Abby. My hand has been forced, and there's only one person in all of this I can look after. If we have any hope in the future, I have to look after *myself. It's the only way I can make sure there's even a slight possibility we can be together one day, years down the line when the old geezer is buried six feet under.*

If she still wants me, then maybe we can finally be together.

It's simple when I think about it. All I have to do is walk away. Walk away and leave my heart in Abby West's hands and hope that one day in the future, she will give it back to me.

For me it's us. Always us.

***

Abby

Jake breaks me from my Dan-induced trance, pulling at my arm a little too roughly.

"Shit, sorry," he says, as I wince and rub my arm. "I didn't mean to hurt you."

"Well, you did," I snap. "What do you want?"

I'm distracted, wanting to watch the remainder of the set and also not wanting to be caught by Dan talking to Jake. If he sees us standing here together, he will know I was lying about things being history between us, especially when Jake's looking at me like he is.

Not giving up, Jake says, "I really need to speak with you."

"What's so urgent that it can't wait?"

"The truth."

As I'm turning back to the stage, his words stop me in my tracks. "The truth?"

The heavens open and rain pours down around us, hitting my skin.

Jake takes a deep breath then says, "The truth ... I'm ready to give it to you."

My eyes dart up to the stage, to Dan. His voice rings out to the crowd, but I know deep down he's singing to me and only me, and my heart aches for what I'm about to do, to both of them.

Looking back at Jake, I drink him in—the raindrops sitting on his dark lashes, the almost overgrown stubble across his jawline and his brown eyes. My breath catches. My gaze flicks back and forth between the two. They're so similar. Tall, dark hair, famous to millions for their musical talents. Yet there are subtle differences, not just that one has brown eyes, and one has blue. Bigger things. One has a habit for flying off the handle but is equally the most passionate and driven person I've ever met. The other humble and kind, considerate of my feelings and history. How could I ever choose between them?

Dan feigns nonchalance for the purpose of his performance, but his face is strained when he looks in our direction.

Jake's face is pale, having finally worked up the courage after all these years to give me the truth and tell me the real reason why we broke up eight years ago.

It's then, as I'm torn between my head and my heart, that I understand I don't need the truth. I could never choose between the two of them because it's not the right time. When it comes to me and Jake, it feels like it never is. Maybe we're just not meant to be.

"It doesn't matter," I say, looking down to the ground.

I refrain from telling him *we're* no longer important, not wanting to give too much away. Now isn't the time or place, standing in the middle of a festival, surrounded by hundreds of people. The fact we're having to shout to each other, proves it. This isn't the sort of news you make public.

His eyes widen. "What do you mean, it doesn't matter?"

It's taken years for us to get to this point, and what do I do ... throw it back in his face. I despise myself for it, but I have no choice. He looks up at Dan, trying to piece it all together.

He frowns. "It's him, isn't it?"

I want to reply, Yes, it's him. It would be the easy way out. I don't want to lie, but I can't tell him anything until I have the answer in front of me. Those two bold lines on a plastic stick are what I need to be certain. I shake my head, hoping he will leave it, as I have nothing else to give. The icy stare I get in return almost breaks me. I can't hold his gaze, so I look around the crowd to avoid it.

If I'd been told eight years ago that I would be the one to stomp all over Jake's heart, not once, but twice, I would have laughed. We're two puzzle pieces that just don't seem to fit.

I don't know how long I'll be able to keep this secret. He deserves to know, especially since he was about to tell me the truth. It could be so easy. Tell him, face the future together. I know Jake. He would drop everything for me. But then all the band's hard work over the years would have been for nothing, and eventually he would resent me for holding him back.

Then there's the issue of trust. Could I trust him not to walk away, again? Not just from me ... from the two of us?

Time seems to slow as Dan continues his performance on stage. When he sees that Jake and I are still standing together, confusion flashes across his face, replaced by anger when Jake takes hold of my arm and pulls me in towards him. His lips find mine. They're urgent and demanding. My knees tremble, and I feel like giving in and saying, screw the consequences, what does it all matter? It's the type of kiss that tears your heart apart in such a way, it's impossible to put it back together.

It hits me like a freight train when I remember why we can't.

I push him away and stumble back. "I can't do this. Not now. Not with either of you."

"If not now, then when?" Jake shakes his head. "When are you going to stop playing games, Abby?"

I wish it were a game. I wish someone would pop up and say, *Just kidding! It was all a joke,* but it's not. This is as real as life gets. "I'm not playing games," I reply. "But I can't do this right now."

I dart through the crowds, stumbling and hearing shouts in the background from Amanda and the other girls, demanding to know where I'm going. There's Jake's voice too, but it all fades away as I block them out.

Jake brought me here this summer, he tampered with my life and this is where it's left us. I need time to process things, and then if there's a decision to make, we make it together.

For once in this whole fucked up scenario, he's wrong. It's no longer *always us*, because there's about to be someone more important than all of us. We're no longer the ones who matter.

Epilogue
Jake

She walked away. She did the one thing I told myself all summer couldn't happen.

And now I have nothing left to play, it's up to her to make the final move and decide how the game ends. What I thought was my winning card—the truth—wasn't enough. She did what I feared and told me it doesn't matter anymore. Deep down, I know why.

She doesn't trust me.

"Penny for your thoughts ..."

I look up, from the ground where I've been sitting, brooding, and find the last person I expect.

Dan Fucking White.

"What do you want?" I snap.

"A word," he replies, albeit with a more civil tone.

"I gathered ..." I pick at the grass, shredding the blades into tiny pieces, keeping my hands occupied with anything that doesn't involve punching him in the face. This is his fault. If he weren't on the scene things might be different. She might've been here with me now.

"Something's wrong with Abby."

He has my full attention now. "What do you mean?" I say as I get to my feet and stand a little too close for his comfort.

Moving back a pace he shrugs. "I don't know … she seems off. Last night when we were together, something wasn't right."

I try not to focus too much on the fact they were together last night when I was worried out of my goddamn mind wondering where she was.

She wasn't alone.

I breathe slowly trying to keep my temper in check. He's right though. There *was* something different about her before. She wasn't her usual pissed off self. She seemed lost. Broken.

"I'll keep an eye on her." I always do, he doesn't need to waltz in trying to be her knight in shining armor. She already has one.

"I'm not the bad guy." He gestures between the two of us. "It doesn't have to be like this. And for the record, I didn't know there was something still going on between the two of you. She said you were history."

I smirk. She didn't tell him. I could. I could tell him every detail, but I won't, because she means more to me than that, and if I did, I'd never stand a chance.

Without realizing, Dan's revealed that the game isn't quite finished. Maybe I didn't play my last card after all, because if she didn't tell him about us this summer it means one thing.

She doesn't fully trust *him* with her heart either.

It's ironic. Last time, John West was the one to seal our fate when he told me to walk away. And now, as his words echo in my mind, this time he's telling me to do the opposite.

To keep on fighting till there's nothing left.

And that's exactly what I intend to do.

Acknowledgements

Never in my life did I ever think I would write one round of acknowledgements, let alone two, yet here we are and shock horror, this won't be the last.

Firstly, thank you to Peter for all the late nights of moral support, never once complaining that I wasn't paying you any attention (well maybe there was a little bit of complaining), and being on Daddy Duty when I needed to, "quickly get a few words done", only to still be writing hours later.

Thank you to my girls, who once again adapted to the crazy scenario that was Mummy writing *another* book during a pandemic and enduring all the extra Hey Duggee time.

Thank you to my Mum, for taking the girls off my hands when you got a chance and giving me the extra time, needed to make this dream a reality.

Thank you to Babs, for once again being the first set of eyes on another piece of my work and giving me your honest feedback and support.

Thank you, Sarah, for ploughing through the proofing even though I'm sure there were a million other things you would have rather been doing. I now owe you at least two bottles of wine.

Finally, thank you to you, the reader and everyone who bought the first book, Always You. Without your encouragement and wonderful feedback, I don't think I would have been as inspired to write another part of Abby and Jake's journey.

I hope you're all as excited as I am to see where life takes them next.

Always

My life's about to change and I can't decide if it's for better or worse.

There was a time when I thought meeting Jake Ross, was fate …
When I thought our love, was written in the stars …
When I hoped we'd find our way back to each other …
Now I'm left wondering if the path I'm about to take, will be one I'll walk alone.
The one I want. The one I need.
Doesn't want me back.
Then the person I least expect gives me exactly what I need.
A break from reality.
But there's only so long I can hide, and when the truth comes out, it's explosive.
They say what will be, will be.

But what if we were never meant to be together?

OTHER WORK BY LIZZIE MORTON

The Always Trilogy:

Always You
Always Us
Always

The Always Series:

Wanting You Always
Needing You Always

Fool Me Series:

Fool Me Once
Fool Me Twice
Fool Me Thrice

Summer Nights Series:

Just One Kiss
Just One Night
Just Once More – Coming Soon